RETRIBUTION

MW01138653

A Special Agent Dylan Kane Thriller

By J. Robert Kennedy

James Acton Thrillers

The Protocol	*Amazon Burning*
Brass Monkey	*The Riddle*
Broken Dove	*Blood Relics*
The Templar's Relic	*Sins of the Titanic*
Flags of Sin	*Saint Peter's Soldiers*
The Arab Fall	*The Thirteenth Legion*
The Circle of Eight	*Raging Sun*
The Venice Code	*Wages of Sin*
Pompeii's Ghosts	*Wrath of the Gods*

The Templar's Revenge

Special Agent Dylan Kane Thrillers

Rogue Operator	*Death to America*
Containment Failure	*Black Widow*
Cold Warriors	*The Agenda*

Retribution

Delta Force Unleashed Thrillers

Payback
Infidels
The Lazarus Moment
Kill Chain
Forgotten

Detective Shakespeare Mysteries

Depraved Difference
Tick Tock
The Redeemer

Zander Varga, Vampire Detective

The Turned

RETRIBUTION

A Special Agent Dylan Kane Thriller

J. ROBERT KENNEDY

ISBN-10: 1975778944

ISBN-13: 978-1975778941

First Edition

10 9 8 7 6 5 4 3 2 1

For Dave Camp, a good friend of the family, and a true fan.
You are missed.

RETRIBUTION

A Special Agent Dylan Kane Thriller

"The National Security Agency/Central Security Service (NSA/CSS) leads the U.S. Government in cryptology that encompasses both Signals Intelligence (SIGINT) and Information Assurance (IA) products and services, and enables Computer Network Operations (CNO) in order to gain a decision advantage for the Nation and our allies under all circumstances."

Mission Statement of the National Security Agency

"We face cyber threats from state-sponsored hackers, hackers for hire, global cyber syndicates, and terrorists. They seek our state secrets, our trade secrets, our technology, and our ideas - things of incredible value to all of us. They seek to strike our critical infrastructure and to harm our economy."

James Comey, Director of the FBI
February 25, 2016

PREFACE

On May 12, 2017, the largest ransomware attack in history began. Dubbed "WannaCry," it rapidly spread through computers around the world, exploiting a vulnerability in the Windows operating system only recently patched by Microsoft, a patch too many hadn't installed. Hundreds of thousands of computers were infected worldwide, and if it weren't for an analyst who discovered a kill-switch built into the code, things could have been much worse.

Individuals, utilities, businesses, and governments around the globe were affected, with Britain's National Health Service (NHS) particularly hard hit. This resulted in postponed surgeries and tests, and clogged emergency rooms. To date, it is not known if anyone died as a direct result of WannaCry, however it is only a matter of time before someone does from an attack of this nature.

What was particularly shocking about this event was that it used a vulnerability discovered by the NSA, a vulnerability allegedly stolen, along with thousands of others, by one of their own.

What follows is fiction, but too soon could become a reality when someone, somewhere, finally has enough.

Albany, New York
One week from now

NSA Special Agent Janine Graf's heart hammered as the events unfolded before her eyes. Events that were now beyond her control. Their two escort vehicles had been disabled, the fate of their occupants unknown, and now she sat, boxed in, with overwhelming firepower directed at her and her team.

But they were alive.

For now.

An SUV rolled up on their position, braking hard, the lone occupant stepping out, weapon in hand as he aimed it at their attackers.

Her heart leaped.

It was Kane, a man she had met only today, who had identified himself as working for Homeland Security.

Something she knew was BS.

"Would it be presumptuous of me to ask all of you to lower your weapons?"

She almost had to stifle a giggle. Was the man ever serious? He was strangely appealing to her. Yes, he was a gorgeous specimen of a man, but it was the confidence he exuded that made him attractive. Too bad she didn't date liars.

Four of the weapons trained on her SUV were redirected toward Kane.

He frowned. "I guess so." He leaned through the window, rather obviously aiming at the prisoner she had been transporting, now out of the SUV. "Shoot me, and I guarantee you he dies."

One of their attackers stepped forward, covered head to toe in black, including his face, a submachine gun aimed casually in Kane's direction. "I think you should mind your own business. You might get yourself hurt."

She drew a quick breath as someone rounded Kane's vehicle from behind. She opened her mouth to warn him, but it was too late.

Kane was down, and their only hope of rescue gone with him.

Ashland, Oregon
Present Day

Franklin Temple careened around a corner, his navigation system giving him turn-by-turn instructions as he split his attention between the road and the back seat.

"Hang on, Angel, we're almost there!"

The tremor in his voice couldn't be hidden, and he reached up to wipe away a tear. His heart hammered as he realized this time he didn't even hear a moan in reply.

Only silence.

His car beeped at him and slowed rapidly. He spun his head and gasped as his car prevented him from rear-ending the vehicle ahead of him. He cranked the wheel and veered around, a flurry of horns protesting as he forced his way through the quiet intersection and the red light that blared at him in the dimness of a small town at night.

But traffic tickets meant nothing to him.

He hammered on the gas and the 621 horsepower shoved him into the back of his seat as the navigation system warned him of an impending turn. He spotted it and turned hard, the lights of the hospital just ahead. He reached back blindly and felt his daughter's tiny arm.

It was cold.

"Oh, God, please don't take her too!"

He closed his eyes for a brief moment, picturing his wife, lost to him a year ago to ALS, then opened his eyes and cranked the wheel as the system announced he had reached his destination. He slammed on his brakes, bringing the Mercedes-AMG S 65 to a shuddering halt. Jumping out the driver's side, he yanked open the rear door and reached in, grabbing the still form of his daughter.

"Somebody help me!" he cried as he pulled her from the rear seat and rushed toward the doors. "Help me! It's my daughter!"

But no one did. They just turned and watched him as he raced inside, one having the audacity to hold up a phone and record his horror.

"Help me! My daughter, I think she's dying!"

The lobby turned toward him, and this time, finally, somebody reacted. Nurses and staff rushed toward him, his precious Angela gently pulled from his desperate grip and taken away, a flurry of questions bombarding him as he followed in stunned shock, his responses automatic, his conscious brain not even realizing he was answering.

"Wait here."

He stood in the emergency room, the bustle of activity coming into focus.

"Have you reached Dr. Karl yet?"

"No. Nobody has his number. Jennifer took my car to go to his house."

"Call her and get an ETA."

Temple stared at the two nurses having the conversation, the words finally registering.

Nobody has a doctor's phone number?

That didn't make any sense. He examined the room around him. There were a larger number of patients than he would have expected for a small hospital, and the nurses appeared overwhelmed. He turned to ask a question when he noticed the computers. Every screen was red, with the image of a large white lock in the upper corner and a box of text to the right.

And nobody was at any of the terminals, except one lone man, pulling at his hair, who didn't appear to be medical staff.

Temple quickly strode around the counter in the center of the room and leaned over. "What's going on?"

The man looked up. "Huh?"

"What's going on with the computers?"

"We've been hacked."

Temple tensed, then glanced toward the doors where his daughter had been taken, and he had been refused entry. "What do you mean?"

"I don't know. I'm in over my head on this one. We've been locked out of every computer on the network. Whoever did it is demanding Bitcoins as some sort of ransom to unlock the machines."

Temple frowned. "What have you tried?"

"Everything I can think of. I've booted from a USB key, and it looks like the files are encrypted. We don't have access to anything. Patient records, prescriptions. Hell, we don't even have the emergency contact info for our on-call doctors!"

"What happened to the doctors on staff?"

"Doctor. He was attacked by a patient about half an hour ago. His hand has been sliced open. He can't treat anybody."

Temple cursed, his hands balling into fists. "Pay the ransom."

The young man's eyes widened. "Are you kidding me?"

Temple leaned further over the counter. "Pay it now. My daughter's in there, and she needs a doctor. Now!"

"I can't pay it! I'm not authorized."

"Terry, is there a problem here?"

Temple glanced over his shoulder at a man in a suit. "Apparently so. I need you to pay the ransom now to unlock these computers."

"Sir, I'm going to have to ask you to have a seat and let our staff work the problem."

Work the problem. This guy I can deal with.

"I'm Franklin Temple." He extended a hand, struggling to remain as calm as he could, his daughter's very life perhaps depending on it. "Do you know who I am?"

The man's eyes widened. "CEO of Temple Technologies?"

"Exactly. I'll pay the ransom. Just tell your man to proceed."

"I-I wish it were that simple, Mr. Temple, but the Board has already given me strict instructions not to pay any ransom. We have offsite backups, and a team is already on its way to wipe the computers and reinstall. We should be up and running by end of day tomorrow."

"And what of my daughter? She's dying now!" Temple clamped his jaw shut, stifling the tirade he feared would erupt at any moment.

"We're transferring all critical patients—"

"We don't have time for that!" He leaned toward the man. "What's your annual budget?"

"Excuse me?"

"I'll double it. You know I can."

The man's jaw slowly dropped. "I-I'll have to convene the board."

Temple threw up his hands in frustration. "It's time to grow some balls! Make a damned decision for once in your life, or I'll sue this hospital for every penny it's got!"

The man took a long breath through his nose, then turned to the young man, Terry, working the computers. "Do it."

"Really?"

"Yes. I'll deal with the board."

Terry's eyes widened. "Cool!"

Temple leaped over the counter and grabbed one of the empty chairs, parking behind a terminal. "Do you know what to do?"

"Yeah, I think so."

"Then let's prioritize. What do we need first?"

"It shouldn't matter. We just need one terminal to access the network. I don't think the network data has been encrypted, just the local. Once we unlock one machine, we should have access to everything."

A rage built inside Temple. "How much are they asking for?"

"It's in Bitcoins, but I think it works out to be about three hundred bucks per computer."

Temple slammed both fists onto the counter. "Are you kidding me! You guys have put all these patients' lives at risk over three hundred bucks!"

Terry recoiled, the blood draining from his face. "Hey, don't blame me. I'm just following orders."

Temple bit his tongue. "Pay it, now."

Terry nodded, his fingers flying over the keyboard, and a few minutes later he smiled, the red screen disappearing. "I'm in!"

Temple rolled his chair over and watched as Terry rebooted the machine, a standard login appearing. Moments later, they were staring at the hospital's interface. "Get whoever needs that machine the most on it, then let's start unlocking the rest."

A nurse rushed over. "Did you get in?"

"Yes."

She shoved Terry out of the way and quickly began typing away. "I've got the numbers!"

The flurry of activity stopped for a moment, sighs of relief briefly replacing the panic. Then it returned almost immediately. Temple and Terry quickly went to work, unlocking the rest of the computers, each requiring payment in Bitcoins, the hackers having provided specific instructions on how to purchase them through conventional means, then how to deposit those digital coins into their untraceable wallet.

It disgusted him with every transaction, but as each was completed, another staff member returned to their computer.

"Dr. Karl will be here in five minutes."

Temple glanced over his shoulder at the nurse. "My daughter?"

She stared at him for a moment. "I'll go check."

He smiled at her gratefully, and took a moment for a silent prayer before returning to solving the problem at hand. It was all he could do. He was a technical expert, not a medical expert. He needed the doctors and nurses to be able to focus on their jobs with the tools they were used to having at their disposal. That was something he could help with, and by doing so, he just might save his daughter's life by allowing the experts to do their job.

The doors to the ER swung open and he glanced up to see the nurse who had left moments ago to check on his daughter.

And her face told him everything.

"Is she...?" He couldn't finish the question as he began to shut down.

"I'm so sorry, sir. There was nothing we could do."

"If there had been a doctor here?"

"I-I really can't say. Perhaps."

Temple's shoulders shook as sobs racked his body. "Oh, God, why? Why both of them?" He felt a hand on his shoulder, but it provided none of the comfort intended. He ignored it, his self-pity almost overwhelming him, until through the tears he saw the blur of the screen in front of him, the red burning through the sorrow, a rage building within.

They're going to pay.

Clayton Hummel Residence
Annapolis, Maryland
Two Years Ago

Clayton Hummel stared at the mirror, the reflection still a shock to him even after decades of disappointment looking back at him. He was what the medical community labeled morbidly obese, what the comedians and public might call a fat bastard, and what he called a disgusting example of a human being.

He hated himself.

It was why he despised having photos taken of himself. If he were in a situation where a camera was out, he was always the one offering to take the photo.

Better to be behind the lens, than in front of it.

There were no photos of himself in his home except from his youth, before the food addiction had taken over, or from the brief period of time when he had lost the weight after bariatric surgery.

But it had all come back.

And more.

He had never wanted the surgery, but the doctors had insisted it was his best and only option. His family had urged him to go through with it, and what few friends he had, agreed as well.

So he had.

And it had worked.

Until he had slowly stretched out his newly shrunken stomach, and eventually put the weight back on.

Much to the dismay—and disgust—of those around him.

But they didn't understand. They *couldn't* understand.

It was an addiction. An emotional crutch. When he was depressed or stressed, he ate. The very act of chewing, of tasting, of swallowing, was a comfort that no person had ever provided him. During those few minutes he was eating, he wasn't alone. It was him and his fork, in front of the television, lost in a world of euphoric satisfaction, where his troubles would be forgotten, where the fact he was chronically alone would fade to the periphery, and for those few brief moments, he was happy.

Until he was done.

Then he'd feel sick.

Stuffed to the point of almost vomiting, disgusted with what he had just eaten, the depression would return as he beat himself up over his failure as a man, as a human being. He hated himself, and he hated what he had become. Yet no surgery, no diet, could possibly work until he addressed the root cause.

And what that was, he had no idea.

He needed counseling, yet was too proud, too much of "a man" to ever submit to such a thing. He never spoke of it to his family, and they never broached the subject anymore. Not since his dramatic failure after the surgery. It was a constant source of anguish for his parents and his sister, and he desperately wanted to stop, but he couldn't.

He wouldn't.

And he didn't know why.

Every single time he overate, he knew it was wrong, even while he was doing it. Even before he placed the online order for a large pizza when all he needed was the small. He wasn't a fool. He wasn't an idiot. He was killing himself, yet he couldn't stop.

And he didn't know why.

God, help me! Please!

He didn't know why he bothered praying for some sort of salvation. And what form would that be? Instantaneous weight loss? The miraculous ability to just say no to the cravings? The sudden ability to love himself for the first time in his life?

He stared in the mirror, then shrugged his 2XLT black pocket-tee over his shoulders and pulled it down over his large frame, yanking at the fibers of the freshly laundered shirt in an attempt to stretch it out so it wasn't so tight.

He glared at himself.

Do you really think the black makes you look any thinner, you fat piece of shit?

His eyes burned and he turned away, sitting on the edge of the bed, slipping on a pair of shorts with an elastic waistband that allowed him to feel thinner than he actually was. Size 44, instead of the probably 50 he needed. He stood and buttoned them closed with a struggle, his held breath bursting as he finally managed to get the button through the hole he had no hope of seeing.

He checked the part in his hair then headed for his home office, and to the only friends he had. The friends he had met online, in a world that had no idea what he looked like, or how he felt about himself.

An electronic world where he could be the man he dreamed of being, and not the pathetic creature he had become.

Ashland, Oregon
Present Day

Franklin Temple sat alone in a room reserved for the families of patients who had succumbed to whatever had brought them here. A call had been placed to his company, and a team was on the way, though with the exception of his personal assistant, none were friends, and none were family.

The last of that died only hours ago.

An autopsy was to be performed, but he already had a preliminary diagnosis from the doctor who had arrived too late, his phone with him the entire time as he had a romantic dinner with his wife nearby, the number known only to a ransomed computer, the nurse's aide sent to his home finding an empty, darkened house.

The doctor's theory was a ruptured aorta, probably from a congenital defect like Marfan syndrome. If he had been here, if any surgeon had been here, they would probably have saved her. But instead, the surgeon on duty had been incapacitated by an irate patient, frustrated by the long waits due to the ransomware attack on the hospital's computers, and the backup had been unreachable.

A confluence of events no contingency plan could have mitigated.

And it wasn't just here. A television in the corner, the volume low, was tuned to a news channel as it delighted in broadcasting the details of what was characterized as the largest ransomware attack in history, with millions of computers crippled across the planet, including government, institutional, corporate, and personal. Talking head experts were advising people not to pay the ransom, as it would only encourage further attacks, and those not impacted were urged to make sure their latest security patches for their operating systems were installed.

He stared at his phone, at the last photo taken of his wife and daughter together. His beloved Clara was having a good day, and if he didn't know when it was taken, he could be forgiven for not remembering the fact her body had been ravaged by an incurable disease, and she was only weeks away from death. His precious angel, his dear, sweet Angela, was hugging her mother, a huge grin on her face, seemingly oblivious to the fate that awaited the woman who had given birth to her too few years ago.

And now they were both gone.

All because a hospital hadn't patched their systems with the latest security updates.

All because a hospital wouldn't pay three hundred dollars to unlock just one machine.

All because some faceless hacker, working on behalf of only God knew who, launched an attack purely motivated by greed.

He put his phone in sleep mode and closed his eyes, his mind racing with what to do next. His team would arrive soon, and they would make things much easier. Being rich had its advantages, and he planned on letting them deal with as much as they could.

His daughter was dead, and there was nothing he could do about it. He would cut a check to the hospital as he had promised, and he would meet with somebody in Washington to find out what they were doing about the attack.

For someone had to pay.

The death of his little girl, the death of the only thing left in this world that he loved, could not go unpunished.

There was a gentle knock on the door and he glanced toward it. "Come."

The door opened slightly and his assistant entered, Tanya Davis' concerned look genuine, the woman always doting on Angela whenever she was at the office. "Sir, I'm so sorry. Are you okay?"

Temple grunted. "What do you think?"

She knelt in front of him and took his hand. "Can I get you anything?"

His shoulders shook and a single tear escaped, rolling down his cheek. "The heads of those responsible."

She reached into her purse and removed a tissue, handing it to him. He took it and gripped it into a ball, leaving the now streaming tears to burn his cheeks. "The team is outside. What do you need us to do?"

"Do whatever is needed to confirm what took my daughter, then arrange the burial."

"Beside her mother?"

He squeezed his eyes shut, finally losing what little control he had, his shoulders collapsing. Davis' arms surrounded him, and he reached out, taking her in his as she shook with her own sobs. The shared pain was strangely comforting, and he felt no shame in revealing his sorrow, his vulnerability, to this woman he trusted implicitly, who had been a friend to him and his wife, and a surrogate mother to his daughter after his beloved's passing.

She *was* a friend.

And she *was* hurting. Just like him.

He gently pushed her away and offered her the balled up tissue. She chuckled, pulling two fresh ones from her purse, dabbing her eyes dry as she handed him the other. This time he wiped his eyes and face, leaning back as Davis stood then sat beside him. He took her hand in his and squeezed as they sat in silence, sniffling.

"Take care of my little girl."

Davis nodded. "I will." She blew her nose. "Anything else?"

"Just deal with my daughter, and arrange a meeting with Washington."

"What for?"

"I intend to make whoever is responsible for this, pay."

Tailored Access Operations Unit, NSA Headquarters
a.k.a. The Equation Group
Fort George G. Meade, Maryland
Two Years Ago

Clayton Hummel sat hunched over his keyboard, an array of monitors sweeping across his desk, his cubicle one of complete disarray to those who didn't know him, yet he knew where everything was in the piles of papers and junk food. As he reviewed the chunk of code designed to exploit a vulnerability he had found in an older version of the world's most popular operating system, he reached absentmindedly to his right, grabbing a handful of Cheezies from the Costco-sized bag sitting in his desk drawer. He stuffed the delicious orange, puffy treat into his mouth, and savored the taste and textures as he let the chips dissolve before he swallowed. Then, in an almost ritualistic fashion, he sucked each digit clean, the sticky orange paste that remained behind, the dessert course of a carb-laden meal.

It was pathetic.

Someone cleared her throat behind him and he reached down, slamming the desk drawer shut, two orange fingerprints left behind, his ring and pinky fingers still covered. He spun in his chair and gulped to see his supervisor, Sheila Stone, behind him. "Wh-what can I do for you, ma'am?"

He could tell Stone was disgusted with him. They all were. Coming to work every day was a struggle. If he didn't make excellent money here, he'd probably have tried to get a job where he could work from home. But he couldn't do that here. Not with this job. This was the National Security Agency. The NSA. Tasked with protecting the nation's secrets from hostile elements both foreign and domestic, they were the people of codes. They created them, and more importantly, they cracked them. They were the agency that monitored the phone calls and emails, that hacked foreign governments and individuals. They were the agency you definitely wanted on your side.

And they didn't allow telecommuting.

"I just wanted to know how that exploit is coming."

Hummel jerked a thumb over his shoulder at his computer. "Just finishing up. It looks good. All we need is for the target to open an email in their browser, and we've got full access."

"And this is new?"

Hummel nodded vigorously. "Absolutely. Redmond doesn't know about this one yet." His eyes narrowed. "Should we tell them? If this gets into the wrong hands, it could be pretty dangerous."

Stone stared at him then smiled. "I thought you were serious there for a moment."

Hummel laughed nervously. "Just joking with you. You know me."

"Yes, I do." Stone jabbed a finger at the monitor. "Keep this one under your hat. We'll keep it for the ToolKit until we see the other side using it, then we'll let the company know. Until then, this is our little secret." She paused. "So, you just need them to open an email, and it installs?"

"Yup. It's just a matter of getting someone on the target's network to be willing to open it. It's too bad people are still so stupid that they open things from people they don't even know."

"Hey, promise cheap Viagra or a larger penis, and you'd be surprised how many people will click on an email. If it didn't work, you wouldn't be receiving ten or twenty of them a day."

"Pathetic."

Stone agreed. "Yup. Let me know when you're done. The Director will want to know about it."

"Will do."

Stone left the cubicle and Hummel turned back toward his keyboard, eying the closed drawer with his Cheezies. He resisted, staring at the code, slowly scrolling through it as his brilliant mind traced the logic line by line, branching off with each possible outcome, tracking it all like a grandmaster chess player plotting seven moves ahead.

He was a failure in life, but not at this. At his job, he was brilliant. You weren't paid six-figures if you weren't. Though he'd never really get any further than he already had. He wasn't supervisor material. Fat bastards like him rarely were unless they were connected, or had become so after they were in the position.

He had always been overweight, and it was his brains that had gotten him this far. He had studied hard, learned his craft, and worked his way up through various subcontractors, eventually put on contract at the NSA itself, a dream job of sorts. His dream was to be a spy. Operational, like James Bond, though more on the cyber side of things. The women, the glamor, the cars, the resorts. It was a lifestyle he wasn't even certain existed outside of the movies, but fantasies never hurt anybody, and it was one that as far as he was concerned, working in this building put him one step closer to.

You're an idiot.

He reached down and opened the drawer, stretching a hand into the greasy mess.

Leroux/White Residence, Fairfax Towers
Falls Church, Virginia
Present Day

CIA Analyst Supervisor Chris Leroux stepped through the door of his apartment and tossed his keys into the bowl beside the entrance, pulling his shoes off with the opposing toes as he dragged his ass toward the bedroom.

He was exhausted.

It had been all hands on deck for the past twenty-four hours as the ransomware attack that had struck the globe spread. Millions of computers had been infected, and it was still spreading as more people turned on their computers, ignorant to the risks.

This one had been different.

Very different.

It had exploited a security hole nobody had known about, so there wasn't a system in the world protected against it. It spread through email, which made it easy to disseminate, and all one had to do was open the email in a browser to activate it. At that point, if proper security wasn't implemented on the machine, which most people didn't have, it was infected, and the hackers could fire any chunk of code they wanted.

In this case, ransomware designed to encrypt all the data on a hard drive, and demand payment for an unlocking code.

Tens of thousands around the world had paid the ransom, though the vast majority hadn't. Those with proper backups simply wiped their machines and restored, and those who kept their data in the cloud did the same.

But there were reports of cash-strapped organizations like charities and hospitals that had been hit, and hit hard. And it wasn't their fault in this case. No one could point to a machine and say, "Hey, you ignored the security updates for two years!"

Nobody had known it existed.

"Is that you?"

He smiled at the sound of his girlfriend, Sherrie White, coming from the bedroom. "No, just an Assembly hit squad that's really too tired to bother killing you today."

"Ha ha. If you're that tired, then I guess I won't be giving you my customary greeting."

Leroux paused. He *was* exhausted, but when Sherrie, a CIA Agent, returned from a mission, she was usually insatiable. Something stirred below.

He stared down at it. "Aren't you tired?"

"What's that?"

He looked up. "Umm, nothing." He resumed dragging his ass toward the bedroom, slowly unbuttoning his shirt. He turned the corner and smiled. Sherrie was lying in bed, a red negligee hugging all the right places, the lamps on low, a bottle of champagne on ice, and a can of whipped cream nestled between her cleavage.

That's new.

"Hungry?"

His stomach growled and he eyed the whipped cream. "You've been surveilling someone kinky again, haven't you?"

She grinned. "Oooh, I've got lots of dirty ideas."

Half-mast.

"Must have been a congressman."

"Close. An ambassador." She smacked her ass. "He was a naughty boy. Are you a naughty boy?"

Leroux gulped, yanking off his shirt as he nodded, a surge of adrenaline fueling him, his lethargy of a moment ago forgotten.

"Then get over here so I can punish you for being such a naughty, naughty boy."

Full mast.

And then some.

He stepped toward her and she reached forward, grabbing him by the belt and hauling him into the bed. She straddled him, grinding him where it counted, and eyed him like he was a pork roast at a bar mitzvah—forbidden but desperately needing to be eaten.

"I just have one thing to say before you receive your punishment."

"What's that?" His voice quivered as he reached for her breasts and she slapped his hands away.

"If Dylan calls, I'm killing him."

With those words, she mauled him like a tiger, and at times he found himself holding on for dear life, whatever she had seen while on assignment truly awe inspiring and deserving of an NC-17 rating.

And whipped cream had never been so delicious.

It felt like hours, though it probably wasn't, but if he ever told anyone about this, he'd claim it was. She finally dropped on top of him, as spent as he was, and he felt her smile, her cheek muscles against his bare chest giving her away.

"Done?"

"For now."

"That was incredible."

"Yes, yes it was." She repositioned so she could look at him. "I think we'll have to do that again sometime."

Leroux picked up the whipped cream bottle and stuck the end in his mouth, spraying some. He swallowed. "Definitely. Dinner, dessert, and a show, all rolled into one."

"I do aim to please."

He leaned forward and gave her a peck. "Oh, you do please. Though that one move did kind of hurt."

"Which one? You screamed I think three times."

"I wouldn't exactly call them screams. More like terrified cries of someone unsure of what the hell was going to happen next."

She grinned and patted his cheek. "Is my little man going to be okay?"

He rolled over, bringing her with him, then wrapped around her, kissing her deeply. "He'll be fine." He yawned. "But now he needs sleep."

She patted his chest. "You've earned it."

Leroux moaned contentedly and closed his eyes, falling asleep within moments, waking up what felt like only minutes later, though the sun was glowing around the edges of the curtains while his phone vibrated impatiently on the nightstand.

Sherrie was nowhere to be found, and the bed smelled sickly sweet from their dessert antics of the night before.

He reached over and grabbed his phone, swiping his thumb across the display. "Leroux."

"Sir, it's Sonya. The Director needs you in for a briefing."

"Regarding?"

J. ROBERT KENNEDY

"Something to do with the attack. An NSA specialist is coming in. Apparently they know something."

"I'll be there in twenty minutes." Leroux's eyebrows rose at a hissing sound from down the hallway. Sherrie stepped into the room wearing a whipped cream bra and panties.

"Make that an hour."

26

Clayton Hummel Residence
Annapolis, Maryland
Two Years Ago

Clayton Hummel sat in his high-back leather chair, a smile on his face as he leaned forward and pecked at his keyboard. This wasn't work, this was entertainment. This was joy.

This was love.

Her name was Melanie Driscoll, and they had met online several months ago in a World of Warcraft chatroom. He had a few real-world friends, though he rarely saw them, most of his communication with them now by email or text, his embarrassment over his weight turning him into a shut-in more with each passing day.

But online, he had lots of friends. He was a cybersecurity expert, and though he couldn't discuss specifics, he was a frequent contributor to discussions—anonymously of course—about all things security related, and was well respected.

And he loved his online games where he could be whatever and whoever he wanted to be. It was there that he had found Melanie, another lonely soul who had screwed up the courage to reach out to him of all people. And instead of ignoring her, this time, this one time, he had responded—though not before reading her profile.

She was his age, from Texas—far enough away that they probably would never actually meet—and loved all things science fiction. Loved Captain Kirk—both versions, Han Solo and Boba Fett, Battlestar Galactica and Stargate—basically his entire hit parade. She read

Heinlein and Asimov, and could quote snippets from all his favorite franchises.

She was his soulmate.

And he had responded with a single word.

"Hi."

Months of nightly chats ensued, getting longer and more involved, and eventually, he had realized he was in love for the first time with a woman who actually knew he existed. He had been in love before, but it had always been from the sidelines, always one way. He had never had the courage to ask anyone out in his entire life, not since a humiliating experience in high school had crushed him, destroying any confidence the chubby senior might have managed to build up.

It had scarred him for life.

But this was different. He could be *not* himself. He could be the man he always envisioned himself to be. Sexy, witty, confident. He told her everything, though at first carefully filtered, and over time, he found himself slowly lifting the veil over his life, letting some of his insecurities through.

Leading to a revelation.

Through a picture.

She had sent him her photo. She was chubby, like him, yet beautiful, unlike him. It had been such a relief. Her avatar online had been of a sexy blonde elf, his a strapping half-human, half-orc—with pecs and abs. She had opened up to him, and who she truly was, was someone he could see himself with.

He had sent her a photo of when he was in college, with a joke about how he wished he still had his college body—despite weighing in at probably 250 in the picture.

She had loved it, saying he was so cute and she wished she had known him back then. Two weeks later, he sent her a real photo of himself, shot from overhead to try and minimize the fat-effect.

And she had called him handsome.

He had cried, this the nicest thing anyone had said to him in years.

And the fact they had continued to talk, to open up completely with each other, with no more filters, no more lies, no more telling each other what they felt the other wanted to hear—just the complete, unvarnished truth—including the ugliness of their lives as overweight people.

Discrimination was frowned upon. You couldn't make fun of anyone for their race, religion, handicaps or disabilities, but there was one thing you could do with impunity—make fun of a fat person. Society did it constantly in its movies and comedy, in the way fat people were frowned upon or pointed at, laughed at or insulted.

Fat people were people too, with the same feelings as any other person, and the pointing, the snickering, the laughing, and the straight out rude comments, hurt. They cut to the bone.

When someone at work made a joke about his weight, he'd fire back with a prepared insult—all fat people have them—that would leave him laughing with the room, yet deep inside he'd be hurt and want to curl up into a ball somewhere dark and alone, to cry away his pain.

And it had happened again today at a gathering after work. He had been invited to an impromptu bachelor party. He hadn't wanted to go, but if he wanted to get anywhere in the NSA, he had to make his appearances. And when the groom had risen to give a speech, albeit fairly drunk, he had thanked everyone, then spoke of how much he loved the woman he was marrying, delivering a line that Hummel was certain the man had thought was hilarious.

"I think I did pretty damned good landing Rita. She's a beautiful woman, and as you all know, I'm the ugliest guy in this group, with the possible exception of Clay!"

The laughter had stung, but he had joined in, raising his glass. "Consider yourself blessed!" More laughter and some back slaps ensued, and he had downed his drink, waiting long enough to extricate himself from the festivities with the excuse that it was his sister's birthday and he had to call. It was a lie, though anything was better than the truth.

He had cried in his car the entire way home, sick of being fat, sick of the constant jokes at his expense, by people too ignorant to realize how wrong it was.

And then to top it all off, Melanie had been offline, leaving him with no one to share his pain with.

A pizza was promptly ordered, a large meat lover's with hot peppers and pineapple—yes, pineapple—and he had sat going through his emails and newsgroup postings while he waited.

And made a mistake.

Angry at his co-workers, all of whom he was certainly at least twenty IQ points ahead of, he had entered into an argument with someone online, and by mistake, tried to prove his point of the government exploiting vulnerabilities in various operating systems, by stating he worked for the NSA and knew damned well what he was talking about.

This had changed the tone, with people piling on asking him to prove it.

And like an idiot, he had.

He delivered up the vulnerability he had been working on over the past few months. Not the specifics, but just the fact it existed, and how, in general, it worked.

And again, they demanded proof.

His pizza had arrived and he ended the conversation, parking in front of The Big Bang Theory on his PVR, and ate away his anger and pain until his laptop, sitting to his right, finally beeped, and he wiped away his tears as Melanie came online. He had pushed his pizza aside, a smile spreading across his face for the first time in hours.

Briefing Room 6A, CIA Headquarters
Langley, Virginia
Present Day

"We're aware of the vulnerability that was exploited."

Chris Leroux's eyes narrowed as he exchanged a glance with two of his staff in the packed meeting, Sonya Tong and Randy Child. "For how long?"

The woman standing in front of a large display scratched her nose, NSA Special Agent Janine Graf appearing uncomfortable with her current situation. "Two years."

National Clandestine Service Chief Leif Morrison leaned forward in his chair, pointing at the chunk of code scrolling on the screen. "You've known about that for two years, and you did nothing about it?"

Graf frowned, shifting from foot to foot. "We thought it was contained. It was the NSA's position that it be kept quiet so it could be used to fulfill our mandate."

"To spy on Americans," muttered the young Child, his brain-mouth filter yet to develop.

Leroux gave him a look, Child dropping his head in an attempt to make himself less conspicuous.

Graf glared at him. "To protect our nation from enemies both foreign and domestic." She redirected her attention to Morrison. "Sir, we've used this vulnerability dozens of times over the past two years to collect incredibly valuable information. Because it wasn't known to the manufacturer, there are no computers using these versions of the operating system that aren't vulnerable unless they have some pretty serious extra security installed. By not informing the company, we've advanced America's interests by leaps and bounds."

"And now infected millions of computers worldwide."

Graf glared at Child. "Does he need to be here?"

Leroux leaned forward as Tong elbowed Child. "He has a point. Because you kept this to yourselves, we're in the middle of this crisis. If no one else knew about this, then we have to assume either someone finally did discover it—"

"And we've found zero evidence of that," interrupted Child, leaning forward so he could be seen past both Leroux and Tong.

"—or you've had a leak."

Graf's eyes darted about the room, focusing on anything but those at the table grilling her.

Bingo.

"Who was the leak?" asked Leroux, Morrison smiling slightly at him.

Graf sighed, dropping into the chair at the head of the table. "What I'm about to tell you is highly classified."

Morrison grunted. "This is the CIA."

Graf gave him a weak smile. "Of course. Two years ago, I was part of a sting operation, targeting contractors in a routine security operation. We identified various targets with vulnerabilities, then tried to get them to violate the terms of their security clearance."

"And one did?"

"Yes and no. Clayton Hummel was identified as a possible security risk, and my partner and I were assigned to him."

Leroux made a note of the name. "What made him a risk?"

"He was a loner who worked on something that could easily be digitally transferred and sold."

"So we're targeting lonely people now?"

Leroux held out a hand, pushing Child back in his seat without looking. "What was he working on?"

Graf stared at him for a moment before turning away. She tilted her head and scratched her temple. "The ToolKit."

Child nearly burst out of his chair, Tong's hand on his arm the only thing stopping him, but it was Leroux who erupted first. "The ToolKit? Are you kidding me? Are you telling us that the ToolKit might have been stolen?"

Graf's cheeks went red, along with her ears. "We now believe that, yes."

Morrison tapped the tabletop, silencing everyone. "What is the ToolKit?"

Leroux turned to his boss. "It's a nickname for all the methods the NSA uses to hack into computers or networks. Essentially, it is all the vulnerabilities they and others have been able to identify, and how to exploit them. It's a how-to manual to access pretty much any computer, anywhere."

Morrison whistled, turning to Graf. "And this is now out there, in the hands of hackers?"

She nodded. "We believe so."

The Equation Group, NSA Headquarters
Fort George G. Meade, Maryland
Two Years Ago

Clayton Hummel closed his eyes as he gripped the memory stick in his fist. The data on it could put him in prison for life, yet he was already in a prison he couldn't stand. For too many years he had wished he was dead, finished with the pain, finished with the embarrassment and humiliation. And when he finally had been given some hope, some faint hope of escape, it had been crushed.

He had fought with Melanie.

It was the night of the bachelor party, when he had been humiliated in front of all his colleagues. They hadn't known what they had done to him, how they had stabbed at his emotional scars yet again, the next day acting as if nothing had happened, the only reference to the events the usual unimaginative clichés. "Great party!" "You left too soon!" and various other statements that merely went unacknowledged.

For he had been completely preoccupied.

He had dumped his heart out to Melanie that night, about the pain, about how his so-called friends on the forum had torn him apart, and she had been at first sympathetic, exactly as he had expected.

He had started to feel better.

But he had continued pressing the self-pity, and had gone too far.

"Why don't you prove them wrong, then, if it's so important to you?"

"I can't. I could get fired. I shouldn't have even said what I did."

"Then stop whining about it. If you can't provide them with the proof, then either you're lying, or you're telling the truth. It doesn't really matter to me nor should it matter to you if you're telling the truth. Just suck it up, be a man, and move on."

It had hurt more than he could ever have imagined.

It was high school all over again.

"Do you think I'm lying?"

"How am I supposed to know? I hope you're not. If you are, then you're not the man I thought you were." There had been a long pause before she continued, the three dots on the screen indicating she was typing and repeatedly editing before sending her reply. It was that delay that made her words so much more painful, as they were clearly well thought out. "I think I love you, Clay, but I can't be with a man who won't stick up for himself. Prove them wrong. Show them what you can do, and that will shut them up, and it will prove to me that you're a man I can be with for the rest of my life."

She had gone offline immediately after, and he had sat stunned all evening, staring at her words, spiraling into a pit of despair unlike any he had previously found himself in. He had actually stared around the room, assessing each item in how quickly and painlessly it might be used to kill himself, to end this suffering once and for all.

Though he was too much of a coward for that.

Instead, he had climbed in his car and gone for donuts. His form of suicide. Slow but sure.

Too slow.

As he chowed down on his fourth Krispy Kreme, licking his fingers clean at a stoplight, he had turned his head to see some teenagers in the car beside him staring, one with the phone held up, recording the fat guy pigging out on donuts.

It had enraged him.

He had thrown open his door and grabbed the tire iron from his trunk, charging at the car as it peeled away, leaving him huffing and puffing from the effort, and several cars honking their horns at him, one driving by and tossing the final straw out the window.

"Get back in your car, you fat piece of shit!"

He whipped the tire iron at the man's car as he pulled away, but it fell short.

Thankfully.

The last thing he needed was to be arrested. He'd lose his security clearance, and his job.

And his future.

What future?

He had returned to his car and gone home, tears streaming down his face, donuts stuffing his mouth, as he felt more alone than ever.

He hadn't heard from Melanie for days, and his messages had gone unanswered. He needed her. Desperately. But there appeared to be only one way to get her back.

And that was to fight.

And that very security clearance he had been so afraid of losing earlier in the week, was exactly how he could get her back.

He had full access to the entire ToolKit, a list of all the vulnerabilities the NSA had at its disposal. Thousands of ways to access every operating system and network imaginable, many known to the companies responsible, but too many not. Even fully patched systems were vulnerable in some cases.

And he had it all in the palm of his hand.

Literally.

He squeezed the memory stick, sweat beading on his forehead. He knew exactly how to get it out of the building. Security was designed to keep people out, to keep weapons and bombs out, but at the end of the day, when the rush of workers was leaving, security was designed to keep people moving, and the higher the security clearance you had, and the longer you had worked there, the quicker you were processed.

He pulled the tiny microSD card from the USB adapter, reducing the size of what he had to smuggle out of the building to something the size of an M&M, yet thinner. He opened his desk drawer, pulling out a roll of Scotch tape, unused in his entire time here, and tore off a piece. He taped the memory card to the back of his watch, then inhaled deeply.

Let's do this.

He wiped his forehead dry with a handkerchief, then rose, struggling to stick to his regular routine as much as he could, the very act of thinking about it making it difficult to remember what he normally did by instinct. He merged with the masses, waiting for an elevator, then piled on amid several frowns and muttered grumblings as he struggled to squeeze his large frame on board, praying the doors would actually close.

They did.

Moments later, he was on the ground floor, the lines of personnel splitting into various tiers as those who needed closer scrutiny joined lines that would hold them up for some time, and others, like himself, that merely swiped their passes, subject to random searches. In his entire time there, he had been taken aside on only a handful of occasions. The chances of today being one of them were slim to none.

Yet today would be the day, the way your luck is.

"Sir, I'll get you to step aside, please."

He nearly peed, the color draining from his face as he turned.

But the guard wasn't talking to him, he was addressing the person behind him.

And now, thanks to his overreaction, he appeared as guilty as sin.

He grinned at the man behind him. "Lucky you."

The man chuckled. "The one day I'm in a hurry."

"Isn't that the way it always is." Hummel grabbed his briefcase off the scanner and headed for the doors then the parking lot, not breathing easy until he cleared the front gates.

And as he headed for home, he began to shake all over, the crime he had just committed unforgivable.

But entirely necessary if he were to prove to Melanie that he was a man worth loving.

Temple Technologies Corporate Head Office
Mountain View, California
Present Day

Franklin Temple regarded the man sitting in front of him, his assistant Tanya Davis taking notes in the corner. Nothing he had heard in the past fifteen minutes had any substance. It was all the standard lines designed to make it sound like one was doing something, when in reality, little to nothing was getting accomplished.

He was being handled in the same way he handled impatient shareholders.

"Mr. Hughes, all you've told me is that you're looking into it, as I fully expect you would be, that you sympathize with my situation, as I fully expect you would, and that you can't discuss the specifics of the investigation, which I fully expect you couldn't. What you don't seem to be grasping is that I have an extremely high security clearance due to the Department of Defense contracts we have, and have resources that can be used to help in this situation. Don't treat me like your average citizen. I am not."

"Of course, Mr. Temple, I realize who you are, and the fact you and your company have been of great help to our nation. That's why I'm here. If we were treating you like anything less than you are, I can assure you I wouldn't have been sent. It's just that, as I'm sure you're aware, just because you have a high security clearance, doesn't mean you get clearance to everything. You only have access to what you need to know."

Temple dropped his head slightly, staring at Hughes. "You're suggesting I don't need to know?"

"As a father and a victim, you need to know when we have something concrete, as in when we make an arrest. But, and I say this with all due respect, sir, you don't need to know the specifics of our investigation. Rest assured that we are following all leads diligently, and are doing everything in our power, in cooperation with our allies, to identify who exactly is behind this unprecedented attack. I have been instructed to tell you, from the White House itself, that when we do have a name—or names—that we will inform you before it is made public."

Temple exhaled slowly and loudly, steepling his fingers in front of his chin as he rested his elbows on the arms of his leather chair. "I suppose I should have expected as much." This was a waste of his time. This man might as well have been an intern, though it wasn't his fault. He had his orders, and he was following them. It was his superiors who were to blame for this brush off, and eventually he'd find a way to make them pay, but not today. He had higher priorities. He rose, extending a hand across his desk. "Thanks for your time, Mr. Hughes."

Hughes leaped from his chair, shaking the hand. "I wish I could have told you more, sir." He lowered his voice slightly. "And as a father, I just want to say, I understand completely your desire to be more involved. If it were my child…" He shook his head. "Well, I would be doing the same."

"Thank you, Mr. Hughes." Temple motioned toward Davis. "Please show Mr. Hughes out." He sat back in his chair and spun toward the window, staring out at the city below him as Davis showed the government lackey to the elevators, his chest growing tighter with each passing moment.

He wasn't sure why he was upset more now than half an hour ago. What had he expected? A complete, detailed update on the progress? A list of suspects delivered to him with a smile? Of course not. Yet he had at least expected the courtesy of a senior level bureaucrat to deliver the brush off, not some low-level paper-pusher.

What was clear to him now, was that no one in the government gave a damn about the fact his daughter had died because of this, and they were taking this as seriously as any other attack upon the nation's cyber infrastructure—not seriously enough. If the government truly cared, they would make certain that these attacks weren't possible. Shut down things like Bitcoin where it was too easy for criminals to hide their money, force machines that had access to the internet to have the latest security patches installed along with anti-virus software.

These things were technically possible, yet the will to enforce them didn't exist, and apparently the death of his daughter wasn't enough to provide that will.

He had to take matters into his own hands.

It would be up to him to find out who was behind this, as he had no faith whatsoever in the government delivering.

The door opened and Davis returned. "So, what do you think?"

Temple frowned. "I think it's exactly as we expected."

Davis nodded, sitting in the chair vacated by the bureaucrat. "Agreed. So what do you want to do?"

"Put a team together. I want every inch of the Internet and Dark Web monitored. Somebody knows something." He sighed, staring at the photo sitting on the corner of his desk of his wife and daughter, the frame a bright white with colorful seashells painstakingly glued in place by his daughter last summer. He reached out and touched her face as tears welled. "I want whoever is behind this dead."

Clayton Hummel Residence
Annapolis, Maryland
Two Years Ago

"I did it."

It was a simple message, the first Clayton Hummel had sent to Melanie in three days. He sat, staring at his screen for hours, waiting for her to logon. Four excruciating hours. He had stolen the data, smuggled it out of NSA headquarters, and wasn't sure what to do with it now that his triumph had been achieved. He now had all the proof he needed to show that he was everything he said he was, that everything he had said was the truth, yet as he sat there thinking about what he had done, he realized there was nothing he could really do with it.

He couldn't upload it to the Internet. That would be the end of him. They would somehow catch him, and his life would be over. He'd be tossed in prison, the key thrown away. And his annoyance at those goading him had passed. He didn't care what those people thought anymore, he only cared about what Melanie thought.

The question was, would this theft be enough proof to her that he was a "man," and worthy of her affections, without having to put it to use?

He prayed it was, because right now he was so terrified, he was absolutely certain he wouldn't have the courage to go any further with this.

His machine beeped and his heart skipped.

"Did what?"

"I got it. The proof."

"What proof?"

"Of everything I said. EVERYTHING."

A smiley face appeared. "I knew you could do it! Did you shove it down those assholes' throats?"

His chest ached and his shoulders slumped. "No. I can't do that. That could put our country at risk."

Her response had him smiling, breathing a sigh of relief. "Good! I wouldn't want you to do that. But how do you feel?"

His smiled spread. "Terrified. Relieved. Kinda proud of myself."

"Do you feel like a man?"

He grinned. "Thor's got nothing on me."

Another smiley face. "I'm so happy you did this."

"I did it for you."

"No, you did it for yourself. You did it to stand up for yourself for the first time in years. I really think this could be a turning point for you...and for us."

His eyes narrowed at the last few words. "What do you mean?"

"I'm in DC. I want to meet you."

His chest tightened as panic set in. He closed his eyes then reached forward, positioning his fingers on the bumps of the F and J keys. "I'd like that."

45

CIA Headquarters
Langley, Virginia
Present Day

"What do you mean we knew about this?"

Chris Leroux frowned at his boss, Leif Morrison, as they sat in the Director's office. "A few months ago, a hacker group claimed to have the ToolKit and offered it for sale. They wanted a million Bitcoins for it."

Morrison cursed. "And someone bought it then did this?"

Leroux shook his head. "No, there were no bidders. It was a ridiculous amount, equivalent to over one hundred million dollars at the time. Frankly, nobody believed them. Neither did we. They gave a sample, but it was all known vulnerabilities. It was as if they didn't really know what they had, so they just released the letter 'A' for example. After a week or so it was taken down, and that was the end of it."

"Until now."

"Yes."

Morrison sighed. "Do we know who this group is?"

"Not much. They're believed to be Russian backed, but have also been linked to the Chinese and Iranians. We believe they're a small group of highly skilled black hatters for hire. They call themselves the Shadow Collective."

"Lovely. And are they behind this ransomware attack? Or does someone else have this ToolKit as well?"

Leroux grunted. "That's the problem with this whole thing. If there was a leak at the NSA, who knows how many people this guy sold it to. Dozens might have it. And that failed auction might not have failed at all. They might have been contacted privately by any number of people who bought it without an exclusivity clause. We just don't know."

"Well, our country came under attack by foreign forces, which makes this at least partially our jurisdiction. I'm not going to just have us sit back and wait for the NSA to try and figure out just how exceptional their screw-up was. These morons actually allowed the data to leave the building. Who the hell does that?"

Leroux shrugged. "In their defense, they couldn't put fake data on the network for him to copy. He knew the ToolKit too well to fall for that. They had to let him copy the information and smuggle it out, though I would have just arrested him the moment he boarded the elevator. They got greedy. They actually were hoping he'd upload it to the Internet so he could show it off to their dummy accounts. That way the charges would be juicier."

"Didn't exactly work out for our country, did it?"

Leroux grunted. "No."

"So, what's your recommendation?"

"We need to know what really happened to that data."

"And how do we do that?"

"I think somebody has to pay a visit to Mr. Hummel."

Morrison nodded. "Have anyone in mind?"

Leroux grinned. "Dylan is in-country and has a valid Homeland cover."

Morrison grunted. "He's not going to be happy if we interrupt his time with Lee Fang."

Leroux rolled his eyes. "With the number of times he's interrupted me and Sher—" Morrison's eyebrows rose and Leroux stopped. "Umm, nothing."

Morrison laughed. "Ahh, to be young again." He pointed at the door. "Go, get your revenge."

Leroux rose with a smile. "Yes, sir!"

Chart House Restaurant
Annapolis, Maryland
Two Years Ago

Clayton Hummel had chosen this restaurant specifically because the tables in the booths could be moved. Too often in his life, he had gone into a restaurant to find he couldn't fit in the booth, the table bolted to the floor. It was embarrassing and humiliating, to say the least. It was why he usually asked for a table if he wasn't sure, never wanting to repeat the humiliation of entering an Outback in Niagara Falls with his sister's family, to leave moments later, battling tears, when he discovered there were no tables, and the booths were too tight.

Now he would scour for photos of any new restaurant online before going, making certain there were either tables, or that those in the booths weren't bolted to the floor.

And this restaurant had been pre-vetted by him, this his go-to place for when any family came to town. It was upscale without being pretentious, perfect for a nice sit-down dinner with family or friends, or in this case, with the woman he loved.

He checked his watch.

Ninety minutes late.

He had eaten all the bread at the table, downed half a dozen glasses of water refilled by the increasingly sympathetic staff, and it was clear he had been stood up.

Something that he had no experience with.

At first, he had been worried, though now he was beyond that.

He knew.

He knew she wasn't coming.

But how long was he supposed to wait before he slunk out of here, humiliated?

An hour ago.

His phone vibrated.

I'm so sorry, my love. I thought I was ready for this, but I'm not.

His heart ached and his eyes burned. He shoved the table away, squirming out of the booth, rushing for the door as he struggled to keep himself together. His waiter opened his mouth to say something but snapped it shut, thinking better of it, about the only thing to have gone right tonight.

Yet it didn't matter.

He would never be back.

He could never return to where he had faced yet another humiliation.

He was done with women.

He was done with it all.

He would never be happy, and because he was such a coward, his only escape would be death.

Tonight he was getting extra bacon on his pizza.

And deleting his social media accounts.

NSA Special Agent Janine Graf pressed her phone tighter against her ear. "He's leaving now. Do you have it?"

"Not yet."

Graf frowned at the response from her partner, Donald Penn, as she watched their target, Clayton Hummel, rush from the restaurant and shuffle down the street toward his car. She did feel slightly sorry for him. After all, she had used him, had made him fall in love with her, and had now shattered his heart. She knew from their long conversations over the past several months, exactly how fragile he was.

It was her job to know.

Thousands of people had been screened before this operation began, and dozens like Hummel had been targeted because they not only had access to sensitive data, but were vulnerable in some way. Some were closet homosexuals still terrified to admit their status to the world, some were gamblers with massive debts they had no hope of paying, and some were lost souls, like Hummel, alone and desperate for love.

He had been assigned to her.

As part of his contract, his online activities were subject to monitoring, therefore finding his digital haunts had been easy. She and her partner had taken over several accounts among the many thousands set up by the NSA for just such operations, giving them instant credibility brand new accounts couldn't.

Men like Hummel were smart, and a new account with no history might make him suspicious. But Melanie Driscoll had been online for years, regularly played World of Warcraft, and her profile only needed some tweaking to fit Hummel's interests.

It had been too easy.

The poor bastard is lonely.

She loved her job, and it *was* necessary as was proven by what was going on this very minute, yet she did harbor some discomfort at what they were doing. The agency ran sting operations like this all the time. Their staff and contractors were constantly tested, tempted, asked casual questions in bars or coffee shops, and the vast majority passed with flying colors.

But Hummel had failed.

Because he had allowed himself to be manipulated, falling for the classic Honeypot trap. If she could manipulate him, then so could a Russian or Chinese agent. And he had given up the goods far too easily. They still weren't certain how he had managed to get the data out of NSA Headquarters, but he had, which meant he had committed a felony.

A lot of them.

He was going to prison, probably for the rest of his life.

He had betrayed his country, all for the love of a woman he had never met.

Idiot.

Why couldn't he have just said no? To his credit, he hadn't posted it on the Internet to prove wrong those who had goaded him into stealing the data in the first place. Fortunately for the country, all those accounts were fake, operated by her and Penn, though there was still the possibility others might have been monitoring.

It *was* the Internet.

No, he hadn't gone that far, but he had still stolen the data, and told her, a complete stranger. If she were a Russian agent, she would have lured him out of his house the moment she found out, then sent someone in to retrieve the data.

Exactly as she had done tonight.

And the damage to the country could be immeasurable.

For this was their ToolKit. What he had stolen was the key to how the NSA gathered its data, how it spied on friend and foe, how it protected the country from harm. If those tools fell into the wrong hands, then their enemies could protect themselves from the snooping the agency was guilty of, or worse, could use those same techniques against America and Americans.

She shuddered at the thought.

"Status?"

"It's not here."

Her eyebrows rose. "Repeat that?"

"It's not here. I can't find it."

"Keep looking."

"There's no point. I've got the USB key right here, and it's blank. Completely wiped."

Graf pursed her lips, watching as Hummel climbed into his car. "He must have moved it to his PC."

"No, I ran a scan. Nothing's been copied on or off since he got home. I'm telling you, it's not here. He must have wiped it."

Graf cursed, starting her car. She pulled from her spot and gunned it ahead, steering in front of Hummel before he could drive away. She climbed out, her phone pressed against one ear, her free hand reaching into her pocket for her badge. She didn't bother with her gun. She knew Hummel. She knew him better than he knew himself.

And he was no killer.

He didn't even own a gun.

"You're positive."

"Absolutely." There was a pause. "Could he have just lied to you?"

She shook her head as Hummel rolled down his window. "No, we were monitoring his station. We know he copied the data. So what the hell happened to it?" She stared at Hummel, his eyes red, his cheeks visibly stained, even in the dim light from the street lamps. "Keep looking." She hung up and stuffed her phone into her pocket. "Mr. Clayton Hummel, I'm Special Agent Janine Graf, NSA. I'm going to need you to come with me."

Hummel blanched as his jaw dropped.

Now that's a pretty guilty look for a man who didn't steal anything.

"Wh-what for?"

"It's about a woman named Melanie Driscoll."

Hummel went even whiter. Any more and she feared he'd pass out. "She w-was supposed to meet me for dinner." His shoulders slumped. "She never showed." He brightened slightly. "Did something happen to her?"

You poor dear.

He was so desperate for any possibility other than having been stood up, that the very thought she might be hurt somewhere actually held some appeal.

Time to end it.

She pulled out a separate phone and brought up the text message she had sent him earlier. She held it up. "I'm Melanie Driscoll."

He stared at the screen, his eyes widening in disbelief, his head shaking. "No, no, no, no, no!" Each successive denial got louder, and Graf took a step back, her hand reaching to rest on her hip holster.

"Mr. Hummel, I'll need you to calm down."

Hummel stared at her, tears rolling down his cheeks, his nose wet and beginning to ooze over his upper lip. "Why? Why would you do that to me? *How* could you do that to me? I did nothing wrong! Why!"

"Standard operation, sir. We were testing you, as per your contract." She motioned toward the door. "I'll need you to step out now."

He pushed the door open and turned in his seat, struggling to lift each leg out as his entire body shook, his shoulders racked with sobs. He shoved to his feet then caught his breath, staring at her. "I didn't mean to do it. I only took it to prove to her, to you, that I was…" His voice faded as he turned away, too ashamed to continue.

But Graf was barely listening anymore.

I only took it to prove to her…

Her eyes narrowed.

So he did take the data.

She stared at him. "Mr. Hummel, where is the data you stole?"

His shoulders slumped and he dropped onto the hood of his car, the suspension protesting. "At home."

"Where? Specifically."

"On a memory stick I took from work. Take me there and I'll show you."

"We already have an agent at your house. He says the memory stick is empty."

Hummel's eyes widened as he looked up from staring at the ground. "But that's impossible. I was going to show it to her, I mean you, tonight, if you wanted to see it." He blushed, turning away. "It was going to be my excuse to get you to come back to my place." His voice cracked. "It was all a lie." He sighed. "I'm going to die alone."

Graf resisted the urge to reach out and comfort him. She felt horrible for him, yet he was guilty of stealing state secrets. Of espionage. Of so many things.

But where was the data?

"You should just move in."

CIA Special Agent Dylan Kane winced as he took a chunk off his chin with his razor. He stared at his girlfriend, Lee Fang, in the mirror. "Huh?"

"You're bleeding."

"You surprised me."

"Judging from the look on your face, I'd have said shocked."

He quickly finished, rinsing off his razor before tapping it dry on a hand towel, sensing this was about to get serious. He loved Fang. She was probably the first woman he had ever truly loved. He had been with dozens if not hundreds of women, but none had captured his heart, and none had ever been meant to be true relationships. As an agent, he slept with lots of women for the job, and as a broken soul, he had used booze and women to drown out his loneliness, his isolation.

Until Fang.

She had healed him, and he had never been happier. He stared at her scar, still fresh from when she had been shot recently, then his eyes drifted to the rest of her naked body as she toweled off.

My God, she is incredible.

She was tight. *Very* tight. Ripped abs, toned all over but not to the point where she looked like a man. She was just in incredible shape. Former Chinese Special Forces, she had been forced to betray her country in order to save it from corrupt generals supporting a coup attempt in the United States. She had been living in here ever since, essentially in witness protection on a grateful American government's pension, going slowly batty until they had recognized in each other their mutual need for companionship—companionship where their secret lives could be shared freely.

He hated the lying.

Especially to his loved ones. His parents had only recently discovered what he did for a living, and it had mended fences with his father broken long ago. It shouldn't have been necessary, but his father was a stubborn ass sometimes—all the time—though their relationship was now the best it had been since he had left the Army to join the cover company arranged for him by the CIA—Shaw's of London. He was an insurance investigator, allowing him to travel the world on business, leading a flashy life investigating multi-million dollar frauds.

All the while actually spying or killing for the American people.

Yet with Fang, it was different. She had been in the business, she understood the need for secrecy, but because he had been the agent sent in to extract her, she knew what he did for a living. It was so nice, at the end of a mission, to come to a place he felt safe, with someone he felt completely comfortable with, and not have to give the cover story of another tedious investigation.

He grabbed Fang's towel and pulled her against him. "Okay, you shocked me. But in a good way."

She stared up at him, her eyes glistening, then she dropped her head, pressing her forehead against his chest. "It was just an idea."

He reached down and tipped her chin up with a gentle press of his thumb. He placed a soft kiss on her forehead. "A great idea."

She smiled.

And goose bumps rushed over his entire body. Not experienced in true love, he wasn't sure if this was a typical response, but he just wanted to make this woman happy. And when he succeeded, it was a euphoric feeling that would envelop him. He smiled back and kissed her on the lips, gently at first, then with a growing urgency. She hopped up, wrapping her legs around his waist, her arms around his neck, and he stepped over to the wall, pressing her back against it as their need became urgent.

She gasped as he found her, his moan drowning her out as they attacked each other with a feral intensity that made it all the more exciting, and all the more rapid. Only minutes later they were gasping for breath, both spent, both totally satisfied, and both needing to shower again.

Fang grinned as she disentangled. "That was fun."

Kane stepped back and leaned against the bathroom vanity. "Oh yeah." He wiped the sweat from his brow. "So, umm, about that whole moving in thing."

Fang picked up the forgotten towel. "What do you think?"

Kane reached out a hand and she took it, stepping closer, but not so close that a wagging participant might say hello. "I practically live here anyway."

"You do."

"When I get back from a mission, I check my mail, grab a few things, and come here."

"If you don't come here first."

"Exactly. I'm basically paying rent for nothing."

"I hate to waste money."

"And it would save me time, so we could actually spend more together."

"Wasting time should be a crime."

He paused. "I wonder if Langley will object."

Fang's glow dimmed. "Would they?"

He shrugged. "I don't know. I doubt an operational agent has ever shacked up with a Chinese special operator on the run from her own government."

She rested her cheek against his chest and sighed. "What if they say no?"

Kane wrapped his arms around her. "Then I'll resign."

She pushed away and stared up at him. "You would do that for me?"

He couldn't believe he was saying it, but he was. He adored this woman, and would do anything to make her happy, even give up a job he loved.

It shocked him.

And frightened him a little.

He smiled. "Absolutely."

She patted his chest. "Let's hope it doesn't come to that. You'd be miserable if you couldn't kill people or blow things up."

He grinned. "I could always become a paid assassin."

She chuckled. "We could partner. The husband and wife hit squad."

He smiled and she flushed. "I like the sound of that."

She pushed away slightly, her cheeks still burning. "Let's try living together first." She dropped her eyes. "But so do I."

He pulled her close again and kissed her. She thrust her hips away and he laughed. "Yeah, yeah, I know. We'll be at this all day if we don't stop now."

She grinned. "I like the sound of that, too." She raised a finger. "But! You promised you were going to help me rearrange the living room."

He paused, pursing his lips. "You know, if we're going to live together, maybe we should get a new place. Something a little bigger." He reached over and put on his watch, snapping the clasp shut. "We could get a two or three bedroom, set up an office, a home gym. A home theatre?" He grinned.

"Sounds good to me. Would we stay in Philly?"

He shrugged. "We can if you want. I like it here, but we could live anywhere. Langley might like me a little closer. And I know my folks wouldn't want me moving any farther away."

His CIA-issued watch sent a discrete pulsing electric shock into his wrist, notifying him of an urgent communication. He frowned.

"What?"

He shook his wrist with the watch, and she nodded. He entered the coded sequence of button presses around the sides. A message scrolled across the crystal.

Contact CL immediately.

He smiled. "It's Chris. Something urgent." Chris Leroux was the best friend he had in the world. Fang was probably closer to him now, though friends and lovers should be in two different categories. He had met Leroux in high school, an insecure, brilliant teenager constantly picked on and bullied. Kane had been the jock, and was struggling with his grades. Leroux ended up tutoring him, and they had become friends, and Kane Leroux's protector. They had lost touch after high school, reuniting by accident at Langley, both working for the Agency unbeknownst to each other.

Leroux was probably his only friend in the world besides Fang. He was friendly with some of his old Delta Force buddies from Bravo Team, though those types of friendships usually fell to the wayside when you became a CIA operator.

But Leroux was someone he always tried to keep in touch with, and with his friend's brilliance recognized through promotions, they often had the opportunity to work together, Leroux sometimes the voice at the other end of his earpiece.

Fang climbed back in the shower as Kane grabbed his phone, calling Leroux. "Hey, buddy, what's up?"

"We need you to pay a visit to someone. Off the books."

Kane grinned. "Those are always my favorite. Send me the details. I've got some business to finish up here then I'll get right on it."

"Already done."

"Great. Talk to you soon." He ended the call then stepped into the shower.

"Am I your unfinished business?"

He smiled, taking Fang into his arms. "Yup."

Clayton Hummel Residence
Annapolis, Maryland
Two Years Ago

Janine "Melanie Driscoll" Graf shook her head at her partner. Teams had been going over Clayton Hummel's house for days, and had turned up nothing. He was squeaky clean. No classified data had been taken home, physical or otherwise, and his computer logs were clean. There was no evidence he had ever possessed the stolen data, or shared it with anyone.

It made no sense.

They had the logs from his work computer proving he had transferred the data to an external device. There was no doubt it had happened. That device had a unique identification code installed by the manufacturer, and it matched the device they had found beside his home computer. There was no evidence it had ever been copied to his machine, which agreed with his own initial statements before he lawyered up. They had even found the small piece of tape he had used to hide the microSD card under his watchband, the tear matching exactly the roll of tape in his desk drawer at the office.

Everything he had told her matched with what they had found.

Except that the memory card was empty.

If he had never stolen the data, was it just pride that made him stick to his story? That might make sense if Melanie Driscoll actually existed, but she didn't. She was a digital fabrication. There was no woman to prove his manhood to, except, perhaps, her. She didn't get a chance to play that card, however, once the lawyers got involved. Now her access was limited, and toying with his emotions was no longer on the table.

But why hadn't his lawyers just said he never stole the data, that it was just a boast to a woman he was trying to impress? That might actually get him out of it. He could have made up a story that he copied the files to do some work elsewhere in the building, then decided against it, wiping the memory card clean. He could have claimed he snuck it out of the building as a security test, and was going to report his findings.

There were so many possible stories he could have come up with, yet he hadn't. He had stuck to his story that he had taken the data, and that it should be on the card.

And without any evidence to back up his claims, their case was going nowhere, fast.

They might even have to let him go.

The embarrassment to the agency might not be worth the effort to prosecute. The man wasn't a national security threat if he didn't work there. He had proven he could be manipulated, so his security clearance had already been revoked, and if nothing had been stolen, her supervisor was already suggesting it all be swept under the rug.

That decision was above her pay grade, but she still couldn't understand what had happened to the data. If he had indeed stolen it, and he hadn't wiped it, then someone had.

But who?

"Penny for your thoughts?"

She glanced at her partner, Donald Penn. "They're worth a hell of a lot more than that."

He chuckled. "Nickle?"

"That's better." She sighed. "I'm just trying to figure out what happened to the data. I mean, we know it was copied onto the device, we know the device is now blank, and we know he continues to claim he not only copied it, but didn't delete it. If we believe him, then someone else must have deleted it."

"Or it never properly copied."

She shook her head. "No, he said he double-checked."

"Maybe he was wrong?"

She eyed Penn. "He's a computer expert. Do you really think he could be wrong about something as simple as whether or not some files had been copied?"

Penn shrugged. "Hey, he was nervous, made a mistake, and the data either didn't get copied, or it somehow got deleted. Maybe he was exposed to a magnet or something."

"No, the techs said the device was deliberately zero-filled. If it were a magnet, it wouldn't be completely uniform."

"So we're back to some mystery person getting in here between the time he walked out the door for his hot date with you"—she gave him a look—"and me arriving ten minutes later."

She frowned. "I can't see any other option."

Penn sighed. "Me neither, if you discount the possibility he's lying, which I don't." He leaned in closer. "I think he's still got the hots for this Melanie chick, and has transferred his feelings to you. I think he wants to impress you with his manliness, then impress his manliness upon you."

"You're a pig."

"That's why you love me."

"I'd as soon go out with Clay before I'd go out with you."

"Oh, 'Clay' is it?" His eyes narrowed and he tapped his chin. "I think you like this guy."

Graf growled. "You're impossible. Can you be professional for once in your life?"

"That's not a denial. How could you possibly be attracted to a man that, well, big?"

Graf surprised herself with the vehemence of her response. "What kind of Neanderthal are you? Who cares if he's overweight? Does that make him any less of a human being? And your wife is black! How would you like it if people discriminated against you guys because of that? Discrimination is discrimination, whether it's racial, sexual, cultural, or physical. Clay—Hummel—is a very nice, very lonely man, who deserves happiness, and we used that against him, and forgive me if I don't feel good about it." Her head spun, glaring at the room of NSA staff that had stopped what they were doing to watch the tirade. "Back to work!"

The room resumed, and Penn leaned in. "Sorry, I was just joking around. You're right. It was wrong. *I* was wrong."

Graf glanced up at him and grunted. "Sometimes you're an asshole."

"Hey, have you and my wife been talking?"

Graf growled then punched him gently on the shoulder. "Let's get out of here. We need to figure out if someone else was in this house. Maybe some neighbors have some cameras."

Alta Mesa Memorial Park Cemetery
Palo Alto, California
Present Day

Franklin Temple climbed into the rear of the limousine, the emotions inside buried deep. The paparazzi hadn't left him alone, despite his office's request for privacy. People loved to see those more successful than them suffer, delighting in the misery of those like him. If it weren't true, then there would be no market for the photos, and the paparazzi wouldn't bother.

It disgusted him.

There were times he felt Western civilization deserved to crumble into the annals of history, and this moment was one of those. If people truly did want to see the photos of a grieving father burying his seven-year-old daughter, then they were disgusting pigs that deserved whatever happened to them. This obsession with celebrity was destroying the West, and this hatred of success, as if he had somehow cheated or stolen from others to achieve what he had, was insanity.

He had worked his ass off, creating his first company when he was twelve years old, selling it at fifteen for over ten million dollars. He was now personally worth billions through hard work and sacrifice. He donated hundreds of millions to charity, yet did it quietly. He paid his people generously, treated them well, and his domestic staff all had good salaries, health coverage, generous paid vacations, and pensions.

He was a good person.

And he was part of the one percent that was vilified by morons who couldn't grasp the concept that most of their jobs and those of their parents, existed due to people like him. They couldn't understand that corporate America, the large corporations like his, needed suppliers. Those suppliers were often medium and small businesses, even the mom and pop shops that these Occupy protesters championed.

Did they not understand that every day his company ordered thousands of doughnuts, thousands of muffins, thousands of pounds of fruit and vegetables for smoothies and juicing junkies? These came from local farms, from small businesses that landed the contract when his company was small, and grew along with him. Big business fueled mid-sized which in turn fueled the small. Wipe out big business, and the economy would crumble.

"Let's get out of here."

"Yes, sir."

His driver put the car in gear and pulled away from the curb, scattering the photographers. He turned his head and smiled as two large black SUVs, owned by his security team, blocked the road behind him, preventing the vermin from following. He leaned his head back and closed his eyes, sighing. The window separating him from his driver hummed closed, giving him the privacy he so desperately needed right now.

His daughter's laughing face was seared on the back of his eyelids, her smile inescapable since the moment she had died, the only image to ever replace it cruelly that of her dying moments.

Why didn't I insist on being with her?

She had died alone while he had played on a computer.

That wasn't fair.

He was trying to save her life in the only way he knew how, yet he couldn't shake the feeling she had died, wondering where her daddy was.

His own doctors had examined her and the autopsy results, confirming the initial diagnosis, and also confirming that she probably would have survived had she received prompt attention when they arrived.

The ransomware attack had killed her.

There was no doubt of that anymore.

His phone rang, automatically paired with the car's Bluetooth, restricted to the rear cabin. He glanced at the display, the caller ID indicating it was Tanya Davis. She had been one of the few permitted at the funeral, and was likely in a vehicle behind him. She had taken a separate car, insisting he needed his privacy, though she would be the only person welcome with him at this moment.

And for her to call him at this time, meant she had something important that couldn't wait.

He reached up and pressed a button on the roof, taking the call. "Yes, Tanya?"

"Sir, I'm sorry to interrupt. But the specialist you wanted has arrived. He has suggested you meet somewhere other than one of your properties."

A sneer at the prospects of what this meeting meant, threatened to mar his face. "When?"

"As soon as you're ready."

"I'm ready now."

Bureau 121

North Korean Cyberwarfare Agency

Classified Location

Two Years Ago

"I have it."

Colonel Park Ji-Sung sat forward in his chair, his phone pressed hard against his ear. "Are you certain?"

"Absolutely."

Park leaned back, a smile spreading across his face. Agent K was his man, his mole within the mighty American's National Security Agency apparatus, and after years of grooming, it was finally paying off.

In a way he could never have imagined.

The ToolKit!

It was an impossible dream. Never could they have hoped to gain access to the rumored set of tools accumulated by the NSA. Yes, agencies across the world used the vulnerabilities in browsers and operating systems to try and steal or monitor data, but only the Americans had the resources to discover those that hadn't yet been acknowledged, at least to the extent they had been thought to.

He had never intended to use Agent K for such an operation, in fact, he had expected he might not be useful for several more years, but they had caught a lucky break.

And now they had the ToolKit.

"When will we have it?"

"You already do. I uploaded it to one of our secure servers as soon as I could. Check your secure email."

Park tapped at his keyboard and entered a ridiculously complex password.

And smiled.

He clicked on the link then began scrolling through the thousands of files. "It will take us months to go through all of this."

"Years, I think, to fully understand it all."

"You have done a great service for your country."

"Thank you, sir."

"Now, what is your status?"

"The Americans have no idea. I say we let things play out for now. As far as those investigating are concerned, they think the data is contained, and at this moment, have no idea there has been a breach. I think I can still be of use here."

"Very well. The moment you think otherwise, execute your extraction plan. We can't risk you getting caught."

"Understood."

Los Altos Hills, California
Present Day

Franklin Temple moved to the far corner of his limo as the door opened. Tanya Davis climbed in, followed by a man who exuded masculine confidence. He was solid, well-kempt in an impeccable suit, and his chiseled face was emotionless.

Just as he was.

"Mr. Temple, this is Mr. Simmons."

Simmons reached out and shook Temple's hand. "Sir, it's an honor."

Temple nodded, the man's voice deep, his manner military. He wasn't surprised. He had requested his security chief find someone who could deal with the problem, and his chief was ex-military. It made sense that he'd bring in someone he knew. "You're aware of the situation?"

"Yes, sir. Your daughter was murdered by those responsible for the ransomware attack earlier this week, and you would like them brought to justice."

Murdered. Good. He understands.

"Yes."

"I just need to know what manner of justice you mean."

Temple kept the smile from his face. This man wanted to know what his Rules of Engagement were. What limitations under which he was operating. But what if his desires went further than this man was willing to go?

72

Then you'll find someone else.

"They'll never see the inside of a courtroom."

"Understood. I have a team that will do the wetwork, plus a tech team. Your security chief and I have already worked out the particulars on our fee, and it's my understanding that all of our expenses will be covered, and there are no limits to those expenses."

"Correct."

"Then, sir, I suggest you let me do my job."

"I want to be kept informed every step of the way."

"If you wish."

"I've had a team set up offsite that are investigating the hacks. They are some of the finest cybersecurity specialists in the world. You will want to coordinate with them."

"With all due respect, sir, the fewer who know I'm involved, the better."

"Agreed. Miss Davis will be your liaison with them. When they discover anything, she will feed the information to you, and vice versa. If you discover some piece of intel that could help, let her know, she'll pass it on to the team." He leaned forward. "Have you done this sort of thing before?"

He nodded. "My team has dealt with problems in the past."

"And you have no problem dealing with whoever is at the other end of this?"

"As long as they aren't children, and aren't Americans, then no. If they are, then you will be provided with their identities and proof of their crimes, and they will be delivered to the authorities, involuntarily repatriated if necessary."

"So you have limits."

Simmons stared at him. "Of course. We're not assassins for hire. We're problem solvers. We kill bad people, and only bad people. If you wanted us to eliminate a business rival, we wouldn't be having this conversation. But that's not the case here. These hackers have been operating with impunity for too long. It's time they were taken down. Permanently."

Temple allowed a smile to form. "I think, Mr. Simmons, that we are on the exact same page." He extended his hand. "I don't think we shall meet again."

Agent K's Residence
Two Years Ago

"You have the sample?"

"Yes. Very impressive. How did you get it?"

Agent K smiled at the screen. Dealing with amateurs was amusing at times, and because of it, dangerous. Just because someone was successful at cybercrime, didn't mean they were wise in the ways of the trade. The world of espionage was dangerous, and his world involved guns and garrotes, brass knuckles and knives, not bits and bytes and chunks of illicit code. These people were in over their heads, but they had money, which was all he cared about.

He had hit the mother lode, and he intended to cash in, securing a future always uncertain under the Dear Leader. He could be recalled to the homeland at any moment, but now that he had stumbled upon one of the most valuable chunks of ones and zeroes in the world, none of that mattered anymore.

He had found the ToolKit.

He tapped away at his keyboard. "Does it matter?"

"No, I suppose not. How do you want to do this?"

"Twenty-five thousand Bitcoins. Half now, half when I deliver the rest of the files."

"Just a second."

He stared at his other screen, his Bitcoin account displayed. It jumped by 12,500 coins. The column showing what that was in US Dollars leaped. Over three million. He leaned closer to his keyboard.

"Received. Stand by." He tapped away, the data rapidly transferring from an encrypted server on the Dark Web to his contact's own server hidden in the illicit cloud. "Transfer complete."

"One moment while we verify."

His knee bounced rapidly and his finger tapped on the palmrest of his ergonomic keyboard.

The Bitcoin account soared again, and he flopped back in his chair.

"A pleasure doing business with you."

The display went dead before he could reply.

He stared at the US Dollar total, his jaw dropping as the realization of what had just occurred set in.

Now the worrying ends.

The doorbell rang.

Penn Residence
Argonne Hills, Maryland
Two Years Ago

"Oh, hi, Janine, come on in!"

Janine Graf smiled at Grace Penn as she stepped inside, closing the door behind her. She sniffed. "My God, Grace, that smells good. What is it?"

"Some good ol' Creole cooking. My grandma's recipe. Now please tell me you have time to stick around and try some."

Graf followed her partner's wife into the kitchen, her mouth watering as she searched for an excuse not to. She hated interrupting family life, and though her partner had no children, Grace's prominent bulge indicated that status was about to change. "I wouldn't want to impose."

"Nonsense. You're my husband's partner. You're family."

Graf smiled. It felt good to hear those words. Her own family was on the other side of the country, and she rarely saw them. And she was chronically single. Few men were willing to put up with a woman who could kick their ass, and was rarely home. She was married to her job, as Penn had been, which was why she was surprised when he had returned from New Orleans a year ago with Grace in tow.

According to him, his annual pilgrimage to the great city had taken place every year since Katrina, interrupted only once during the outbreak a few years ago where the containment failure had threatened the entire planet. The city had bounced back once again, and Penn's

77

annual trips had resumed. Little had she known he had been going down to see a woman.

Grace was fantastic. Everything she imagined Penn would be attracted to, and they certainly seemed happy. They had been married shortly thereafter, Graf the best "man," and now there was a bun in the oven.

The perfect family.

Graf leaned over a pot of something wonderful and inhaled. "Okay, there should be a law against something that smells that good. What do you put in it?"

"I think it's fentanyl. The damned stuff is addictive."

Graf chuckled at Penn as he rounded the corner. "Whatever it is, she's a genius."

"Don't I know it." Penn gave his wife a quick kiss then smiled at his partner. "What brings you here?"

She gestured toward the stove. "Your wife's cooking."

Penn sat on one of the stools lining the breakfast bar, and Graf did the same.

"Actually, I have news."

Penn's eyes narrowed. "What?"

"You're not going to like it."

Grace paused. "Should I leave?"

Graf shook her head. "No, it's okay." She turned back to Penn. "The case has been dropped. He's been released."

Penn's eyes shot wide. "Are you kidding me!" He flicked his hand toward her. "Well, you called it. What was the reasoning?"

"Not worth the embarrassment to the agency. He's being allowed to resign from his contracting agency rather than be fired, and he won't be allowed to work on any government contracts for the rest of his life, but, essentially, he's a free man."

Penn sighed, shaking his head. "Unbelievable. The bastard's guilty, and we're just letting him go."

Graf grunted. "It's not the first time, and it won't be the last."

"So what are we going to do?"

Graf shrugged. "I don't know about you, but I'm going to loosen my belt and tuck into your wife's cooking."

Clayton Hummel Residence
Annapolis, Maryland
Two Years Ago

Clayton Hummel picked up the pace slightly, there nothing more annoying than a doorbell rung a second time. He opened the door and smiled.

"Hey, Clay, we were beginning to worry about you!"

Hummel's eyebrows rose as he took the pizza from the delivery man. "Huh?"

"Well, you haven't ordered for a couple of weeks. Some of us at the shop were thinking we should call the police."

Hummel forced a chuckle. "I was visiting family." He began to close the door and was given a thumbs up.

"Next time warn us!" The young man laughed and Hummel closed the door, locking it. He carried the box into the family room and sat it on his ottoman as he snapped open a can of Diet Pepsi, pouring it over the already waiting glass, filled to the brim with ice. He pressed the button on his remote control, a missed episode of Game of Thrones resuming. He pulled the ottoman closer then lifted the pizza, placing it on his legs as he rested them on the cushioned surface. Flipping open the lid, he smiled at the cheesy perfection in front of him.

Life was getting back to normal.

To hell with Melanie, or whatever her damned name was. He didn't need a woman in his life. He had everything he needed here. And now he had money. Enough to keep him going until the day he died.

And as he took his first bite, savoring the burst of flavors, he had little doubt that day would be coming soon.

Clayton Hummel Residence
Annapolis, Maryland
Present Day

Dylan Kane examined the front porch of the nondescript home his subject lived at. According to the file sent to him, Clayton Hummel had lived here for over ten years, paid his taxes on time, and his only blemish was the fact he had been suspected of leaking the NSA's ToolKit to persons unknown.

Yet they had never actually found any evidence of the crime beyond the copying of the files.

And his confession.

The classic Honeypot operation probably stretched back to when the first Neanderthal cave decided to spy on the next. It was effective if you targeted the right person, and from the file photo he had seen, he could understand why it had worked. What was interesting was the variation employed by the NSA agent in charge, Janine Graf.

Hummel had never met her.

Had never seen the sexy woman at the other end of the conversation.

Instead, he had seen a larger person, like him, and had fallen into the trap.

Graf was good.

She had recognized that for Hummel, it wasn't sex that would work. It was the promise of companionship, of the end to a crippling loneliness. He actually felt kind of bad for the guy. Everything he had read suggested he was a model employee, a little arrogant online, perhaps a little overconfident in his abilities, though his evals had all been excellent, so perhaps his confidence wasn't misplaced.

But as was too often true when it came to techies, he was a loner. Kane thought of his friend Leroux, and how lonely he had been before he had met Sherrie. And Sherrie was the classic Honeypot. Director Morrison had given her the task of seducing Leroux, to see if he would spill his secrets in exchange for sex with an incredibly gorgeous woman. If he failed, his career was over. If he passed, he'd be promoted.

He had passed.

How, Kane would never know.

But in the process, Leroux had fallen in love with Sherrie, just as Hummel had for the imaginary Melanie Driscoll. The difference was Sherrie had developed feelings for Leroux as well, even requesting to be taken off the assignment. When Leroux had discovered the betrayal, he had holed up in his apartment, bitter and hurt. Kane had forced the two of them back together, and the rest was history.

Leroux had passed the test.

Hummel had failed.

He rang the doorbell again, this time adding several firm raps to the door. Hummel was home, Langley confirming his phone of record was located there, and his Netflix account was active on a device identified as his Smart TV. The fact the man wasn't answering wasn't much of a surprise, loners rarely coming to the door voluntarily.

He heard a noise, then the curtain covering the window moved.

"Clayton Hummel, I'm Special Agent Kane, Homeland Security. I need to speak with you."

A deadbolt clicked and the door opened slightly, a large man peering at him. "Yes?"

Kane held up his ID. "Special Agent Kane, Homeland. May I come in?"

"Umm, do you have a warrant?"

Kane smiled pleasantly. "No, we don't need to get the courts involved. I just have a few questions to ask you, then I'll be on my way."

Hummel began to close the door. "Come back when you have a warrant."

Good thing I'm not actually Homeland.

Kane shoved the door open, stepping inside, pushing Hummel backward with a palm to the chest. He closed the door behind him, locking it.

"What the hell do you think you're doing? I have rights, you know!"

"Yes, and so did the victims of this week's cyberattack."

Hummel froze. "What does that have to do with me?"

Kane smiled, stepping deeper into the home, all the blinds closed, all the light artificial including the glow of the large television, Stranger Things on pause. "Oh, I think you know what I'm talking about."

"I have no idea." Hummel followed him, his anger morphing into near panic as Kane continued through the house. It was surprisingly tidy, Hummel likely employing a maid service, and judging by the stack of four pizza boxes on the kitchen island, she was due in three days.

"What do you do for a living, Mr. Hummel?"

"I'm in cybersecurity."

"Really? Where?"

"Umm, I'm currently between jobs."

Kane sat in one of the kitchen chairs, removing his Glock and placing it on the table. He motioned toward it. "I hope you don't mind, it's been bugging me all day."

Hummel's eyes widened, but he said nothing.

Kane resumed their conversation. "You've been between jobs for two years now, haven't you?"

Hummel leaned against the island, his face turning red, beads of sweat forming on his forehead.

Is he nervous, or just out of shape?

"What of it?" Hummel sat with a huff, the chair creaking, Kane glancing at the legs for a moment.

"You seem to be leading a fairly comfortable lifestyle for someone who has been unemployed for two years."

Hummel flushed, his eyes darting away, and this time Kane knew it had nothing to do with his lack of conditioning. "I have savings."

"Yes. I checked your accounts. It looks like you had a very large deposit made two years ago into your account. Care to explain that?"

Hummel stared at the linoleum, the pattern a tacky design straight out of Leave it to Beaver.

"Well?"

"I, umm, can't."

"Maybe I can." Hummel stole a quick glance at him before returning his attention to the floor. "I think you sold the data you stole, and that deposit was your payoff."

Hummel's eyes widened, and he stared at Kane for a moment. "No! That's not at all what happened."

"I don't believe you."

Hummel bit his thumbnail. "I-I don't care what you believe."

Kane moved the gun an inch to the right, the barrel aimed directly at Hummel's prodigious stomach. "You should."

Hummel stared at the weapon, unblinking. "Listen, I really want to help you, but I can't. I'm"—he sighed, reaching up and massaging his temples—"I'm not allowed to."

Kane resisted the urge to react. It was an unexpected response. An interesting response.

Not allowed to.

The word "allowed" was the key here. "Allowed" implied he had been told by someone not to talk about it, but "allowed" also implied by telling him, Hummel would be breaking some sort of rule or law. If a criminal told you to not tell anyone, you wouldn't tell a law enforcement official that you weren't "allowed" to tell him anything, you'd say you "couldn't" or you "can't" or even more specific, "*they* said I couldn't" or the ever-popular "*they'll* kill me."

But no, Hummel had specifically said, "I'm not allowed to."

Kane stared at him for a moment. "Who told you you're not allowed to tell me where you got the money?"

"I-I can't say." He bit his nail again.

"Was it who you sold the data to?"

Hummel shook his head. "I never sold it."

"But according to the agent you were ready to spill your secrets to, you admitted to stealing the data, then plead ignorance as to what happened to it after you left the building."

His eyes widened, and he stared at Kane. "She said that?"

Kane nodded. "Yes."

"I-I didn't think she'd be allowed."

There was that word again. "Allowed." But why would it apply to an NSA agent? It made no sense. Not in the context of Hummel being a traitor to his country.

Kane paused, a thought occurring to him.

And he smiled.

"They gave you a deal, didn't they?"

Hummel looked away, biting his nail again.

Bingo.

"You stole the data, they covered it up, but couldn't let you work there anymore, so they gave you a deal to keep your mouth shut."

Hummel continued the silent routine, though his lack of denials was enough confirmation for Kane.

"You're aware of the ransomware attack?"

"Of course."

"Are you aware that the method used was the very one you developed two years ago, and was included in the ToolKit you stole?"

He nodded.

"Do you have an explanation?"

He shook his head.

"Care to theorize?"

Hummel glanced at him for a moment, then back at the floor. "Well, umm, if I had to hazard a guess, I'd say someone discovered the vulnerability, just like I did, and decided to exploit it."

"Using the exact same code you developed?"

Hummel's eyes widened. "Excuse me?"

"You developed the code that could exploit the bug. Are you telling me they not only discovered the bug, but created, line for line, the same code to exploit it?"

Hummel's jaw dropped and he stared at Kane, his tasty thumb forgotten. "Are you serious?"

Kane nodded. "Yes."

Hummel stared at the gun as Kane watched, the man clearly reevaluating everything. He let him play it out rather than interrupt him, Hummel finally figuring out more was going on here than he realized.

He looked at Kane. "Someone else must have stolen the ToolKit."

"I've been assured that is now impossible."

"Of course they'd say that."

Kane smiled. "Of course they would, but they assure me that the current version of the ToolKit code surrounding this attack doesn't match, and hasn't matched since you left. Someone else on your team modified it. That means that the version used this week, is the version you wrote, and it was the copy you stole."

Hummel rose, heading for the fridge. He opened it and pulled out a Diet Pepsi. He held it up. "Want one?"

Kane shook his head. "I'm a Diet Dr. Pepper man myself."

Hummel reached in the fridge and produced a can of Kane's preferred soda, sliding it across the table toward him. Hummel returned to his chair, opening his can with a hiss, Kane doing the same.

"Thanks." Kane took a long swig, his Adam's apple bouncing greedily. He hadn't realized how thirsty he was until presented with the opportunity to quench it.

"You do realize what this means, don't you?"

Kane stared at Hummel. "Let's pretend I don't."

Hummel chuckled. "*If* we assume it was my copy of the data that was used to perpetrate the attack, and *if* I didn't sell it to anyone, and *if* the agent who searched my house and claimed that the memory stick was blank is telling the truth, then someone stole the data between the time I left the house, and the time the agent arrived."

Kane nodded, already having come to that conclusion, though there were too many ifs in there for his liking. "And you didn't tell anyone you were doing this."

"Of course not, I'm not an idiot."

Well, yes, you are. You fell for the trap.

Kane let it go. "Then how did anyone know to actually be here at that precise moment, with the equipment necessary to not only copy the data, but wipe it as well." Kane leaned forward, pushing the Glock aside. "And why bother wiping it at all?"

Hummel drained his soda. "I've been asking myself that very question for two years."

Kane leaned back in his chair. "And have you found an answer?"

"I didn't until today."

Kane put his can on the table. "What changed?"

Hummel stared at him. "I've figured out the motive."

"Which is?"

"Two years ago somebody wiped the memory stick. That made it look like I was lying about either stealing the data, which they had proof of, or what I had done with it after I left the building. The fact it had been wiped was the only inconsistency that I couldn't explain. It made me look like I was lying."

"And?"

"And now, here I am, two years later, getting a visit from someone who is *definitely* not Homeland, accusing me of selling that same data."

"So you're saying—"

"Someone stole the data, and wanted to plant the seed, two years ago, that I lied, so that I'd be blamed when it was eventually used."

Kane grunted, Hummel's theory plausible. "Any idea who?"

"I've got an idea, but you'll never believe it."

"Humor me."

When Kane heard who Hummel thought was behind this, he pursed his lips, staring at the man. "I think you might be right."

Bureau 121

North Korean Cyberwarfare Agency

Classified Location

Colonel Park Ji-Sung looked up as his aide entered his office. "So? What have you found?"

Captain Tann closed the door, glancing around the room as if to make sure they were alone. "Colonel, you were right. It *is* the same code from the ToolKit retrieved by Agent K two years ago."

"Are you certain?"

"Absolutely. There is no doubt. One of the previously unknown exploits had a tool written to make use of it, and that code was found, line for line, in the infected computers we've analyzed."

Park leaned back in his chair, pinching the bridge of his nose as he removed his glasses. "Could there have been another leak?"

"Possibly. Without Agent K at the NSA anymore, we can't be sure. Our other operatives have had no indication of a breach, but it's not like the Americans would publicize this."

"They may have no choice."

Tann's eyes narrowed. "What do you mean?"

"I think the Americans need to be taken down a peg, as they might say."

A smile slowly spread across Tann's face. "You're going to leak the story."

Park nodded. "We've already prepared for this eventuality. Execute the option that makes it look like the Russians leaked the story. I want this in the hands of every news organization in the world before the hour is out."

"Right away, sir."

Park raised a finger as Tann headed for the door. "And send a team to collect Agent K. It's only a matter of time before the Americans figure out he's behind this. It could get uncomfortable for us should he be questioned."

Tann paused, his eyebrows rising. "You want him brought here?"

"No. Take him to one of our safe houses in America for debriefing."

Tann clicked his heels. "Yes, sir!"

Park leaned back in his chair, tapping his chin. "I wonder…"

"Yes?"

He frowned, staring at Tann. "Could the leak have come from within?"

Tann's eyes widened. "From within the Bureau?" He lowered his voice. "I suppose anything is possible. More likely it would have come from one of our subcontractors."

Park leaned forward. "Go on."

Tann approached the desk. "Well, we've deployed some of the ToolKit to our hacker collectives for targeting exploits. I don't think we've let this particular tool outside of our own staff, but a mistake might have been made." He sucked in a deep breath. "I'll check."

"Do that. But first I want that story leaked."

Tann bowed. "Yes, sir."

Operations Center 2, CIA Headquarters
Langley, Virginia

"So what do we know about these agents?"

Chris Leroux stared at his screen, creating an executive summary as quickly as he could while Kane sat in his car on the other end of the headset. "Not much at all. I can tell you she's still with the NSA, clean record, though her career trajectory seems to have taken a hit two years ago."

Kane grunted. "Probably because the fake leak became an actual one. What about her partner?"

"We don't even have his name. She never gave it during the briefing, and since there appear to be no records of the investigation that we can find, I'm not sure how we'll find out short of asking her point blank."

"We might just have to do that."

"What if she's involved?"

"It's a risk we'll have to take, but I don't think so."

Leroux's eyes narrowed. "Why?"

"Gut feeling."

"You saw her picture, didn't you?"

He could almost hear the grin through the headset.

"Umm, no comment."

"Uh-huh. Well, don't let Fang find out."

Kane chuckled. "It's always okay to look."

"Not always."

"This is true. But in the privacy of my own car, it is." Leroux heard Kane tapping a keyboard. "Get one of your people to contact Agent Graf. We need to find her partner before he gets nervous."

Leroux snapped his fingers and Sonya Tong nodded, immediately going to work. "Do you think he knows it was used?"

"Maybe. But somebody knows, and depending on who it was, they might want to tie up loose ends."

Leroux paused, leaning back in his chair. "You think it could be government?"

"It wouldn't be the first time the Russians, Chinese, or North Koreans did something. Or the Iranians for that matter."

Leroux spun in his chair, Randy Child smiling at him.

"Addictive, isn't it?"

Leroux dropped his foot, stopping the spin. "I can't see a foreign government doing a ransomware attack. It makes no sense. Some sort of attempt at pulling data or attacking our infrastructure, sure, but not a ransomware attack that appears almost random in nature."

"Sir, I can't reach her."

Leroux turned to Tong. "Where is she?"

Tong pointed at the large set of displays wrapping around the front of the room. "I've got her cellphone in Albany. Stationary."

"Can we get an image of her?"

Tong pecked away at her keyboard, accessing a database of millions of cameras they could tap into, including a disturbing number of private cameras installed in homes, with either no security, or with security left on the default settings by their owners.

"I've got an angle." An image appeared from a veranda, a porch swing blocking part of the view. Leroux rose and stepped toward the displays, examining the area. Nobody was visible, though there were several cars parked on the street. It was too dark to see inside. He pointed blindly behind him at Tong. "Dial her number again."

"Yes, sir." He heard Tong's keyboard. "It's ringing."

Something glowed inside one of the cars and Leroux smiled, pointing at it. "That's her."

"Okay, send me her number and location," said Kane. Leroux glanced at Tong who nodded, sending the information. "Okay, got it. I'm about an hour from there. Update me if she moves."

"Will do."

"Holy shit!"

Leroux turned toward their youngest team member, Randy Child. "What is it?"

Child tapped at his keyboard then pointed to the displays, dozens of websites appearing.

"What am I looking at?" But he didn't need to wait for the answer as his brain caught up with his eyes. Website after website was repeating the same or similar headline.

NSA Leak Responsible for Ransomware Attack

"They've got everything including Hummel's name, Agent Graf's, and her partner."

Leroux spun toward Child. "What is it?"

"Donald Penn."

"Find him." Child nodded, going to work as Leroux pressed his headset a little tighter against his ear. "Did you hear that?"

"Yeah, I'm looking at it now. You've got to find out who leaked that story. The timing is too coincidental and the details too specific. This is someone with insider knowledge."

"Do you think Graf could have leaked it?"

"Possibly, but I doubt it."

"Because she's hot?"

Kane chuckled. "No, because if it were her, she'd be preparing for blowback, not sitting on a residential street somewhere on a stakeout."

Leroux stared at the image of the car. "What makes you think she's on a stakeout?"

"She's involved in investigating the biggest ransomware attack in history, yet she's sitting in a car in Albany. That's a stakeout."

"Found him."

Leroux turned to Child. "Where is he?"

"You're not going to believe it, but"—he pointed at the image of Graf's car—"he lives about two houses down from where she's parked."

A victory cry erupted from Kane. "I told you! She suspects him too!"

"What do we know about him?"

Child quickly read off the highlights. "It looks like he's no longer with the NSA. Left about a year and a half ago."

Leroux sat, chewing his cheek. "So, not long after the leak."

"Right. According to the IRS, he's self-employed. I can't find anything indicating what he's self-employed at, though."

Kane beat Leroux to it. "Sounds to me like someone took a payoff and quit the daily grind. Listen, is there any way you can send me some backup? My Spidey senses are telling me I'm walking into something."

Leroux agreed. "I'll have to talk to the Director. Technically you're not legally operational."

"Hey, I thought I was Homeland?"

Leroux chuckled. "You're Homeland until someone at Homeland discovers that fact. Then you're grassed ass."

"Maybe you shouldn't tell the Chief."

Leroux's eyebrows shot up. "Huh?"

"Well, if you tell him, then he's going to want me to play nice and obey all kinds of inconvenient rules."

Leroux grinned. "Since when did rules ever stop you?"

"This is true. I'm on my way to Graf's position. Don't call me if he says to play nice."

The line went dead, leaving those in the room who didn't know Kane to wonder if he was serious. Fortunately, most of them knew him all too well.

He turned to Tong. "Contact the Director's office. I need to see him ASAP."

"Yes, sir."

He turned to Child. "Who leaked the story?"

Child shrugged. "Don't know yet, but RT News leaked it first."

Leroux frowned. "The Russians."

Outside Penn Residence
Albany, New York

Janine Graf stared at her phone, vibrating with another message from the office, urgently requesting she contact them. By ignoring all their calls and messages, she could plausibly say she had left the phone in her car, or elsewhere.

Because right now, she couldn't let them know where she was.

It had been a shock when Penn had announced he was leaving the agency, though his explanation had been reasonable. The two of them had been essentially demoted after the stolen data had "disappeared" into the ether. She knew the whispers in the corridors were that the data had been handed off to someone else, and that they had screwed up royally.

She didn't believe it.

Or at least, hadn't until a few months ago when a segment of it showed up for sale on the Dark Web. But it wasn't until this week that she truly questioned everything.

The ransomware attack was the number one priority at the NSA— everyone that could be spared was working on it. Because of her familiarity with the case, she had been brought in—against the better judgment of her bosses, she was certain—and was privy to much of what was going on. It had been confirmed that the exploit used was the one identified by Hummel, and the version of the tool used to exploit it was identical to the one Hummel wrote two years ago.

And she knew it wasn't Hummel behind it.

She believed him. She believed his story. He had been in love with her, and merely wanted to prove himself to her so that she'd take him back. This had nothing to do with betraying his country, of theft for profit or gain, and everything to do with love. She wouldn't even have characterized it as lust, which was what most Honeypot stings relied upon. Get a man worked up enough, obsessed enough, and far too often he could be manipulated with ease, where the word "love" only entered into it when followed by "to slam you against the headboard."

And men weren't the only ones guilty of falling for it, though from her experience, women were more apt to fall in love than lust—though not all of them.

But not Hummel. For him, it was purely love, and to this day, she still felt a little guilty about it. You couldn't spend hours every night chatting with someone, even if it was from behind a keyboard, and not develop some sort of attachment to them. When she had revealed the truth to Hummel, and their communication had been terminated permanently, she had discovered a hole that she still hadn't filled. Her evenings were empty without him in them, and even though most of what she fed him were lies, all part of the intricate cover developed for her by NSA staffers locked away deep inside Fort George G. Meade, there were elements of truth to it.

When she had a bad day at work, or an encounter with some idiot at the grocery store, or trouble with her mother, she vented to him, and he was the sympathetic ear she didn't have in her real life. Agents didn't share their problems—it made them look weak. And as a woman, she couldn't have any male think of her as weak—it would just confirm in their sometimes sexist minds that the only reason she had the job she did was because she had tits and had slept with the right person.

And if she had confided in her partner, she might have been confiding with a traitor.

She stared at Penn's house, her chest tightening as she relived the moment she realized it had to be him behind it all. He had been the one to "volunteer" them for the ToolKit assignment, and he had been the one to insist the data had to actually be removed from the building for there to be no doubt a crime had been committed.

And he had been the one to contradict Hummel, by claiming the memory stick was blank.

It had never occurred to her that Penn could be lying. It had also never occurred to her that Hummel could be lying. Why would a man, accused of treason, stick to his story when the government itself was claiming the memory stick was blank? All he had to do was say he had wiped it after copying the files, deciding it wasn't worth breaking the law to impress a woman.

Yet he hadn't, even after finding out the woman he was trying to impress was a liar, with no interest in him whatsoever.

They both couldn't be telling the truth, which meant, until a few days ago, that Hummel had screwed up somehow.

But now she didn't believe that for a moment, and never really had. He was too good.

Yet if Penn had been lying, if he had found the data and copied it, then wiped it himself, Hummel's story fit. And so did Penn's actions afterward. If he stole the data and sold it, he'd probably have collected a tidy sum. And that meant he wouldn't need to work. He waited long enough before resigning so no one would suspect the two events were related, then moved, so any changes in lifestyle wouldn't be noticed by his neighbors, and he would have an excuse to not keep in contact with his former colleagues.

She hadn't seen him in well over a year.

And the house he now lived in was easily half again as big as his last, the Jag a lot nicer than the Hyundai he had been driving while at the agency, though proof that money didn't mean brains.

His wife had a business, and she could have become a success, though it was difficult to tell from a website. She couldn't access any type of records on him or her without raising flags, so she had to rely on her gut.

And her gut told her this bastard was dirty.

He had made a fool out of her, destroyed her career, and now was living the life of Riley while she toiled away, struggling to rebuild her reputation.

Her phone vibrated again and she glanced at it.

Mom?

Her mother never called at this hour, which meant something was wrong. She had to take it. She swiped her thumb. "Mom? What's wrong? Is everything okay?"

"I'm supposed to be asking you that question. Are you in trouble?"

Graf's eyes narrowed. "No. Why?"

"Well, your name is all over the news."

Her eyebrows shot up and she leaned over, activating her iPad and pulling up CNN's website. "What are they saying?"

"They're saying you were part of some operation that went bad, and valuable data was stolen."

Holy shit!

She tapped on the lead story and cursed.

"You *are* in trouble, aren't you?"

She quickly scanned the article, the entire op laid bare, along with all the names involved.

How could they have possibly found out?

"Honey, answer me."

She tossed the iPad on the passenger seat and closed her eyes. "No, Mom, I'm not in trouble. Whoever leaked the story will be, but I didn't do anything wrong."

"That's not what they're saying."

"Who, the idiots posing as reporters? You know never to listen to them."

"I don't have to. I can listen to any channel or read any website. They're all talking about this. *Every*one." There was a sigh. "Oh, dear, I'm so worried about you. You know the way things are these days. They always look for someone to blame, and I think they're trying to blame this whole computer attack thing on you."

Damn right they are, but who is "they?"

"I've gotta go, Mom, I'm working. But don't worry about me. I'll be fine."

"Call me later?"

"No promises tonight, but I'll definitely call if I get a chance tomorrow. Love you."

"I love you too, take care of yourself."

Graf ended the call, scowling at Penn's house. With the story out, there was little doubt he either already knew his name was public, or soon would. And if he was involved, he would be going to ground, and could do it at any moment.

Her phone vibrated again.

I have been told to tell you to call or kiss your career goodbye.

She frowned. It was her new partner, Mulgrew, whom she had told earlier she was taking the night off. She sighed, then dialed her number.

"Oh, thank God! Do you know what's going on?"

She smiled at the panic in Mulgrew's voice. She was good people. "I just found out."

"Where are you? Gordon has been on my back all evening to find you. He wants you to come in, now."

"I'm at his place."

There was a pause. "Whose?"

"Penn's."

Mulgrew's voice dropped to a harsh whisper. "Are you crazy? What are you doing there?"

"If you think I'm crazy, then you already know."

"You think he's the mole?"

"Yes."

"Is that Graf?"

Graf's stomach flipped at the sound of Gordon's voice in the background.

"Give me the phone." There was a burst of static then her boss' voice came on the line. "Graf, is that you?"

"Yes, sir."

"Why the hell have you been ignoring my calls?"

"I haven't been, sir, I just turned—"

"Bullshit. We're the damned NSA, we can tell when your phone is on or off. Never mind that. I want you in here, now."

"I can't do that, sir."

"Why the hell not?"

"I'm at Penn's house. I'm going to—"

"You'll do nothing! Understood? I've already got a team on the way to bring him in." There was a pause. "Wait a minute, what the hell are you doing there?"

"I figured it had to be him, sir. He had to have been the one to steal the data. He's the only one who had the opportunity, and if you could see his house and car, you'd know he's behind all of this."

Gordon calmed slightly. "Yeah, that's what we just figured out on this end too once that news story broke." He sighed. "Listen, wait for the team, don't do anything stupid, understood?"

"What if I see him leave?"

"Then follow him. But do *not* engage. Do we understand each other?"

"Yes, sir."

"Good. And once he's been picked up, get your ass in here. *No* excuses."

"Yes, sir."

The call ended and she drew a long breath.

My career just might survive the night.

Temple Technologies Corporate Head Office
Mountain View, California

"Are you watching this?"

Tanya Davis waved her iPad as she stepped into Franklin Temple's office. "I think everyone in the country is. I've already had half a dozen media outlets request interviews, and security says there are several camera trucks setting up downstairs."

Temple stood, pacing back and forth along the windows of his corner office, his hands clasped behind his head as he battled the rage. He spun, jabbing a finger at the chair occupied earlier that week by the lackey sent to placate him. "That little shit sat right in that chair and lied to me! They knew all along that they were responsible for what happened to my little angel, but they didn't have the balls to admit it."

"It would appear so."

"My own damn country killed my daughter!" He resumed his pacing, staring at the ceiling as Davis sat in her customary seat, working her tablet.

"You're getting quite a few emails from your friends and business associates. They're expressing their anger at the news, and wondering how they can help."

"Where's Simmons?"

"I'm not sure."

"Well find out."

She nodded, pulling out her phone as she rose. He heard a whispered conversation before she turned to him. "He's already on a plane. Apparently his team caught wind of the leaked NSA story a couple of hours ago. They're already on their way to interview the suspect involved in the theft two years ago."

Temple smiled slightly.

He's good.

"Excellent. Have him contact us as soon as he knows anything."

"Yes, sir."

Davis returned to her conversation then ended the call. "With this new information, we might be able to actually make some progress in the investigation."

Temple stared at her for a moment. "To what end? Our government is responsible."

"Ultimately, yes. But they didn't launch the attack. Someone else did, and now maybe we can find out who."

Temple sighed, dropping into his chair. "You're right. I'm not thinking straight. This entire situation is complete and utter bullshit. If that story is right, they allowed this ToolKit, or whatever the hell they called it, to be stolen, all as a loyalty test! Who the hell does that?"

"The American government, apparently."

Temple grunted at Davis' calming smile. "Thank God I have you, Tanya, otherwise I think I'd go insane."

"Let me snap, sir, you're too important."

He chuckled, staring at the photo of his wife. "She always liked you, you know. She trusted you."

"I always liked her too, sir."

He sighed, spinning his chair toward the windows, the sun low on the horizon. He drummed his fingers on the arms, rhythmically calming himself. The NSA was responsible for the leak, and there was nothing he could do to them. Hopefully, he could apply pressure through his own connections and those of his friends now expressing support, so some heads would roll. Some might lose their jobs, though he doubted any would actually see the inside of a prison.

But Davis was right. They weren't who launched the attack. Their crime was incompetence. Idiocy.

The man who stole it, he was responsible. And Simmons would soon have him. The problem was that if this man was still free, then for some reason the NSA hadn't been willing to press charges, giving him time enough to sell his secrets, and somehow remain free.

Hopefully, Simmons will break him.

The ToolKit was sold to someone, and they needed to find out who. Some hacker or hackers, somewhere, had used what was stolen to launch the attack that had killed his daughter. These hackers were responsible, and they had to pay.

With their lives.

He was sick and tired of hackers operating with impunity, protected by borders and foreign governments unwilling to take action.

It had to stop.

And there was only one way he could think of accomplishing that.

"You said there are camera trucks outside?"

"Yes, sir. Three at last count."

He rose, stepping toward his bathroom, discretely hidden behind a false wall. He entered, examining himself in the mirror, straightening his hair. He stepped back out and headed for the door. "I think it's time to make a statement to the press."

Davis leaped to her feet. "Is that wise? What with Simmons out there and all?"

He held open the door for her and she stepped through. "That's precisely why. The world knows how angry I am. If I don't say something, now that this story has broken, they'll wonder why. If people start winding up dead, someone might just figure out I'm behind it."

They boarded his private elevator. The doors closed and Davis stood before him, confirming he hadn't missed anything in the mirror.

"How do I look?"

"The very model of a modern major-general."

He chuckled. "Don't make me laugh. I'm the grieving father and widower, remember?"

"Of course, sir. But I think as soon as you start talking, that won't be a problem." Her face clouded over. "Just be careful, sir. No one must know what we're doing."

The doors opened, and he smiled at her through thin lips. They stepped through the lobby, a gaggle of press outside the doors, held back by building security, the flashing lights of police arriving suggesting his staff feared they would be overwhelmed. He stepped through the revolving doors, coming to a stop in the small cleared area in front of the building.

The reporters erupted.

He held up his hands, remaining silent until they finally calmed down. "Thank you, everyone, thank you for coming. I'm going to make a brief statement, and I won't be taking any questions. Interrupt me, and my statement ends. Understood?"

Dozens of microphones and cameras edged forward, but silence reigned.

"Good. As you are aware, the recent revelation that the NSA itself was responsible for the leak of what I believe they are calling their ToolKit, is both shocking and outrageous. How our own government could be so irresponsible is beyond me, and I intend to take my concerns to the highest levels, I assure you. I will also be consulting with my lawyers to see what legal action might be possible against those responsible.

"The question still remains as to who actually carried out the attack that murdered my daughter, my little angel, and now I must trust that the very government that is ultimately responsible for her death, will bring to justice those who took advantage of their incompetence." His voice finally cracked, and he held up his hand, holding off the horde while he regained his composure. He drew a deep breath, staring at the crowd, his eyes glistening as he pictured his daughter's body, lying on a slab in a cold morgue, all the joy she had brought to the world forever gone. He closed his eyes and sighed.

They have to pay.

An ember sparked inside, kindling a rage that slowly built, giving him the strength to finally continue. He opened his eyes, glaring at the cameras. "Unfortunately, I have very little faith in our government's ability, or willingness, to bring these people to justice. Just look at their track record. Why is it, when something is done using a computer, people assume there are no victims? Why do we have an entire generation that believes it is morally acceptable to steal digital content? Does that content not have value? If you wouldn't go to Best Buy and steal a DVD, then why is it okay to steal a digital copy? Why is it okay to pirate movies, music, software, or books? They still have value, despite being digital ones and zeroes stored on the Internet somewhere.

Someone still worked hard to create those, spent money to produce the end product. Why do so many people feel it is their right to take that for free? Why do so many people think that if you charge more than they think it's worth, then they should be able to steal it? If you think the car you want is overpriced, would you just steal it off the lot? Of course not, because that's a physical product, and copying or streaming a digital product from the Internet isn't, and for some reason, our society has decided that isn't a crime, at least not one worth punishing."

He stared at the confused reporters, deciding he had better make his point, and focus his anger where it truly needed to be. "Now take our government. We are constantly being hacked by countries like China, Russia, North Korea, among others, yet what is done? These hacks cost our economies millions if not billions, put our citizens at risk, yet what does our government do? They sometimes retaliate through our own cyberattacks, but carefully make sure we don't cross any lines that might actually harm someone.

"And that's only when we know for certain who did it. Too often, these countries hire out the work so it can't be traced back to them. We often know who these perpetrators are, but they're safely ensconced in countries where we can't touch them, and we know damned well who's financing them. We don't go after them because nothing *physical* happened, just digital. And that's just as wrong as stealing digital content."

Temple stared at the reporters, then glanced over his shoulder at Davis, whose eyes widened slightly as she recognized the expression on his face. She knew he was about to crack.

She knows me better than I know myself.

"In the past, when our country was attacked with bombs and guns, we mobilized and defeated our enemies. But today, when we are attacked through computers, we do nothing. It's time for that to end. And I don't just mean government sponsored hacking. This entire concept that digital crimes are victimless crimes is nonsense, and our society has to change its views on this. If the governments meant to protect us won't defend us from these criminals, these terrorists, then it's time we defend ourselves. I say it's time for an eye for an eye. I say it's time these hackers are tracked down and captured, and if the government won't imprison them, then they should be summarily executed."

A round of gasps erupted.

"Perhaps if some vigilante justice takes place, these hackers, sitting in their parent's basement, or in some state-sponsored office, will think twice before they actually launch their next attack. I say we kill them, and end this problem, once and for all. It's time for our society to seek retribution against those who seek to destroy it with impunity!"

He turned away from the cameras, his fists clenched, his chest heaving as he struggled to regain control. Davis led him toward the revolving doors as the reporters surged forward, dozens of questions screamed at him. He stepped through and strode toward his elevator, Davis silently at his side. He stepped on, Davis pressing the button to take them to the top floor. The door closed.

Davis turned to him. "Are you insane?"

He glared at her. "Absolutely!"

"You could go to jail for this."

He shrugged as he pulled in huge lungsful of air, the rage almost blinding. "I don't care. No other father should have to go through what

I'm going through, because anonymous people behind keyboards feel they can operate with impunity." He glanced down at her. "Don't worry, I don't think it will take more than a few dozen deaths before we see a real change."

Her eyes narrowed as she stared up at him. "Are you okay? I'm being serious. Are you feeling okay?"

He drew in a quick breath as the doors opened and he stepped out, staff huddled in groups, breaking apart, avoiding eye contact. Temple entered his office, walking over to the windows, his hands on his hips as he stared out at the city below, the view calming.

"I've never been better. I know what I have to do now."

Penn Residence
Albany, New York

Donald Penn stared at the television then his laptop, his attention split between the two devices streaming him different details on the top story across the nation, and around the world. Whoever had leaked the facts of what had happened two years ago, had too many details. It had to be somebody well connected.

It had to be his former employer.

Someone on the inside had leaked it. It was too accurate. The news channels had his name and Graf's, as well as Hummel's. They had every detail as if they had read the mission debriefs. He had left Maryland to get away from all that, to start a new life, and now it was all about to fall apart.

His wife entered the room, holding the baby. Her smile disappeared as soon as she saw his face. "What's wrong?"

He snapped the laptop shut and turned off the TV. "I need you to take the baby and go to your mother's."

Grace's eyes widened then she batted a hand at him. "Are you kidding me? I've got an important meeting tomorrow with my biggest client, lunch with Jill, then a doctor's appointment. Besides, you know how Mom hates being dropped in on."

Penn rose and approached her, taking hold of her shoulders as he stared into her eyes, trying to convey the seriousness of the situation. "Do you remember two years ago when I told you that we might need

113

to pick up and leave at any given moment because of something that happened while I was at the agency?"

Grace's face clouded over, her eyes widening with fear as she paled. "Yes."

"Well, this is that time."

Tears filled her eyes, and she held their son a little closer. "Are we in danger?"

He closed his eyes for a moment, sighing. He opened them, rubbing a thumb over her cheek, wiping away a tear that had escaped.

"Yes."

Outside Penn Residence
Albany, New York

Kane pulled up in his government issued SUV and parked about half a block down from where Special Agent Graf held vigil. He surveyed the neighborhood through his tinted windows, searching for anything out of the ordinary besides Graf's vehicle, but saw nothing.

He dialed Leroux. "Got anything for me?"

"Just that the NSA is sending a team to pick up Penn. They're less than thirty minutes out."

Kane pursed his lips, staring at the home of his suspect. "Any movement from Graf?"

"Negative. She's stayed put, but she had a conversation with someone at Fort Meade. She was probably ordered to sit tight."

"Are locals involved?"

"No. Not even the FBI field office has been notified, as far as I can tell. I think they're trying to contain this."

"Well, they're doing a bang-up job, if the radio's any indication."

"Yeah, this story is everywhere. I wouldn't be surprised if the press is on Penn's doorstep before the NSA team arrives."

Kane frowned. That would be a distinctly bad thing, at least for what he had planned. "Okay, I'm going to have to act fast." The porch light flicked on at the Penn residence. "Wait a minute. I've got activity. I'll get back to you."

The garage door opened and Kane watched Penn and his wife rush out, Penn loading a baby into the back seat of their car, his wife tossing two large suitcases in the trunk. Hugs were exchanged, then she pulled out of the driveway, speeding off as her husband waved. Penn looked about, then went back inside, the lights flicking out as the garage door closed.

He's going to ground.

Two SUVs turned onto the street, their headlights dimming as they pulled to the side and parked. Kane cursed and reached up, pressing the button to suppress the dome light. He opened the door and closed it quietly, dropping low as he crept along the opposite side of the street to the new arrivals. He reached Graf's vehicle and tapped on the window.

The woman nearly jumped out of her skin.

She lowered the window, her eyes wide, her cheeks flushed, her chest heaving. "Sir, I'm going to have—"

Kane held up his Homeland Security ID. "Special Agent Kane, Homeland."

Her eyes widened further. "What the hell are you doing here?"

"I was going to pay a visit to your former partner, but I think we've got bigger problems."

Her eyes narrowed. "What do you mean?"

Kane nodded toward the SUVs, eight doors opening. "When's your team due to arrive?"

"How do you—"

"Just answer the question. We don't have any time to waste."

"Not for at least another twenty minutes."

Kane sighed, drawing his weapon. "Then I think we have to assume these guys aren't friendly."

Graf cursed, reaching for her phone. "I've got to call this in."

Kane shook his head. "No time." He watched the team deploy, leaving little doubt this wasn't some amateur hit squad inspired by Temple's plea for vigilante justice. These were pros, probably sent by whoever had instructed Penn to steal the data in the first place.

"Then what are we going to do?" asked Graf.

"Our jobs."

Graf's eyebrows shot up. "You don't propose to take out eight men alone, do you?"

Kane laughed. "Of course not. You're going to help."

He watched as the team deployed, four covering the front, four the back. He reached into his pocket and retrieved a suppressor, screwing it into the end of the barrel of his Glock. Graf's eyes widened.

"You're not Homeland, are you?"

"All you need to know is I'm on your side." He repositioned two feet to the left, using the hood of the car and the front tires as cover. He rested his forearms on the front of the vehicle and took aim at the first target, positioned by a large oak tree at the front of the house.

He squeezed the trigger.

The man dropped, the suppressor doing its job, but only as good as a suppressor could be counted upon. As his targets looked to see where the sound had come from, he already had the next one in his sights, two men now on the porch. He fired then adjusted, firing again.

Two more down, the fourth covering the front spinning and now opening fire with an assault rifle, randomly spraying the street as he raced back toward the SUVs. His magazine spent, Kane heard the man reload. Kane popped up and put two into his target as four weapons rounded the corners of the house, barrels blazing.

Kane dropped back behind the tire as Graf cried out. He reached over and pulled open her door, the agent pouring out onto the sidewalk. He pushed her to the rear of the car. "Get behind the tire!"

She scrambled for the limited cover as Kane listened, his expert ear blindly following the movements of their attackers. He raised his gun over the hood, aimed without looking, then fired the remaining rounds in an arc.

Somebody cried out as Kane reloaded. He glanced over at Graf. "You okay?"

She nodded.

"Then start shooting!"

A steady stream of lead continued to shred the car, the tires on the opposite side flattened, the windows shattered. Kane lay prone on the ground, directly behind the tire as the gunmen continued forward, now less than ten feet away.

He peered out from behind the tire and underneath the car. He could see a set of feet approaching when the muzzle flash of someone positioned in the middle of the road, prone like him, erupted. He jerked back behind the tire as the curb was torn apart where his head had been a moment before.

These guys are good.

If it hadn't been for the element of surprise, he'd be dead now. But there were still three of them, with vastly superior firepower, and they seemed determined to kill him as opposed to escaping.

This isn't going to end well.

Another gun entered the game, a pistol, probably a Beretta if Kane's ringing ears were still to be trusted. One of the guns fell silent as he heard the thud of a body hitting the pavement, and the distinct pings of lead slamming into their car stopped, suggesting those that remained were refocusing their attention.

He leaped to his feet, pumping two rounds into the backs of each of the men, then redirected his aim at the porch where Donald Penn stood, weapon in hand.

"Homeland Security! Drop your weapon!"

"Bullshit! Show me some ID!"

Kane glanced at Graf. "He's your partner, talk to him."

Graf gave him a look. "Ex-partner." She rolled over onto her knees. "Don, it's me, Janine!"

"Janine?" Penn lowered his weapon slightly as Graf tentatively rose. "Holy shit! What are you doing here?"

Kane kept his weapon trained on the man. "Drop your gun, and she'll be happy to tell you."

Somebody groaned to the left, one of their targets rolling to his knees.

Three weapons put two rounds each into the man, the standoff resuming.

"Drop it now. There are two of us, and only one of you."

Penn raised his hands. "Okay, okay." He slowly crouched, placing the weapon on the porch.

"Kick it onto your lawn."

Penn gave it a boot, the weapon scraping along the concrete of the porch then thudding onto the grass. Kane surged forward as sirens in the distance grew, the locals on their way. Graf joined him, and moments later, she had her former partner in cuffs, much to his annoyance.

"What the hell is going on? Why am I under arrest?"

"You know damned well, why. You stole the data!"

Penn shook his head vehemently. "That's bullshit, and you know it. The data had already been wiped."

He's going to stick to his story, and there's no time for a proper interrogation.

Kane left the porch, pulling out his phone, quickly snapping photos of the eight dead answers lying on the street and Penn's front lawn. He sent them to Leroux as he headed for his SUV.

"Where are you going?"

He glanced over his shoulder at Graf. "It's best if I'm not here when the locals arrive."

As if on cue, the first squad car tore around the corner, rapidly approaching before brakes were applied. Kane hopped into his vehicle, starting it up and gently pulling away from the curb, executing a U-turn before accelerating slowly away. There was no hope of the police unit following him—there were too many bodies in the road, but it didn't matter. They were already distracted by Graf approaching them, her hands in the air, one holding her ID.

He turned the corner and accelerated quickly to the speed limit before executing several more turns, in case a description of his vehicle had been put out over the radio. He spotted a Home Depot, and pulled into the parking lot, wedging between two pickup trucks.

He dialed Leroux, his friend answering immediately.

"Control Actual here."

"What can you tell me about them?"

"We're running them now. You'll be happy to know they weren't the NSA team. They're still en route."

Kane smiled at Leroux's tone. "That's a stroke of luck."

"Uh-huh. You got lucky. We watched most of it on the neighbor's security camera. If Penn hadn't come out when he had, you'd be dead. Kind of makes you wonder whose side he's on, doesn't it?"

Kane grunted. "Never mistake self-preservation for loyalty."

A whistle erupted through the phone. "Now that's interesting."

Kane pressed it tighter against his ear. "What?"

"You'll never guess who one of your guys is."

"Who?"

"The son of the North Korean ambassador to the United Nations."

Clayton Hummel Residence
Annapolis, Maryland

Clayton Hummel scrolled through his ridiculously long list of movies on his Apple TV. Whoever had designed the interface should have been flogged with a rubber hose years ago, the piss poor categorizations, search functionality, and complete lack of customizable organization capabilities suggesting it had only ever been tested with catalogs of a few dozen movies.

He had over one thousand, and it made finding anything ridiculously time-consuming.

But at least there were only seven buttons on the remote, four of which were arrow keys.

Elegant, and useless.

"I'd suggest The Ghost and the Darkness. Great movie."

Hummel spun in his chair to see four men, all in black, standing behind him.

Heavily armed.

His bladder loosened and he kegeled down, saving the day. "Who-who are you?" he cried as he struggled out of his chair. The men spread out casually, Hummel noticing all exits from the room now blocked.

One of the men, his face covered by a ski mask, nodded toward the screen. "I agree with my partner. The Ghost and the Darkness would make a great choice. Val Kilmer in his prime before he chunked out, Michael Douglas before he wrinkled out. Lots of action, great acting. My favorite was lion number two."

A large man to the right grunted. "I always thought number one was more committed to the role."

Hummel stared, dumbfounded at the conversation. "Who *are* you people?"

The man apparently in charge held up a hand, silencing the others. "Concerned citizens. Any minute now, dozens of reporters are going to be descending on this place, and if you're really unlucky, which I have a feeling you are, at least one vigilante will come here to collect some justice on behalf of a grieving billionaire."

Hummel's eyes narrowed. "You're not government?"

"As I said, we're concerned citizens."

Hummel's chest tightened and his heart raced as his mouth went dry. "If you're not government, then get the hell out of here before I call the police."

The leader tapped his machine gun. "I think we'll leave them out of this for now." He took another step closer. "Cooperate, and nobody needs to be inconvenienced at all. You won't even have lost any time, since we saved you so much by recommending a movie for you to watch."

Hummel still couldn't believe what he was hearing. It was so odd, it was almost comical.

If it weren't for the guns and body armor.

"What do you want?"

"I want to know who you sold the data to."

Hummel sighed, shaking his head. "This again? Like I told the other guy, it wasn't me. I never sold the data. The NSA lied when they said the memory stick was wiped."

"That's quite the accusation. Do you have any proof to back it up?"

Hummel gave a toothy grin, his eyes widening slightly. "Umm, my word?"

Chuckles erupted from the men gathered, and Hummel relaxed slightly.

"Forgive me if that's not enough."

"Listen, like I told that Agent Kane or Crane or something, I think it was the NSA agent who came here to retrieve the data while I was at the restaurant. I think he stole—"

He was cut off by a raised hand.

"Who did you say was here?"

"Some Homeland Security guy, but I don't think he was actually Homeland. Maybe he was like you, you know, private contractor or something. I don't really remember his name. I was too busy trying not to shit my pants." He clenched.

Like now!

"And you think it was the NSA agent who stole the data?"

"Yes. It had to be, right? My lawyers said that he was watching my house, waiting for me to leave for the restaurant to meet his partner. As soon as I was clear, he entered the house, and was there until I was arrested. That means nobody had time to copy it and wipe it. So, it was either blank when I left, or he wiped it, and I know it wasn't blank."

"So you say."

"Why the hell would I stick to a story that makes me a traitor in some people's eyes? I could just—"

The man held up his hand. "Forget it, I've read your file."

"All of it?"

"All but the sealed portion." The man stepped forward. "Care to share?"

"I-I'm not allowed."

The machine gun was tapped once again. "I think they'll forgive you."

Hummel sighed as a stream of urine ran down his leg, his battle lost. His eyes burned and he closed them as his shoulders and chin sank with shame. "They forced me to resign, then paid me a lump-sum pension to keep silent about the breach."

He heard footsteps then the back door. He looked up, opening his eyes, finding himself alone in a puddle of his own urine and shame.

Temple Technologies Corporate Head Office
Mountain View, California

Franklin Temple attacked his stair climber, his body glistening, his tank top dripping. If every square inch of his workout wear wasn't a different shade by the time he finished, he hadn't worked hard enough.

But tonight he wasn't challenging himself physically, he was beating down his inner demons.

He had crossed the line.

And it was stupid.

Though he didn't really feel any regret for calling on people to murder hackers around the world, he did feel bad that he had put those who worked for him in an uncomfortable position. Outside the building, there was already a cordon of police and private security holding back the reporters and a growing group of protesters, mostly millennials and professional agitators, organized on social media to picket any building around the world associated with his company.

And that would be dozens. Hundreds if the subcontractors were included.

He found it almost comical how the mainstream media characterized these as spontaneous protests, where people were so incensed by something that they simply showed up, and lo and behold, there just happened to be dozens if not hundreds of others equally incensed.

It was bullshit.

These protests were usually organized by professional agitation groups, funded by the Soros of the world, who had agendas to suit their needs. Why was the great wizard against Keystone? It wasn't because of the environment, it was because he had bought into the railways currently used to move the oil. Where did the money come from to fly the same people around the world for G7 and G20 protests, to bus them in from around the country, to make sure they had places to stay?

That took logistics, and logistics took money.

Something millennials supposedly didn't have.

There was no way you were against globalization and in favor of the Occupy movement, if you could afford to fly to the protest.

Yet somehow they did.

And he knew how, and the MSM did as well, but it wouldn't make for good TV to expose the truth.

In a preemptive move, he had sent all his non-essential employees home, with instructions to monitor their email to see if they should come in tomorrow. Tomorrow was a Friday, so he was already leaning toward just giving them all a paid long weekend. By Monday, things would have calmed down, and at the rate things were moving, he might already have the justice he wanted.

For the outrage of the public was building.

And it was in his favor.

Millions had been impacted directly and indirectly by the ransomware attack, and millions more had been hit with viruses and malware over the years, with no recourse. He had become a rallying point for the common man, pissed at having to put up with increasing attacks, increasing levels of inconvenient security, of inboxes overflowing with spam.

The common man was behind him, despite the fact he was a rich one percenter.

He was speaking their language.

"Kill them all!" had become the rallying cry on the news broadcasts with the courage to cover what the common people were thinking, and his company's social media accounts were flooded with messages of support, funding campaigns already raising hundreds of thousands of dollars, pledged to pay rewards to those who brought hackers to justice.

He fully expected those to be shut down shortly, but it was encouraging.

He had allowed Tanya Davis to deal with the fallout, the lawyers already issuing a press release that these were the words of a grieving father, overwhelmed by the loss of his daughter, and not the words of the CEO of Temple Technologies, nor should anyone actually act on the words.

His only condition on the backpedaling, was that there be no apology. For he wasn't sorry he had called for the deaths of those who held the world hostage through viruses and malware, through cyberattacks and ransomware. They deserved to die. Every last one of them.

Davis entered his private gym, hidden behind another discrete panel from his main office. "Sorry to interrupt, sir, but Simmons is on the line."

Temple killed the machine and stepped down, grabbing a towel. "Put it on speaker."

Davis complied as he toweled off. "You're on with Mr. Temple."

"Sir, I have an update. We've just interviewed Mr. Hummel. I'm confident he didn't sell the data."

"What makes you so sure?"

"I tapped my weapon and he pissed himself. This is not a brave man, sir."

"I guess not." Temple exchanged a glance with Davis. If Simmons had done the same to him, he wasn't so sure his reaction wouldn't have been unlike Hummel's.

"Mr. Hummel did have an interesting theory, however, as to where to look next."

Temple's eyebrows rose as he sat on a nearby bench, Davis handing him a bottle of ice-cold water from the mini-fridge. "What?"

"He believes that the NSA agent who came to his house stole the data then wiped the memory stick. I believe the news reports have him as one Donald Penn."

Davis nodded. "Yes, that's the name. You think he's right?"

"He certainly believes it, and it makes sense. If he did indeed steal the data—which if he didn't, why would he stick to the story—then someone had to have, and Penn is the only one who had the opportunity."

"Pick him up."

"We're already on the way, sir. ETA twenty minutes."

"Good work. Keep me posted."

Davis ended the call and Temple drained the bottle, tossing it into a recycling bin twenty feet away.

"Nothing but net, sir."

He grunted. "I'm not just a pretty face." He stood, grabbing a Gatorade from the fridge, holding it up for his assistant. She shook her head and he cracked the seal, taking a swig for himself. He slowly paced the room, cooling down from his workout, his mind racing.

"Penny for your thoughts."

He glanced at Davis. "Sure you want to know? If you have to testify in court, you might have to perjure yourself."

She smiled. "Sir, all the orders have been issued in my name, all the invoices paid with my signature. You're completely insulated from this, as long as you don't give any more press conferences."

He stopped, turning toward her. "Why did you do that?"

She turned away slightly. "I'd do anything for you, sir."

He smiled slightly. He knew it was nothing romantic, no infatuation, nothing tawdry.

It was loyalty.

Pure, unadulterated loyalty.

And that kind of loyalty was extremely hard to find today, especially in the civilian world. He walked toward her and stopped in front of her. "I'd give you a hug, but you'd have to change your clothes."

She looked up at him, her eyes slightly red, and smiled. "We wouldn't want that, now, would we?"

"So what do we do now? Has our team made any progress?"

She nodded as he headed toward the shower. "Yes, actually, they have. They've identified the group that tried to sell the ToolKit a few months ago."

Temple stepped behind a screen, stripping to his birthday suit. "I thought we already knew that."

"We knew what they called themselves, but not who they actually were."

Temple's eyebrows rose, and he poked his head out from behind the screen. "You know *who* they are? Like actual names, not Cyberbob?"

"Oh, we only know handles at the moment, but we now know where they're located."

"How?"

"Our guys are good. I didn't bother asking."

Temple stepped into the shower, turning on the water. "Where are they?"

"The Ukraine."

"Not much of a surprise there. Get the location to Simmons. I want his team over there ASAP."

"And if he finds them?"

"Tell him to follow his own rules."

If they're not kids, or American, then kill them.

Operations Center 2, CIA Headquarters
Langley, Virginia

Chris Leroux stared at his display, reading the dispatches pouring in after Temple's call to action against hackers. He could understand the man's pain, despite not having children of his own. He just had to imagine how his own parents would react if something happened to him, and nothing was being done about it.

But that was the problem. Something *was* being done about it, though perhaps not what Temple wanted. Temple wanted his interpretation of justice, and that wasn't necessarily the right thing. Everyone had teams of specialists that hacked their enemies. It was the new way to fight a war. And like the Cold War, where people died, it was the measured response that was key. If America or the Soviet Union had overreacted every time one of their agents was killed, the planet would be a smoking mess right now.

And the same was true with cyberwarfare.

If bombs and rockets were the response to hack attacks, the world would be in far worse shape than it currently was.

But that wasn't what had happened here, at least that's what was generally believed in the cyber community.

This was not a rogue state launching an attack.

This was black hat hackers.

Criminals, pure and simple.

And for those people, he sort of agreed with Temple. Killing them wouldn't start a war, though it might just curb the enthusiasm of others not yet on a grieving father's radar.

Though it would appear he was on theirs. Reports were now coming in that all of Temple's web assets were under attack, more and more of those he had called for the death of, piling onto various types of assaults, mostly Denial of Service attacks where they overwhelmed the company's servers.

But what was interesting was the response.

None.

At least none that was evident. Normally a company would take action to thwart the attack, yet it appeared nothing was being done at all. Instead, Temple websites were down around the globe, the company doing nothing about the attack. The press was reporting that the night shift staff had been sent home early, and it left Leroux to wonder if that might be the reason nothing was going on.

There was nobody manning the store.

"Holy shit!" Leroux turned toward Randy Child's workstation. "Sorry, boss, but, I mean, holy crap!"

"What?"

"Look at this." He pointed at the displays in the front of the room, a map of the world appearing as Child tapped at his keyboard. It zoomed in on the Ukraine, various numbers and charts appearing.

"What am I looking at?"

"The Internet was just shut off in the Ukraine."

Leroux's eyebrows shot up as the room became silent. "What?"

"Not completely, but about ninety percent of their traffic just died."

Leroux rose, stepping toward the display. "What happened? The Russians?"

"I don't know, but it's like someone just threw a switch and killed the bulk of their bandwidth."

Leroux tapped his chin for a moment then turned to Tong. "Have you been able to figure out where most of the attacks against Temple Technologies are coming from?"

She nodded, pointing at a new chart on the screen. "Ukraine is number one, Belarus number two."

"Belarus just went down."

Leroux glanced at Child. "How the hell are they doing it?"

"No idea. Do you think it's Temple?"

"That would be pretty ballsy if it was them. It could put some people in jail."

"The dude just called for people to murder hackers. I don't think he cares about going to prison."

Leroux sighed then snapped his fingers. "Wait a minute. What's Temple known for?"

"Widower. Daredevil."

Leroux shook his head. "No, the company, not the man. They're a tech company."

"Yes."

"Routers, communications, satellites…"

Child whistled. "Holy shit. Do you think they spiked their own hardware?"

Leroux shrugged. "I would if I were him. Hell, I would if I were *them*. Your company is being attacked using your own equipment. Shut it down."

Tong cleared her throat. "But wouldn't that mean they had built a backdoor into their equipment? Would that be legal?"

"Depends on where it was manufactured and where it was sold. Remember, they subcontract out a lot of the work. If the subcontractor technically did it, and performed the installation, then Temple might just be able to come out of this looking clean. And don't forget, our own government might have had his company insert the backdoor on these foreign sales."

Child whistled. "I'm checking all my hardware when I get home."

Leroux chuckled. "Me too." He returned to his station. "Which raises an interesting question, though."

Tong looked at him. "What?"

"If they're able to shut down their hardware remotely, can they monitor what's going through it? If they can, then they might actually know exactly where these attacks are coming from."

Child spun in his chair, staring at the ceiling. "Whoever they are, they better hope somebody doesn't start publishing their home addresses."

Temple Technologies Corporate Head Office
Mountain View, California

Temple looked up as Davis entered the room, waving her tablet computer, a smile on her face. "It's working."

He stared at her. "What's working?"

"Your idea to retaliate. Our external team we set up—untraceable back to us, of course—just essentially shut down the Ukraine and Belarus."

Temple smiled. His company's servers received millions of hits a day if not billions, and a large proportion of them were cyberattacks, fishing expeditions by automated tools designed to test for vulnerabilities. He knew from their own internal reporting where the bulk of these attacks came from, where the disproportionate number of these attacks came from—countries like the Ukraine and Belarus.

Countries, curiously, with heavy ties to Russia.

These countries, among others, had become the hub of illegal cyber activity. Not necessarily because the hackers were located there, but because their governments looked the other way rather than prosecute, so traffic was directed through them, especially the Russian portion of the Ukraine.

But not today. Not anymore.

The countries would suffer, and he'd probably never get another contract there, yet he couldn't care less. He couldn't care less if he ever received another contract from one of the too many countries turning a blind eye to digital crimes.

"How long will they be down?"

"Days at least, unless we intervene."

"Let them drown. Maybe then the governments will take action and clean up their own backyards."

"Doubt it."

Temple grunted. "You're probably right." He eyed her. "You've got more, don't you?"

She grinned. "Yup."

"What?"

"Our guys have been using the backdoors to access the ISP records. We've pulled hundreds of physical addresses from their databases."

A smile climbed half of Temple's face. "So we know who's behind the attacks on us?"

"We know where the attacks are coming from. They might be victims as well through viruses or malware, but it should be simple enough to find the true source. It's just going to take some time."

"Good. Keep Simmons informed, but I get the impression there's too much work for one team." He paused, tapping his chin. "Dox them."

Davis' eyes widened. "Sir?"

"Publish the list. Anonymously. Indicate that it's a suspected list of hackers' home addresses."

"Sir, it could be a bloodbath!"

"That's the idea."

Davis paled slightly. "Sir, there could be innocent people caught up in this. We don't know who's actually the hacker and who's just being used by them."

He stared at her for a moment. "We don't have time to wait to figure out who's who. I want that list published."

"No."

He glared at her. "Excuse me?"

"Sir, I can't let you do this. You won't be able to live with yourself. What if some kid, some little girl like your Angela, is playing on her computer and it's been infected by something she knows nothing about. What if some vigilante storms into her house and starts shooting, because he thinks he's going to get some reward from a billionaire on the other side of the world?"

He sighed, glancing at the photo of his daughter. "You're right. But we can't sit on this. What do you suggest?"

"Let me put everybody we can on this. We'll say it's a cybersecurity operation to determine who's behind the attacks on our servers. We'll provide the info to the FBI as we go, but that list will be leaked as well. We'll say we were hacked and didn't know it."

He smiled slightly as he stared at her. "I'm glad you're on my side."

Bureau 121

North Korean Cyberwarfare Agency

Classified Location

Colonel Park glanced up at the knock on his door. "Enter."

His aide stepped inside, Captain Tann's expression grim as he closed the door behind him. It was a rough time for all of them. The situation with Temple was getting out of control, and though it had nothing to do with him or Bureau 121, things were getting uncomfortably close to assets they had employed in the past.

"What now?" he asked, tossing his glasses on the desk and massaging the bridge of his nose.

Tann sat in one of the chairs in front of the desk and sighed. "Our team failed."

"What?"

"They were wiped out when they attempted to retrieve Agent K."

Park's jaw dropped as he sank back in his chair. "All of them? Dead?"

"Yes, sir."

"The ambassador's son?"

"Dead."

Park paled. "Does the ambassador know yet?"

Tann's eyes darted toward the door. "Umm, I was leaving that for you."

"You're fired."

Tann shrugged. "At least I'll still be alive."

139

Park sighed. "I wouldn't count on it. I never should have agreed to let him go on the mission."

"You know how he is. And with his connections, any type of contradiction means a labor camp or death for us and our families."

Park tensed, the very thought of either possibility horrifying. North Korea was his home. He loved it and their Dear Leader, but it wasn't what the people thought. He had been shocked when he first left North Korea on deployment for Bureau 121 ten years ago. Bureau 121 was the cyberwarfare arm of the Korean People's Army, thousands of highly trained specialists whose sole aim was to conduct digital warfare against the enemies of their country.

He was one of hundreds deployed around the world, disguised as diplomatic staff, or for those under deeper covers, as South Korean business people, tourists, or immigrants. One of the greatest advantages they had over America was the fact their enemy welcomed immigrants into their country. White Americans roaming around Pyongyang would be noticed immediately, but North Koreans in Washington?

Nobody would blink an eye in a multicultural society.

He had never been to America, though hoped to go one day. Russia had been an eye opener, even more so than Beijing, his first encounter with a foreign country. China was incredible. There were so many people, living in harmony, with the modern and ancient fused together. It had been stunning to see how much more advanced they were than his home was, where the government told them day in and day out that they were the most advanced country in the world, that their enemies beyond the gates were starving and weak, desperate to take what North Korea had accomplished through hard work and sacrifice.

It was all a lie.

Though he would never admit that.

At least once a week he was interrogated by his own government, his loyalties tested. His standard answer when challenged about how what he saw contradicted what he had been taught, was that it was an imperialistic trick meant to deceive, and that he wasn't allowed to see the truth, that those outside of this small microcosm of Western life were actually miserable.

Moscow was a lie.

Beijing was a lie.

Home was the only truth.

He had even believed it for a while.

But it was bullshit.

Yet knowing that didn't diminish his loyalty to his country or his Dear Leader. He loved his country and its people, and the leader chosen for them by divine right. Whatever problems his country had, were clearly caused by the corrupt West, and he could understand why the people back home had to be lied to.

If they knew the truth, if they knew they were suffering and their enemies weren't, there could be chaos.

And their enemies would be upon them.

He couldn't allow that to happen, even if it meant death for him and his loved ones. For the leadership never tolerated failure, and never accepted blame.

But now the son of the ambassador to the United Nations was dead, his father well connected, a second or third cousin to the Dear Leader. And someone would be made to pay.

And as the Americans might say, shit always runs downhill.

He looked at his aide, sitting across from him, concern on the man's face. He might plausibly pin it on him, but he still risked being held accountable for his underling's screw-up.

No, there would be no sacrificial lamb for this one.

"Is there any way we could pin it on the Russians?"

Tann's eyes shot wide. "Umm, I'm not sure. None that I can think of, anyway." Tann leaned forward, lowering his voice. "Do you really think it needs to come to that?"

Park stared out the window for a moment, the flag of his great nation slightly visible. Pride and fear surged through him. Agent K was *his* man, and he was responsible for his actions. Someone had stolen the same data Agent K had, and had used it to perpetrate a massive ransomware attack around the world. If Agent K revealed his involvement to the Americans, then North Korea would be blamed for the attack, and that was unacceptable.

He had to die.

He turned back to Tann. "Terminate Agent K. Do whatever it takes."

Albany, New York

Janine Graf sat in the passenger seat of the SUV carrying her former partner, two others completing the mini-convoy. It had taken almost two hours to straighten out the mess, the locals not too trusting, despite her credentials. It wasn't until the NSA team had arrived in full tactical gear that she was actually believed.

And then the real hassle had begun.

She wasn't supposed to have been there, and she wasn't supposed to have engaged, but as she had explained, it was the Homeland agent who had taken out seven of the hostiles, Penn the eighth. She had no clue who they were, and though she was pretty sure Penn didn't know them personally, she was confident he knew who sent them.

Because she didn't believe a word coming out of his mouth. He continued to proclaim his innocence, to claim the memory stick had been blank, and that Hummel must have transferred the data before he even reached the house.

That was a possibility.

But then who had just tried to kill him?

If Hummel was the bad guy here, then shouldn't these assassins be after him?

No, the only thing that made sense was that her former partner was the guilty party here, though convincing her superiors might be a challenge, since Penn's theory that Hummel had transferred the data before even getting to his house was plausible.

The problem was she knew Hummel.

In all the ways that mattered.

He had loved her, had told her everything, had shared his most intimate secrets with her, and she believed him.

He did it for love, not for profit, which meant he would never have done what Penn claimed.

And none of Penn's claims explained the team sent to either collect him or kill him.

She frowned.

And who the hell was this Kane guy? He had taken off as the police arrived, but not before making sure she was safe. He definitely wasn't Homeland, otherwise he would have stuck around. Who was he? Who did he work for?

He was good. She had never before seen anyone operate so smoothly, so confidently. Penn had saved them, but she had little doubt Kane was about to.

Eight to one odds didn't seem so far-fetched with someone like that.

She turned in her seat and stared at Penn. "Why did you do it?"

He shook his head, his eyes wide. "I didn't do anything wrong! Why won't you believe me?"

"Oh, I don't know. Maybe the house you're now living in, the Jag in the driveway."

"Hey, don't look at me. That's my wife's car. Her business is doing really well now. When we moved, we upgraded. Since when has that been a crime?"

"Then why did your wife take off with your kid just a few minutes before that hit squad arrived?"

Penn paused.

Got you.

"It was all planned."

"Bullshit." Graf wagged a finger at him. "You forget, I know you too well. And I know her. Nothing was ever last minute with her, it was always planned precisely. I watched what happened. That was a panicked exit, completely unplanned. She was running from something, and you know what it is."

Penn said nothing, instead staring out the window.

"Don, please, come clean with me so I can help you. Who's trying to kill you?"

Penn's head spun toward her. "Are you kidding me? Did you see that press conference that lunatic gave earlier? My name is out there, and a billionaire is calling for my death! Every damned nut-job in the country is going to be trying to kill me." He jutted his chin at her. "And you too! Our lives are over!"

Her phone vibrated and she glanced at the display, an unknown caller indicated. Somebody had been calling her for the better part of an hour, but she had been busy fielding calls from too many known numbers to bother with the unknown.

Though something in her gut demanded she take the call this time. "Hello?"

"For Christ's sake, it's about time! Special Agent Graf, this is Special Agent Kane. You need to learn to answer your damned phone."

Graf's defenses went up. "Yeah, well, I don't take calls from unknown numbers, and I definitely don't take them from imposters. If I give Homeland Security a call, will they have even heard of you?"

"Who I am is irrelevant. There's something you need to know."

Her eyes narrowed at his change in tone. "What?"

145

"One of the hit squad was the son of the North Korean ambassador."

Graf's stomach flipped. "What!"

"This has nothing to do with Temple, and everything to do with who your partner sold the ToolKit to."

Graf spun in her seat, staring at Penn, her former partner finally showing some discomfort. "You're working for the North Koreans?"

The radio attached to the dash squawked, cutting off any retort from Penn.

"Sierra Three here. We've picked up a tail."

Graf spun in her seat to look out the rear window as she grabbed the radio off the dash. "This is Special Agent Graf. I've just been informed that the North Koreans are involved. We need backup, now!"

Kane shoved the accelerator to the floor as he dialed Leroux. His call with Graf had been cut off in a burst of static he recognized—a cellphone jammer had been deployed. They were highly illegal, but criminals and governments used them to prevent cellphone signals from being sent or received for various reasons. Troop convoys used them to prevent remote detonation of IEDs, and people like him used them to prevent calls for help from being transmitted.

And that was exactly what he feared was happening here.

He had heard someone say a tail had been spotted, and it had to be a backup team, already in position in case the primary failed. Whoever it was had balls. To attack an NSA convoy in New York was insanity, though the North Koreans were never known for levelheadedness. He had little doubt in his mind now that they were behind this—there was no way the North Korean ambassador's son would be working for someone else. He was clearly on a mission for his government, trying to earn his bones so he could move up in the bureaucracy.

His family was already obviously highly respected and trusted, plum assignments outside the country rare and only going to those most loyal to the ruling family. But those assignments could also be very dangerous. Any suggestion of impropriety, of disloyalty, of wavering from the Stalinist state's beliefs, could mean recall and death.

Something told him heads would literally roll after tonight's failure, though if the secondary team succeeded, perhaps fewer might.

But since he had no skin in their family feud, he was content to disrupt their plans once again, though this time he feared they would be shooting first, and not sticking around to answer questions.

Leroux finally answered his call. "Leroux. What's your status?"

"Returning to the scene. Do you have a twenty on the NSA convoy with Penn?"

"Just a sec." There was a pause. "Six miles from your position. Route guidance being sent to your phone now."

Kane glanced at the display, the phone mounted on the dash. "Got it. Get backup to the area. I think they're about to be hit again."

"Copy that. North Koreans again?"

"That would be my guess. Why? Do you have any other suspects?"

"Any number. With Temple putting out a call for hackers' heads on the chopping block, I'd say pretty much any whack-job in the world is out looking for people who own a computer."

"Any reports yet?" Kane took a sharp right, leaning on his horn as he blasted through a red light.

"Some things showing up on the secondary press sites. Mostly in the Ukraine. I guess people are pissed their Internet is down, so they're beating up their neighbors."

Kane frowned, pulsing his horn several times then swerving into the opposing lane, headlights in front of him scattering. "Sounds like it's going to get ugly."

"Randy says you've got a rig coming from your right at the next intersection."

Kane checked right and spotted the truck going full steam and smiled. Obviously, someone under Leroux's command was on the ball, monitoring his progress. "Hold on." He said it more to himself than Leroux, hammering on the gas, taking advantage of a break in the traffic, still on the wrong side of the road. "It's gonna be close!" He gripped the steering wheel, blasting through the intersection and jerking to the right as the cabin was filled with the blinding lights of the rig, its horn blaring as the sound of air brakes locking up were barely heard over the din.

He cleared the bumper of the massive beast, clipping the curb, sending him into a slide, his backend kicking out to the right. He cranked his wheel, steering into the skid, letting the laws of physics trim some speed rather than hammering on his brakes. Suddenly traction kicked back in, and he found himself heading in the right direction again for a brief moment. He let the wheel spin, aligning the tires with the backend then hammered on the gas, surging him toward where he wanted to go. He checked his rearview mirror and saw the rig was just coming to a stop, unscathed, though he had to think the driver's undies needed a swapping or swabbing if no spare was available.

"You're insane."

Kane grinned. "You saw that?"

"Yeah, we did. You're three minutes out. Still no sign of—wait a minute. We've got something." Leroux cursed. "You better hurry."

Graf readied her weapon, stuffing her useless phone back in her pocket. She glared at Penn. "You better hope they kill me first, because I'm going to put a bullet in your damned skull the moment you step out of this vehicle."

Penn stared at her, wide-eyed. "You don't really think I have anything to do with this, do you?"

"Well, somebody does, and citizens on patrol don't send two hit teams to take out one guy they heard about on the news. You're working for the North Koreans, and they've decided they want you dead."

"I'm not. I swear it!"

"Nobody believes you anymore, Don." She glanced around the vehicle. "He doesn't leave this vehicle alive, understood?"

Heads bobbed, the other agents prepared for whatever was about to come. She had no intention of killing Penn, she'd probably go to prison if she did. But if she planted the seed, he might not be so quick to run should the opportunity present itself. And it just might. She couldn't be sure these people were here to kill him. It might be a retrieval—the North Koreans could simply be extracting their spy.

She stared at Penn for a moment, thinking about the day she had first met him. She had been surprised by the Asian man stepping into the briefing room, his name suggesting he was anything but. Sean Penn had popped in her mind the first time she read his name, the only Penn she knew, and he was as white as milk.

"Adopted when I was a baby. I think my birth parents were Korean, but I'm not sure." That had been the answer to the unasked politically incorrect question.

And it had been a lie.

It was clever. Use a traditional sounding name, and on any paperwork, nobody would ever think he might have ties to a foreign power hostile to all things American.

"What the hell is this?"

Graf spun in her seat to see the lead vehicle's brake lights blaring at them, her own driver killing their speed as she spotted someone on the side of the road, a spike strip deployed. She held the radio up to her mouth. "Keep going! Keep going! We've got run flats!"

The brake lights dimmed, but it was too late. The man deploying the strip raised what appeared to be an MP5 and shredded both tires on the driver side, bringing the vehicle to a halt as the man sprinted up the side of the road, firing at the team behind them.

Why isn't he shooting at us?

Her driver hammered on the gas, pulling around the now dead lead vehicle. She twisted around and peered out the rear window to see the trailing vehicle now disabled, the assailant diving into the back of one of the vehicles following them.

They were alone.

And there was no doubt who they were after.

Brake lights lit the night ahead, the entire roadway slowing to a crawl. Kane cursed, searching for a way out of the mess he was about to find himself in. The last intersection before the gridlock was just ahead.

"Two of the NSA convoy vehicles have been taken out ahead of you. You're not going to be—" Leroux cursed as he figured out what Kane was about to do. "Please don't, Dylan."

"Sorry, didn't catch that." He cranked the wheel, skidding over into oncoming traffic once again, laying on his horn with the hazards flashing. He picked a trajectory straight down the middle of the two lanes, giving any traffic an easy choice as to what to do. In a perfect world, everyone would just move a little to the side, and he'd barrel on through unscathed. But experience told him that was never the case.

Too many people panicked when they saw a set of headlights coming at them.

And that meant he'd be the one who would have to swerve, putting him into the direct path of whoever was behind the panicked driver.

Like the jackhole flashing their lights at him.

He pressed harder on the accelerator, putting more of his vehicle in their lane, causing them to finally veer to the right and slam into the guardrail. He didn't bother looking to see if they were all right—they would be, definitely more so than anyone who might suffer a head-on collision should he take his eyes off the road.

"Don't look, but you're passing the two disabled NSA vehicles now. Traffic is clear beyond them."

"Any casualties?"

"None reported. The cellphone jamming seems to be localized to the vehicle containing the prisoner. In two hundred yards, you've got an intersection. Please, for the love of God, get back on the right side of the road."

Kane grinned at Leroux's pleading tone, his friend clearly as frightened as Kane should be. But this wasn't the first time he had done this, and it wouldn't be the last. He spotted the intersection, the lights just turning green. He floored it again, jerking to the right as a crescendo of horns greeted him.

"Thank you."

Kane laughed. "You're welcome. How far?"

"You should be able to see them ahead. Three vehicles. The one in the middle is the NSA vehicle. Looks like they're boxing them in."

"Backup?"

"En route, ten minutes."

Kane cursed. "This is gonna get messy."

"Don't let them box us in!" cried Graf as one of their pursuers overtook them, darting in front and locking up his brakes. They caught his rear bumper as their driver cranked the wheel to avoid the trap, but the vehicle in front was just as quick, and with their speed almost killed, their fate was sealed.

"Is this thing bulletproof?" asked Penn from the back seat.

"It better be." Graf checked her watch. "We've got ten minutes before backup arrives."

They shuddered to a halt, the vehicle behind them hitting their bumper, their SUV now wedged between the two hostiles. Eight men appeared almost immediately, four from each vehicle, MP5s aimed at them, nothing said. One man on either side rushed forward, slapping something on each of their windows. She stared at the tiny round device six inches from her face then gasped.

"Everybody down!"

There were half a dozen small pops, their glass shattered into thousands of tiny pieces, but holding. Something slammed into the window beside her, poking through. It appeared to be a small dart, then the end suddenly expanded, three prongs spreading out. There was a yank, and the bulletproof window was pulled clear.

A weapon was jammed in her face as the process was repeated all around her.

"Drop your weapon."

She nodded, lowering it, then tossing it on the floor. She wasn't going to die, not today, not for Penn. "Do what he says."

Three more thuds were heard, and something was said by one of the hostiles in a language she didn't recognize, but if she had to hazard a guess, was Korean. She spun in her seat, glaring at Penn. "Traitor."

Someone reached in and opened the rear door, more Korean spoken.

Penn shrugged at her. "Sorry, it's been a slice."

It took everything she had to control the urge to grab her weapon and empty it into the bastard, but that would simply mean her own death, and that of the others.

Penn was led toward the lead vehicle as another arrived from behind, screeching to a halt. Someone stepped out, using the door as cover, his weapon aimed at the hostiles.

"Would it be presumptuous of me to ask all of you to lower your weapons?"

Kane aimed his weapon at Penn. He was why everyone was here, and was apparently valuable enough to the North Koreans to risk two international incidents in one day. Shoot him, or at least threaten to, and it might delay things enough for that backup to arrive.

Four weapons swung toward him, the other two still trained on the SUV full of NSA agents.

"I guess so." He made a show of aiming at Penn. "Shoot me, and I guarantee you he dies."

One of the men, all in black, his face covered, stepped toward him, an MP5 aimed casually at Kane. "I think you should mind your own business. You might get yourself hurt."

Kane's eyes narrowed, his jaw dropping, when he heard something behind him.

Graf cried out as Kane was taken down from behind, two of their attackers having disappeared as soon as he arrived, unnoticed by her, and him, until it was too late. Penn was loaded into the lead vehicle, and inexplicably, they took Kane with them as well, tossing him into the back seat of the second vehicle. Within moments they were gone, though not before several dozen rounds were put into their engine block.

She picked up her weapon, uselessly, as the driver called in descriptions of the vehicles. But there would be no catching them. Their backup was five minutes out, and these guys were long gone, probably already on their way to switch vehicles and casually leave the area.

But at least one thing was now certain.

Penn, or whatever his name was, was working for the North Koreans.

And they wanted him alive.

Footfalls startled her, and she calmed once she realized it was their agents from the other two SUVs arriving on foot, spreading out to secure the area in case there was evidence that might provide proof of who was behind this. Though she wasn't sure it really mattered. If the North Koreans had done this, they weren't the kind of country that would care if they were accused of something they had actually done. They would vehemently deny any wrongdoing and proclaim their innocence, threatening war and Armageddon against anyone who would dare make such accusations.

She needed Penn. It was the only way to prove what was going on.

Though the body of the North Korean ambassador's son might be enough proof, at least in covert circles. She had a feeling that bit of information might never see the light of day. By withholding his identity from the press, they might use the body as leverage against the North Koreans.

To what end, she wasn't sure.

What was left to do?

The ToolKit had already been stolen, and was obviously in North Korean hands. They now knew how it had been done, and the North Koreans had Penn. He would be either executed or whisked out of the country before the sun rose the next morning, never to be seen again, or paraded in front of the cameras when safely back in Pyongyang, hailed as a hero of the North Korean people.

So what was left to do?

Penn was gone, the data stolen, the security breach identified and no longer a threat.

Her phone vibrated, her supervisor's name appearing.

Shit.

There *was* one thing left to do.

Salvage her career.

Temple Technologies Corporate Head Office
Mountain View, California

"We got him!"

Temple glanced up from his tablet as Davis entered, waving her phone in the air, triumph on her face. He loved seeing her this way, her smile always brightening his day. Neither of them had smiled much this week, and it was a welcome sight.

If not a fully explained one.

"Who?"

"Simmons just called," she said, dropping into her regular perch. "They had to take out an NSA team to get him, but they got the former NSA agent, Donald Penn."

Temple's chest tightened slightly. "By take out…"

She waved her hand, dismissing his concerns. "Don't worry, nobody was hurt. But they have him and will begin interrogation shortly. We should know who's behind this any minute now."

Temple smiled. "Excellent. I just hope it's someone we can get to."

Davis' smile faded. "What if it's a foreign government?"

Temple stared at her. "What do you mean?"

"Well, we've been assuming he stole the data and sold it to some hackers. What if that wasn't what happened?"

"I thought we already had proof that the ToolKit was in hackers' hands?"

"We do. But we don't really know for sure if he put it there, or if someone else he gave it to, did."

Temple leaned back, rapidly drumming his fingers on the arms of the chair as he contemplated Davis' last statement. She was right. The news reports indicated that the code used for the ransomware attack that had murdered his little angel was from the ToolKit. Of that, there was no doubt. They were almost certain this former NSA agent was the one who had actually stolen it—he believed Clayton Hummel's story.

What they didn't know, what they couldn't know, was whether Penn stole the data as a crime of opportunity, selling it on the black market, or as part of his job as a mole within the agency, stealing it on behalf of a foreign government.

But Simmons would find out the truth.

Yet the question still remained. What do they do if they're actually up against a foreign government?

He pursed his lips, returning his attention to the only person in the world he trusted right now. "Let's cross that bridge when we come to it."

Albany, New York

Kane moaned, rubbing the back of his head. "Why the hell did you hit me so hard?"

"I had to make it look real."

Kane frowned at Sergeant Carl "Niner" Sung, driving the SUV he now found himself in. "A little too real."

"Well, I *was* the lead in my school play."

Kane frowned. "I think you and Cuba Gooding Jr. went to the same acting school."

"What are you trying to say?"

"You overacted."

Niner grinned. "Yet still an Oscar winner. That's pretty good company."

Kane grunted. "You're lucky I recognized BD's voice and dreamy eyes, or I'd have dropped you the moment I heard you coming behind my vehicle."

"Who you kiddin'. I was silent as a, umm, as a—"

"Ballerina?" rumbled a deep voice that Kane felt through the seats. He laughed at Sergeant Leon "Atlas" James' insult, and Niner's indignant reaction.

Kane held up a finger, cutting off the verbal portion. "What the hell are you guys doing here?"

Atlas shrugged. "Kicking your ass, apparently."

Command Sergeant Major Burt "Big Dog" Dawson turned from the passenger seat to face him. "Rather easily, too. You've gone soft at the CIA."

Sergeant Jerry "Jimmy Olsen" Hudson grinned beside him. "Dylan, buddy, are you gonna take that?"

Kane grunted. "It's four against one. I'll wait until there's at least five of you so I can make it fair." He rested his head against the back of the seat and closed his eyes for a moment. These were his former brothers in arms from his days in America's elite fighting unit, the Delta Force, officially known as 1st Special Forces Operational Detachment—Delta. He had spent a brief stint with these men, known as Bravo Team, before recruitment into the CIA.

They were good, loyal soldiers.

And that didn't explain what the hell they were doing assaulting an NSA convoy and kidnapping one of their prisoners.

He opened his eyes. "I'll ask again, what the hell are you doing here?"

Dawson grunted. "Long story. Short version is the head of security for Temple Technologies is ex-Rangers. You've heard of Franklin Temple?"

"Is Niner emasculated just by the mere presence of Atlas?"

"Hey!"

Atlas' impossibly deep voice responded. "You bet the little man is."

Kane smiled, missing the comradery of the Unit. "What about Temple?"

"Well, his daughter died as a result of the ransomware attack earlier in the week."

"I heard."

"What you haven't heard, is that he asked his security chief to find someone who would be willing to do whatever is necessary to bring those responsible to justice."

"And by justice, you mean…"

"He wants them dead. Every one of them."

Kane whistled. "Don't really blame him, though it could cause some problems if it turns out to be the Russians or some other rogue state."

"Exactly. Which is why their security chief called us, and I was sent in as 'Mr. Simmons.'"

Niner twisted around and stuck his tongue out as far as he could while extending un-trademarkable devil horns at him, à la Gene Simmons of Kiss.

Atlas groaned. "Little man, I've seen baby cows with longer tongues."

Niner gave him a pout then returned his attention to the road.

Kane ignored the exchange, still processing what Dawson had said. "So he thinks he's hired an international hit team, but instead he's got the American government doing his dirty work."

"Exactly."

"That's nuts!"

Dawson chuckled. "That's what I said, but it makes sense if you think about it. Delta is the only unit allowed to operate on American and foreign soil, and by actually playing his game without hurting anyone, we stop him from hiring someone else who might not have the same scruples we do."

Kane rubbed the back of his head. "I'm not sure about that not hurting anyone bit, but I get it."

Niner grunted. "Sorry, but like I said, I had to make it look real. And besides, you were about to blow our cover."

"I was not!"

"You so totally were! I saw your jaw drop as soon as you recognized BD's voice. What were you going to say? 'Hey, aren't you the talented and handsome Bravo Team from America's finest group of soldiers, the Delta Force?'"

Kane gave him a look. "You know me so well."

"Told ya." Niner grinned at Atlas in the rearview mirror. "He thinks I'm handsome."

Atlas eyed him. "Yeah, that's the takeaway here."

Kane returned his attention to Dawson. "So, what do you do when you actually have targets to eliminate?"

Dawson shrugged. "Control will decide if they should be eliminated, extracted, or left alone."

"Will that be good enough for Temple?"

"We've faked deaths before. He'll never know. But that's not really the problem anymore."

Kane's eyes narrowed. "What do you mean?"

"After his press conference, there're reports coming in now of vigilante killings all across the Ukraine and the former Soviet Union. Even China has been trying to block any access to the press conference."

"Any innocent victims yet?"

"Oh yeah. It's being used to settle old scores. Like in the Philippines when Duterte basically declared open season on drug pushers and users. People started killing people they had beefs with, then tossed a bag of weed on the body. You can't just declare a segment of society fodder, then turn a blind eye to whether or not someone is actually a member. What Temple hired us for initially, I can understand. Identify who was behind the attack, and bring them to justice. His press conference? That's totally different. Too many innocent people are going to get caught up in this."

"Have they confirmed he's the one who took down the Internet in the Ukraine and Belarus?"

Dawson shook his head. "Not yet, though there's little doubt. Right now, I'm more concerned with who Penn was working for."

"You heard about the North Korean hit team, I take it?"

"Yeah, Control informed us on our way here."

"I think your Control and my Control should talk, then there might not be so many surprises." Kane rubbed his head again.

Niner, a Korean-American, turned back, leaving no hands on the wheel. Dawson cursed and reached over. "Next time, I'm driving."

"I told Penn to get out of the car in Korean, and he did. His file says he's adopted and unilingual, but I don't believe it. He speaks the language."

Kane nodded then pointed ahead of them. "Red light."

The vehicle slowed perfectly, Kane's eyes narrowing as he tried to figure out how Niner was managing it. He glanced to where Niner was staring then pulled Jimmy's sunglasses off, the view ahead reflected in the lenses.

"Hey, you trying to get us all killed?" cried Niner as he turned around to face the front, swatting Dawson's hands off the steering wheel. "I've got this!"

"Are you sure?"

Kane handed Jimmy his glasses back, worn to protect the eyes during an op as opposed to looking dashing. "Expecting trouble?"

Jimmy shrugged. "My Spidey senses are tingling."

Kane's eyes narrowed. "Wrong franchise, dude."

He shrugged again. "I never asked to be pigeonholed with a nickname from Superman."

"Uh-huh." Kane turned back to Dawson when Niner cranked the wheel and they rapidly slowed.

"We're here."

"Good." Dawson threw open the door and stepped out. He leaned back in. "You waiting for an engraved invitation?"

Kane shook his head. "It might be best if Penn doesn't see me cooperating."

Dawson nodded. "Good thinking." He slammed the door shut, leaving Kane glancing around the now empty SUV. The engine of a truck started and he leaned forward, peering out the windshield to see Niner hop in the cab of a delivery van, everyone else, including Penn, climbing in the back. It pulled away moments later.

"Did those bastards just leave me in the middle of nowhere?"

His phone vibrated and he saw Niner wave out the driver's side window, a phone in his hand. Kane peered at the display, a string of emoticons shown.

Waving hand.

Puckered asshole.

Flipped bird.

And a toothy grin.

Dawson glanced around at the others, giving them a look that told them to not ask any questions. Kane was undercover, and they still didn't know how things would play out. "I'm sure you're all wondering what happened with that agent we took. Turns out he knew nothing worth knowing." He nodded toward Atlas. "Our hulking friend here put him out of his misery." He turned to Penn, sitting between the massive Atlas and Dawson's best friend, Master Sergeant Mike "Red" Belme. "Now, it's time for you to talk."

Penn's eyes narrowed. "Umm, you're, umm." He appeared confused, evidently thinking he was among friendlies until this very moment. "Wait, who the hell are you guys? I thought you were sent to extract me?"

"We work for Franklin Temple. Heard of him?"

Penn nodded. "Of course, everybody has. What the hell does he have to do with this? And if you're not...who the hell are you?"

Atlas leaned closer to Penn, squishing him between his shoulder and Red's. "I'd say your worst nightmare, but I hate clichés."

Dawson stifled a smile. "Mr. Penn, we have been contracted by Mr. Temple to bring justice for his little girl who died as a result of the ransomware attack earlier in the week. An attack you are responsible for."

Penn shook his head vehemently. "Bullshit, I had nothing to do with that."

Dawson smiled slightly. "Mr. Penn, we both know you stole the NSA's ToolKit after Mr. Hummel copied it to woo your former partner, Special Agent Graf."

Penn again shook his head. "Never happened."

"Cut the bullshit, Mr. Penn," snapped Dawson. "My colleague spoke Korean to you, and you followed his instructions. According to your official NSA file, you don't speak Korean. So how the hell did you suddenly learn?"

Penn said nothing, instead matching Dawson's glare.

Clearly scaring the man wasn't going to work. He was obviously a loyal foreign agent. But everything was pointing to hackers having launched the ransomware attack, not a foreign government, which meant the ToolKit had been sold by someone, and Dawson's money was on the man sitting across from him.

And that meant he was also motivated by greed.

"Mr. Penn, you seem to be operating under the false assumption that you're being held by the American government."

This caught Penn's attention, his eyebrows rising slightly.

"We are private contractors, hired to bring those responsible to justice. If you cooperate, not only will you live, you might even receive a generous reward from Mr. Temple, should your information prove useful. All we need from you is confirmation of things we already know to be true."

Penn said nothing, but he had visibly relaxed in the last few seconds, especially once Atlas leaned away from him.

"So let's be quick about this. You are working on behalf of the North Korean government."

Penn said nothing, instead staring at the floor.

Dawson flicked a wrist at Atlas. "Shoot him in the knee."

"With pleasure." Atlas drew his sidearm, and Penn's eyes bulged as he pushed away from the big man.

"Wait!"

Dawson held up his hand. "So you do speak. Answer the questions, and you walk out of here. Don't, and you crawl."

"Yes, I work for the Democratic People's Republic of Korea."

"Sleeper agent?"

"Yes. I've been here for almost a decade. Made my way into the NSA. I was activated when I found out I'd have access to the ToolKit due to the loyalty test we were conducting on Hummel."

"So you copied the ToolKit then wiped Hummel's copy."

"Yes."

"Why?"

"To make it look like he was lying, and that it had never actually left the building. That way, nobody would think to keep looking to see if it made it on the market."

"So you sold it."

"Yes."

"For how much?"

"Twenty-five thousand Bitcoins."

Red whistled. "That's a lot of dough if you held on to it."

"I still have most of it. It's worth ten times what it was when I sold it."

"Who'd you sell it to?"

"The Shadow Collective."

"The same ones who put it up for auction a few months ago?"

Penn nodded.

"Did you sell it to anyone else?"

"No. I didn't need to. I had enough money to live comfortably for the rest of my life." He shrugged. "And I couldn't risk my handlers finding out."

"And where are they."

"Not here."

Atlas pressed the barrel of his Glock against Penn's knee.

"Okay, okay! They're in Moscow."

Dawson's eyebrows shot up. "Moscow?"

"Yes."

"What the hell are they doing there?"

"You wouldn't believe me if I told you."

"Try me."

"One of Bureau 121's largest operations is in the North Korean embassy in Moscow, right under the noses of the Russian government."

Temple Technologies Corporate Head Office
Mountain View, California

"Do you have him?"

Temple stood in the window, staring down at the rapidly darkening city, his phone pressed to his ear, the knuckles on his other hand turning white as he tightly gripped the back of his chair, awaiting Simmons' response.

"Affirmative. We have him."

He grinned at Davis, giving her a thumbs up as she listened on another handset. She smiled back, though he sensed she wasn't as happy as he was. He could tell she was having doubts. They had crossed a line tonight, a line he never thought they would have to. His team had assaulted American government officials just doing their job, in order to capture the traitor Penn so they could interrogate him.

It was wrong.

It was illegal.

And it meant they could all go to prison if traced back to them.

He just prayed Simmons was good at his job, and that wouldn't become a possibility.

"What has he said?"

"He's confirmed everything. He copied the data Hummel stole, then wiped the memory card to make it look like Hummel was lying, and he sold it for twenty-five thousand Bitcoins to the Shadow Collective."

"Why did he do it?"

"Money."

168

"No foreign government involvement?"

"No."

Temple sighed with relief, their lives suddenly much simpler. With no foreign governments involved in what had happened, all they had to do was make sure Hummel, Penn, and the Shadow Collective were brought to justice, and this would be over. He paused. "You said he sold the ToolKit for Bitcoins?"

"Yes."

"Get his private key from him. I want to drain whatever he has left."

"Consider it done."

Temple stared at Davis. "Then I want him dead."

Her eyes went wide and she shook her head vehemently, but he ignored her.

"You know my rules," said Simmons.

Temple tensed. "I'm fully aware of your rules. And he's not a child, and he's not an American."

There was a pause. "Why do you say that?"

"Because he's a traitor to his country. He stole our secrets and sold them to a hacker group with known ties to the Russian government. Do you believe for a second that they didn't turn around and give it to their masters in Moscow?"

Another pause. "Agreed. He'll be dead before morning."

A smile crept up the side of Temple's face. "I thought you'd see it my way. Once that's done, I need you in the Ukraine as quickly as possible. I want this Shadow Collective wiped out before the end of day tomorrow."

"With pleasure."

Temple ended the call and returned the phone to its cradle, sitting down in his chair. "You don't look happy."

Davis shook her head. "I'm not."

"Why?"

"I think you know why."

"Explain it to me."

"I don't care if Penn dies. He's a piece of shit. At the very least, he's a criminal, and most likely a traitor. He was going to prison for the rest of his life, no matter what we did tonight. But your team—our team— assaulted United States Federal Agents. Somebody could have been hurt, or worse. That crime alone can put us all in prison for as long as Penn. If it ever gets traced back to us—"

Temple held up a hand. "If it ever gets traced back to *me*. Don't worry, as far as anyone is concerned, you have nothing to do with this. This is all my doing."

She threw her hands up in the air. "That's not true! I talked to Bill and had him arrange Simmons. I set up the team tracking down the hackers' locations. The paperwork is all in my name. That's all on me!"

"Not at all. *I* had you talk to Bill to bring in a security team. You didn't know what *I* was going to use them for. You set up a team to track down the hackers. There's nothing wrong with that. You had no idea that I would then take that information and pass it on to Simmons to then eliminate them. All the paperwork is simply to pay invoices. Nothing on it says 'Payment for hired assassins.'" He smiled gently at her. "Tanya, you're covered. If push comes to shove, you know I'll confess to everything. You'll be protected."

She sighed, removing her glasses and massaging her temples for a moment. "Tell me one thing."

"Anything."

"When Penn is dead, and the Shadow Collective are dead, will that be enough to settle your bloodlust?"

Temple drew a slow breath then turned his chair slightly toward the window, staring at the minions below. Would it be enough? He wanted every hacker in the world dead so this couldn't happen again, but that wasn't realistic. *That* would be insanity. Who had murdered his child? Hummel had stolen the data to impress the undercover female NSA agent Graf. Graf had done nothing wrong, merely doing her job, so he saw no need for revenge against her now that he knew Penn had been behind everything and Graf was an unwitting victim, not an incompetent fool who had let Hummel hoodwink them.

Penn had stolen then sold the data. He was clearly guilty. He had sold it to the Shadow Collective, and they were the same people they had already connected to the ransomware attack, probably designed to recoup some of the money they had spent purchasing the ToolKit.

With Hummel, Penn, and the Shadow Collective gone, he would be satisfied. The fallout of the events would hopefully be enough to make hackers the world over think twice before again doing anything as foolish as what had been done earlier in the week.

He turned back to Davis. "Yes, I think so."

"Then let's put an end to this." She motioned toward the television mounted to the far wall, CNN on a loop of chaos in the Ukraine, then held up her tablet. "Do you realize there are dozens of confirmed dead already? People are killing their neighbors just because they own a computer."

Temple frowned, a hint of a pit forming in his stomach. "Yes, I've seen the reports. It's unfortunate."

"Unfortunate?" Davis closed her eyes for a moment, regaining her composure. She stared at him. "Those people are dead because of you. You went off half-cocked and gave a press conference when you shouldn't have, and called for just this."

"I'm fully aware of that. It was a mistake. I got caught up in the moment. I was thinking about Angela…" His voice cracked. "I'm sorry."

Davis rose then rounded the desk, putting a hand on his shoulder. "*I* forgive you. Now how about we make things right?"

He stared up at her, his eyes burning. "How?"

"We call a press conference, tonight. Put out a statement where you apologize for what you said, tell everyone it was a moment of weakness caused by your grief for your murdered daughter, and that you still want those responsible brought to justice, but not through vigilantism."

He reached up and squeezed her hand on his shoulder. "What would I do without you?"

"Go to prison, apparently."

He laughed, letting go of her hand. "You're probably right." He pointed toward the door. "Now go organize that press conference. I want to get this over with before we hear back from Simmons."

"Yes, sir."

Bureau 121—Moscow Station
Embassy of the Democratic People's Republic of Korea
Mosfilmovskaya Street, Moscow, Russian Federation

Colonel Park cursed, slamming a fist on his desk, causing the contents to rattle, and Captain Tann to flinch. "That bastard! I can't believe he has Agent K!"

Tann nodded as he tried to relax. "It is indeed unfortunate. Mr. Temple's resourcefulness continues to impress."

Park ignored his underling's obvious observations. "We need Agent K back before he talks."

"What if he already has?"

Park paused, pursing his lips. "You don't think he would crack so easily, do you?"

Tann stared about the room, at anything but his superior.

"Speak!"

Tann flinched again. "Yes, sir. Well, sir, I believe we lost Agent K years ago."

Park's eyes narrowed. "What do you mean? He delivered us the ToolKit only two years ago."

"Yes, this is true, but, well, he took a wife, sir! Without sanction. Then he left the NSA—"

"Out of necessity. His career had been stalled because of the botched"—he delivered air quotes—"Hummel investigation. We put him on ice until we could figure out what to do next."

"Yes, and I said we should have brought him in right then."

"And *I* said that would be unwise, as a former NSA agent suddenly disappearing, married with a child, would cause too many questions to be asked. It could start a mole hunt within the American government, and we couldn't risk that."

"Yes, and at the time, that sounded like the right thing to do. But now, here we stand, with Agent K in the hands of mercenaries hired by a madman, who don't have to follow any laws. They could be torturing him as we speak, and he could be confessing to everything."

Park couldn't deny Tann's logic. In retrospect, he should have terminated Agent K the moment he broke protocol and took a wife without permission. It created ties that couldn't easily be broken, making extraction almost impossible. Without a family, Agent K would have simply resigned then moved without leaving a forwarding address beyond a mailbox. He would be back in North Korea, and none of this would be happening.

Yet that wasn't true, was it?

If they had extracted him after the Hummel operation, he still would have come under investigation, and when he was found missing, the Americans might have figured out he was a spy regardless.

But at least he wouldn't be in the hands of Temple.

"We need to get him back, or at the very least terminate him."

Tann nodded. "But how?"

"We need leverage over Temple."

"What could we possibly do? He has no family left, he's worth billions, and recent actions suggest he couldn't care less if he dies or goes to prison."

Park jabbed a finger at the computer, the listening device he had a team plant in Temple's office after his press conference, proving invaluable. "Haven't you been listening?"

"Sir?"

"There's one thing he still cares about."

Tann's eyes narrowed. "Himself?"

Park chuckled then stared out the window for a moment before sucking in a deep breath, committing to something that might just seal his fate. "Send the West Coast team in immediately. We can't leave Agent K in Temple's hands any longer."

Tann's eyes widened. "Yes, sir! But what's the mission?"

Park shook his head. "You really haven't been paying attention, have you?"

Albany, New York

Kane now sat in the driver's seat of the SUV Bravo Team had abandoned him in. Thankfully, Niner had left the keys in the ignition, which had surprised him a little, the bastard known for playing pranks, and what better one than to leave him stranded with two vehicles wanted in relation to an assault on an NSA convoy?

He had already relocated, now in a restaurant parking lot about five miles away, with little chance of anyone stumbling upon him. A new vehicle was already on its way, its ETA less than five minutes. Once it arrived, he'd inform Graf that he had woken up on the side of the road, apparently dumped by those who had kidnapped Penn.

At least then they wouldn't be searching for him, though he knew she had questions he couldn't answer. At least not now.

A car backed in beside him and he glanced over as the door opened and a long, smooth leg appeared. He smiled in appreciation, then followed the lithe figure to the mockingly judgmental face of Sherrie White.

"Do you stare at all women like that?"

He grinned. "Only the ones I know."

"Uh-huh." She jerked her head toward the car. "Come on, let's go."

She climbed back in, closing the door as he stepped out and rounded the rear of the vehicle, sitting in the passenger seat. Sherrie pulled out, quickly putting distance between them and the Bravo Team's vehicle.

Kane glanced at Sherrie. "So what are you doing here?"

She shrugged. "You needed off the books backup, and I was available."

"And this dress you're wearing?"

She gave him a quick look. "It was girls' night, and you interrupted."

He gave her another once over. "Now that's something I'd like to have seen."

"Hey, you've already got a girl. And I'm your best friend's girlfriend!"

He laughed. "Which one upsets you more?"

She paused. "I'm not sure." She harrumphed, a decision made. "Both."

He laughed again. "Your buttons are too easy to press sometimes."

"Uh-huh. So where to?"

"Let's just keep driving." He pulled out his phone, dialing Leroux, putting it on speaker.

"Control Actual here."

"Hey, buddy, it's me. Guess who just picked me up for a night on the town?"

Sherrie leaned toward the phone. "Hey, sweetie, love you!"

"Umm, you're on comms with, like, the entire Ops Center."

Sherrie grinned at Kane. "Okay, I love you all!"

Laughter could be heard.

"That's very nice to hear, Agent White, as I'm certain the NSA and White House representatives on this call will concur."

Sherrie slapped a hand over her mouth and gave Kane a mortified look at the voice of Director Morrison. Kane deflected some of the attention from her.

"Well, Director, you already know *I* love you, and I don't care who knows it. I assume you're aware of what just happened?"

"Yes. The Delta team has Penn in custody and are bringing him in for a formal debriefing by NSA personnel. Right now, we have two concerns. One is the fact Franklin Temple has called open season on anyone who owns a computer, and second and more important, is that Bureau 121 has been operating out of Moscow with impunity."

"Are we confident they had nothing to do with the ransomware attack?"

"No. We do know that the Shadow Collective has been used by the Russians before, and are operating on the Russian side of the Ukraine conflict, essentially under their protection."

Sherrie slowed for a stop sign. "What about the North Koreans? Have they used them?"

"We have no information to suggest they have, but there's so much overlap in these groups, anything is possible."

Kane pinched his chin, thinking. "Sir, I think we have to assume the North Koreans didn't know Penn had sold the data, otherwise they would have extracted or eliminated him long ago."

"Agreed."

"We have to assume they're going to make another play for him."

"Agreed."

"How long before he's secure?"

"Any minute. Delta is inbound with him on a chopper as we speak."

Kane sighed with relief. If Delta had him in a helicopter, there was little chance of interception. He winked at Sherrie. "Sir, I'd make sure you keep Niner away from him. He is, after all, Korean. Who knows where his loyalties lie?"

Somebody coughed.

"I'll take that under advisement, Special Agent."

Kane grinned at Sherrie who punched him in the shoulder. Hard.

"Sir, with Penn secure here, I'd like to request permission to visit Moscow."

"To what end?"

"I haven't seen Red Square in a while, and it might be nice to plant the American flag there in case we need it."

"You've got a girlfriend. You better not be planting anything over there," muttered Sherrie.

Somebody laughed on the other end, Sherrie slapping her hand over her mouth.

"Very well. We'll arrange it," replied Morrison.

Kane glanced at Sherrie. "I'd like to suggest Agent White accompany me." She grinned eagerly. "It would be a good opportunity for her to practice her Russian."

"Agreed. She can act as chaperone. I'd hate to have to train a new agent after Fang gets through with you should anything get planted in the wrong place."

Well done, sir!

"Good thinking, sir."

"Anything else?"

"No, I'm good. Can I pick you up anything while I'm there? Borscht? Vodka?"

The line went dead.

Kane looked at Sherrie. "Do you think I went too far?"

She eyed him. "Umm, yeah?"

He grinned. "Good. Though I do think your flag planting joke was the highlight of the conversation."

She stared at him, aghast. "I really need to find new friends. Hanging around with you is making me do stupid things."

Director Morrison's Office, CIA Headquarters
Langley, Virginia

"The domestic side of this is no longer our concern, and officially, it never was."

Leroux nodded at Morrison. "Understood. Did you catch any flak from Washington for Dylan being involved?"

Morrison chuckled. "No more than usual when it comes to him. If it wasn't for the fact he saved Special Agent Graf's life, and kept Penn alive, the story might have been different. Right now, Washington is happy with his cover as a Homeland agent should anything go public about his involvement, and Homeland is happy to have a hero on their payroll, though his name and picture will never be released."

"Good to hear." Leroux shifted in his chair. "Umm, I know you don't like me being Control when Sherrie—I mean Agent White—is involved, but, umm, well, I was wondering, who did you have in mind?"

Morrison regarded him for a moment, his steepled fingers bouncing off his chin. "I need my best on this, and you and your team fit the bill." He held up a finger before Leroux's smile spread too far. "But! And it's a big but! Sonya takes over the moment she feels it's necessary. Understood?"

Leroux nodded. "I agree completely, but it won't."

"Good. I've already spoken to her, and I've made it clear that despite any feelings she might have for you personally, she must not hesitate to take over. If she does, I'll have her transferred off your team."

Leroux blushed. "Umm, I'm, umm, sure that won't be necessary."

Morrison chuckled. "Two gorgeous women after you." He shook his head. "Ahh, to be young."

Leroux burned hot, staring at the floor. "It's not all it's cracked up to be sometimes."

Morrison leaned back in his chair, laughing. "Son, one day you'll be sitting in this chair, looking at the young whipper-snapper you've been mentoring for years, and give everything to be that young just for one more day."

Leroux smiled shyly, glancing at Morrison. "Yeah, I guess it's not so bad."

Morrison pointed at the door. "Go, before I get too jealous." He leaned forward, picking up his phone. "And see what you've done?"

Leroux rose, his eyes narrowing. "What?"

"You've made me feel guilty. Now I have to call my wife and prove I'm still a good husband."

Temple Technologies Corporate Head Office
Mountain View, California

"So to reiterate, I apologize for anything I might have said that some misinterpreted as a call to action to kill hackers. Those were the words of a grieving father. Yes, when I said them, I did want them dead, but I didn't mean that they should actually be killed. If I said I wished every pedophile in the world were dead, I would mean it, but it wouldn't mean that people like you and me should go out and kill them. Let's leave the justice system to do its job."

"Mr. Temple, Kate Enright, KPLA. What do you say to the families of the dozens who have already died? We have reports that scores have been murdered, mostly in the Ukraine. What about those people who have already fallen victim to your call for vigilante justice?"

"To them, I say I'm sorry for their loss."

"But aren't you responsible?"

Davis stepped forward, leaning toward the array of microphones. "Mr. Temple in no way accepts responsibility for the actions of those who felt taking the law into their own hands was somehow justified by what he said. Next question."

Temple gave her a slight smile, Davis once again saving the day.

"Is your company responsible for the Internet outages in the Ukraine and Belarus?"

Temple shook his head. "No, we're not. Once again, we're the victim here. As you are aware, since my previous press conference, Temple Technologies has been the target of near constant cyberattacks.

This has spread to our subsidiaries and subcontractors as well. In this case, my company has provided much of the backbone hardware in these countries, and hackers have targeted the Internet Service Providers, the ISPs, in these countries to try and embarrass our firm. We're confident they will be back up and running in short order. Last question."

"Sir, my sources in Washington tell me that former NSA Special Agent Donald Penn has been arrested and is now being questioned for his involvement with the ransomware attacks. Will you be testifying should he go to trial?"

Temple's heart slammed as he processed the words. If Simmons had Penn, then how the hell could he be in custody? Was Simmons lying to him? He hadn't seen any proof that Penn had been captured, so it was possible. He glanced over his shoulder at his security chief, who appeared slightly flushed and was avoiding eye contact.

Could Simmons be government?

Had he been betrayed?

He looked at Davis who appeared as shocked as he was by the statement, though she was covering it well, probably better than he was.

He turned back to the cameras. "I'm sorry, but you caught me off guard with that piece of good news. If progress is being made in the case, then I applaud the government's efforts, and should Agent Penn prove to be guilty, I hope our courts deliver a long, punishing sentence. Good night."

He turned, striding toward the doors of the office tower, dozens of questions shouted at his back. He cleared the revolving doors, heading for his private elevator. He glanced over his shoulder at his security chief, Bill Garvin. "Come with me."

Garvin nodded, stepping onto the elevator with Temple and Davis. They rode in silence, then exited at the top floor, Temple leading the way into his office. Davis closed the door as Temple turned on Garvin.

"What the hell is going on?"

Garvin stared at him, wide-eyed. "Umm, I'm not sure what you mean?"

"I just spoke to Simmons, not two hours ago, and he told me they had Penn in custody."

Garvin raised his hands slightly. "Sir, I have no idea. I haven't spoken to Simmons since I arranged the initial meeting. I thought it was best I keep out of it, just in case something went wrong."

Temple stared at him, his chest heaving as he sucked in each enraged breath. "Why should I believe you?"

"Sir, I don't know what to say, except before we go any further, can we at least confirm this reporter's story? You know how the press are these days."

Davis stepped forward, the voice of reason. "He's right, sir. We need confirmation. I suggest we call Simmons, and demand proof that they have Penn."

"But I told him to kill him."

"Then he can send us a photo of the body."

Temple sighed. "Very well. Make the call. Now."

FBI Field Office
Albany, New York

Command Sergeant Major Dawson watched through the two-way mirror as Penn was grilled by two NSA interrogators, the floodgates opened after their brief ride together. It appeared Mr. Penn would be a veritable fountain of information.

Atlas' impossibly deep voice rumbled. "I get the sense he doesn't want to return to Korea."

Niner held his hand up, making a show of squeezing his thumb and forefinger together, as if squishing Penn's head between them. He glanced at Atlas. "*North* Korea."

Atlas shrugged, casting his line. "North. South. What's the difference?"

Niner's eyes shot wide as Dawson exchanged knowing looks with the others. "Are you kidding me? There's a huge difference!"

Atlas stared through the glass. "What? A bunch of little people I don't understand, eating rice."

Niner's head tilted forward. "I'll have you know, the average Korean is almost as tall as the average American."

Atlas gave him a look. "Oh, so you're the exception rather than the rule?"

Jimmy snorted. "Someone call the burn ward!"

Niner spun on him. "Don't you start. I'm liable to get all verklempt."

Jimmy made a show of searching his pockets. "Sorry, I'm all out of tissues."

"And tampons," added Atlas, the rest of the room erupting.

This elicited an over the shoulder glance from one of the interrogators. Dawson raised his hands. "Okay, settle down. Apparently these walls are thin."

Atlas pressed a hand against the wall separating them from the interrogation room. "Must not have a lot of beatings here."

Niner eyeballed him. "One's about to happen if someone doesn't keep his mouth shut."

Atlas reached out and grabbed Niner, bear hugging him, Niner's arms and legs splayed out like a bug on a windshield. "It's okay, little man, I'm sorry."

"Can't. Breathe. Killing. Me."

Atlas let go, Niner collapsing to the floor.

"Who needs enemies when you've got friends like him?"

Dawson's phone vibrated. He pulled it from his pocket and cursed. "Everyone quiet. It's Temple." He swiped his thumb. "Go ahead."

"This is Davis. We've had reports here that Penn is in custody in Washington."

Dawson frowned.

We've got a leak somewhere.

"I'm sure you know better than to trust the press." He pointed at Niner and Atlas as he covered the microphone. "Get him in here, and keep him quiet."

"Of course, but Mr. Temple will require proof that you have Penn."

Atlas and Niner left, and Dawson watched as they entered the interrogation room, grabbing Penn, Atlas holding out a massive hand, ending any protest by the shocked agents.

"Our orders were to kill him."

"Have you?"

The door opened and Penn was hauled inside, Atlas' hand clasped over the prisoner's mouth. "Not yet."

"Why not?"

"We're still trying to get the private key information for his Bitcoin account." He flicked a finger and Atlas moved his hand. Dawson landed half a dozen quick blows until Penn's nose was broken and bloodied.

"What was that?"

"The interrogation is ongoing. Just a second." He activated the camera, taking some video of Penn, blood running down his chin, tears pouring from his eyes. He sent the video to Davis' number. "I just sent you some video."

There was a pause then a gasp. "Okay, umm, understood. I'll get back to you."

"Copy that."

Davis' voice faded, as if speaking to someone else. "Excuse me. Can you do that later?"

A man shouted, then a woman screamed.

Temple Technologies Corporate Head Office
Mountain View, California

Temple gasped as he backed away, raising his hands as a man shoved aside the janitor cart he had pushed through the door, but not before pulling a gun from the wastebasket. Three others followed, drawing weapons from the cart as well, all dressed as members of the cleaning staff.

Bill Garvin stepped forward. "Hey, what the hell is this!"

Davis screamed as Garvin was cold-cocked. He crumpled to the floor, unmoving, and Temple instinctively took a step toward him as Davis dropped her phone. One of the men stomped a steel-toed boot on it, shattering the device as he grabbed Davis by the arm.

Temple held out his hands, pleading with the men. "Listen, I'll give you whatever you want. Just let her go."

None of the men said anything, instead operating with military precision as one kept a weapon calmly trained on him, one held Davis in place with a gun to her stomach, and the other two removed what appeared to be heavy black bags from the cart.

The two men quickly donned the bags, which appeared to be backpacks of some sort. It finally occurred to him what they were when harnesses were fit around their legs and waist.

Parachutes!

His eyes narrowed as the two men swapped positions with their comrades, who then repeated the process, all four soon sporting chutes.

189

What the hell are they going to do with parachutes?

He glanced at the large windows lining his office and gasped. "Hey, wait a minute, you're not going to jump off this building, are you?" He stepped closer to Davis as a second man approached her. Each held one of her arms out as the third fit a harness around her. A harness without a parachute.

They're here for her!

That had to be what was going on. They would be fitting him first, if it weren't the case. He should be getting fit with the harness in case something went wrong, in case they had to leave quickly.

But why her?

It made no sense. He stepped toward the men, his arms out, when the one holding a gun on him spun, firing half a dozen rounds into Garvin. Davis screamed, and Temple backed away as the weapon was retrained on him.

"Okay, okay, I'll keep back. But please, don't hurt anyone else. Take me instead. I'm the one you want. I'm the one with the money."

He stifled a gasp as Davis' harness was snapped to one of the men, the other two stepping back and drawing their weapons. Their muzzles flashed as they belched lead in Temple's direction. He dropped to the floor, covering his head.

"Please stop! I'll do whatever you want!"

The windows behind him shattered, wind whipping through the office, loose papers on his desk picked up in the vortex as the firing stopped. The man with Davis attached to him grabbed her in a bear hug, carrying her to the window as Temple rose, watching in horror as he leaped out the window, the other three sprinting past him and disappearing from sight.

He rushed to the window, grabbing onto one of the support beams as he leaned out, staring at the city below. He saw nothing at first, then finally spotted four dark rectangles as they floated toward the ground. Screams and shouts caught his ear, and he leaned out even further, staring down at the ground below, the press still gathered, delivering their live reports from the news conference over not ten minutes before. He couldn't make out what was going on, but it was clear from the sounds that the glass had fallen on the reporters.

A gust of wind caught him and he was nearly swept out the window. He gripped the column as hard as he could as shouts erupted from behind him.

If I just let go now, it'll all be over. I can be with them.

He closed his eyes, the tears burning.

Just let go.

He loosened his grip when powerful hands grabbed him, hauling him inside.

"Sir, are you okay?"

It took a moment for him to get reoriented, half a dozen members of the security team now in his office, one kneeling over the body of Garvin, the others with their guns drawn as he was led from the room.

"Sir?"

"I-I'm fine." He glanced over his shoulder at Garvin. "Is he dead?"

The man examining him nodded.

Temple sighed, closing his eyes for a moment. "They took Tanya."

"Who took her?"

"Four men, dressed as janitors. They came in, shot Bill, put on parachutes, strapped Tanya to one of them, then jumped out the window. It was over in a couple of minutes."

"We saw them on the security cameras. We sent a team right away, but, well…"

Temple shook his head. "They were too fast."

"Did they say anything?"

Temple shook his head. "Not a word. But if the police hurry, they might be able to get them before they land."

The man doing the talking pulled out his radio. "What did they look like?"

Temple's eyes narrowed as he struggled to picture them. "They all looked pretty much alike. Asian, dark skin, short dark hair, short, slim builds."

The man nodded as he activated his radio. "They almost sound military."

Temple's chest tightened as he remembered the photo of Donald Penn he had seen on a news report. He was Asian as well. Korean-American apparently.

Could there be something more going on here?

Davis screamed until a hand was slapped over her face, her lower lip painfully crushed. The sharp sting silenced her, and the hand was removed as she floated toward the ground, her captor strapped to her back. She glanced over either shoulder, trying to spot Temple, but couldn't see anything at first until her eyes adjusted, soon spotting the three other parachutes, lone occupants dangling under each as the ground rapidly approached.

They had taken her, and her only.

At least he's safe.

Yet why? Why had they taken her? She was nothing. Yes, she had money. Through a generous salary from Temple, along with stock options, she was technically a millionaire. But Temple was a mega-billionaire. If they wanted money, they should have taken him, not her.

And who were they? They all appeared Asian, perhaps Korean or Chinese, maybe even Japanese. She was ashamed to think they all looked alike to her, though at this moment she chastised herself for being concerned with political correctness instead of her life.

But they were all short.

Uniformly short.

North Korean?

Penn was supposed to be Korean.

She had met a lot of business people over the years from Asia, and the stereotype of a short Korean was BS. They weren't short at all. But *North* Korean men were, something to do with malnutrition during childhood.

Could the North Koreans be involved somehow?

But involved with what? If Penn were North Korean, then there must be more going on here than a simple ransomware attack perpetrated by Ukrainian-based hackers who bought the tools from a corrupt NSA agent.

If the North Koreans were involved, then *countries* were involved.

And if that was the case, then this thing just became a lot more serious than either she or Temple had thought only twenty minutes ago.

Oh God, what have we got ourselves into?

Then it dawned on her what was going on.

They wanted Penn.

And we have him.

And they took her so that they'd have leverage over Temple.

Yet why would they think that would work? She was nothing to him beyond an assistant. A damned good assistant, but an assistant nonetheless. She cared for him, and she knew, deep down, that he cared for her too. She had been there during his wife's illness, had helped him through the grieving process, repeating it with his daughter, a young girl whom she had spent so much time with after her mother's death, she almost thought of the little angel as her own.

She squeezed her eyes tight as she realized that the Temple family was her own family. She was single, her parents lived on the other side of the country, and she had no siblings. Her friends were all from the office, and it was hard to call them friends, as she was so tight with Temple, she was pretty sure they only invited her so they could pump her for information, or try to impress her in the hopes she might mention their name to the big man himself.

Temple was her life.

But what was she to him? Would he give up Penn to save her?

If the roles were reversed, she would in a heartbeat. Yet the roles weren't. He wanted his revenge. He *needed* his revenge. And Penn was the man who had caused so much pain around the world, and in Temple's heart.

Gunfire erupted to her right and she yelped, spinning to see what was going on. Tires screeched below as they neared the ground, a news van careening away from them as bullets tore into the pavement. A stream of vehicles behind came to a halt as her captor banked hard to the left, around a building and out of sight of the camera crews.

"Lift your feet."

It was the first words said the entire time, and they startled her.

"Now!"

She complied, lifting her knees as high as she could as the sound of the chute changed above her. They hit the pavement, her captor maintaining his balance as two men, again Asian, rushed toward them. She was quickly unhooked then shoved into the back of a black van idling nearby. They pulled away, and she watched through tinted glass as the four men who had kidnapped her shrugged off their chutes before climbing into another vehicle.

She turned to see two men in the back with her.

"What's the meaning—"

She never finished her sentence, something sprayed in her face causing her to lose consciousness within moments.

Bureau 121—Moscow Station
Embassy of the Democratic People's Republic of Korea
Mosfilmovskaya Street, Moscow, Russian Federation

Colonel Park's heart pounded as he and Captain Tann waited for word on the highly risky operation now being carried out in California. If it went bad, he'd be dangling from the end of a rope before the week was out.

If they even bothered with a public execution.

They were already looking at an international incident with the first failed attempt to retrieve Agent K. Though none of the soldiers dispatched could be traced back to North Korea, the UN ambassador's son could.

There had been no way to deny his participation. The man—the boy—wasn't even twenty-five, yet because of his family ties, he was in charge of all clandestine operations on American soil. The retrieval operation had gone through his office as a matter of protocol, and the bastard had attached himself to the unit.

All in search of glory.

The young man clearly had designs on a future leadership position, and proving himself on foreign soil would be one sure way to draw attention.

And he had certainly done that.

The Americans had to know who he was by now, yet there had been no contact. He had made a call to the ambassador's residence, but had been refused permission to talk to him. He hadn't protested, not really wanting to be the one to deliver the bad news.

Instead, he sent an encrypted message to Pyongyang, informing them of the failed operation, and that it was his belief the ambassador's son might have taken part.

It passed the buck, but only slightly. Everyone would know that the son would be in charge of the mission, so if it failed, it was his fault. It would all depend on what the Dear Leader decided. If he agreed, then Park might live. If he didn't? He was as good as dead.

Unless he could somehow redeem himself.

And that could only happen if he retrieved Agent K, then convinced Pyongyang that the man was a traitor, and *he* was responsible for the young man's death.

It was a long shot. Even if he did convince the leadership that Agent K was a traitor, and was responsible for the death, he still might be eliminated.

The phone rang, and both he and Tann flinched. He grabbed it. "Speak."

"Mission accomplished. No complications."

The line went dead and Park hung up the phone, a smile spreading. He looked at Tann. "We have her."

Temple Technologies Corporate Head Office
Mountain View, California

Temple sat in the office of his senior vice president, surrounded by police and his own security, as well as at least two FBI agents who had taken charge of the entire operation.

Standard protocol, if his movies hadn't been lying to him all these years.

All he had gathered was that the men had arrived in a vehicle stolen from the janitorial service employed by his company, the four men assigned to the vehicle yet to be found, though they were presumed dead. They had used their IDs to gain access to the underground service entrance, fooled the building security staff by staying in character, and arriving during the confusion of the press conference.

After killing Bill Garvin and escaping out the windows using parachutes, they had shot up at least one press vehicle, then disappeared. Traffic cameras had picked them up, but they had already switched cars somehow, the two vans found abandoned, holes cut in the floor. It was presumed they had used the city's sewer system to escape.

In other words, Davis, the only person left in the world that he actually cared about, was gone without a trace.

Equipment had already been set up to record and attempt to trace any call that might come in, a ransom demand expected at any time.

And that terrified him.

He was almost certain they weren't about to ask for money.

They were going to ask for Penn.

And if that were the case, how could he explain that demand to the FBI now standing not five feet from him?

But the kidnappers would know that too, wouldn't they? They had to know such a high-profile kidnapping would draw attention, that the police would arrive even if they weren't called, and that they'd be listening in, refusing to cooperate not an option as it would raise suspicions.

These were professionals, and they had to have taken this into account.

Hadn't they?

His cellphone, sitting on the desk in front of him, rang.

It was Davis' number.

"It's her!" He reached for the phone, excitement gripping him, when one of the agents held out a hand, preventing him from grabbing the phone.

"Didn't you say her phone had been destroyed?"

Temple frowned, his hopes dashed that she had somehow escaped. One of their attackers had crushed her phone under his heel. But how was it showing as her number?

The agent looked about the room. "They've cloned her phone somehow. It's them. Are we ready?"

The personnel in the room nodded, everyone falling silent.

"Remember, try to keep them on as long as possible, and try to get proof of life."

Temple answered the phone. "Hello?"

"A phone has been delivered to the front desk. You will take it in your car, alone. You will receive a phone call in fifteen minutes. No police, no traces, or she dies."

The call ended before he had a chance to respond.

He stared at the agent, already on his phone. "Confirmed. A package arrived for you only a few seconds before the call."

"They must have been waiting for the electronic delivery notification," said someone manning a laptop. "I'll see if we can trace that."

Temple rose and headed for the elevators.

"Where do you think you're going?"

He didn't bother looking back at the FBI agent. "I'm going to follow their instructions. To the letter."

John F. Kennedy International Airport
New York City, New York

"You two seem happy."

Kane grinned at Sherrie, planting a passionate kiss on her lips before turning back to the ticket agent. "Disgustingly so, right?"

Sherrie jabbed him playfully in the ribs. "We're newlyweds. This is our honeymoon."

The agent's eyebrows rose slightly. "Moscow? Interesting choice."

Kane shrugged. "Hey, if my baby wants to go to Moscow, we go to Moscow."

Sherrie squeezed his cheek. "Ooh, you're so good to me!" She took her passport back from the agent. "My great-grandfather is from there, and I've always wanted to go. Dad said I better do it before all hell breaks loose over there, so"—she shrugged—"why not?"

Kane squeezed her tight. "Why not, indeed!" He held up their boarding passes. "Thanks!" He planted another kiss on Sherrie, then they headed for security, hand-in-hand, both the picture of careless bliss. Kane drew her in a little closer so they could whisper sweet nothings in each other's ear. "Do you think Chris is watching?"

She laughed as if he had said something funny. "If he is, he's going to put a hit out on you."

Kane chuckled. "I wouldn't blame him. You're a fantastic kisser."

"The CIA trained me well."

"They do have an amazing program, don't they?"

"Uh-huh."

"I, of course, didn't need any training. I was a natural."

Sherrie patted his cheek. "I'm sure you thought you were."

"Ouch. I guess I'm just going to have to prove myself when we get to the honeymoon suite Langley booked us. Or do you want to join the mile-high club and skip the formalities?"

"You are very sure of yourself. I see why Fang loves you."

"Confidence is but one of my many virtues."

She slid her hand down his chest toward his crotch, Kane's libido taking over. She stopped, poking a finger into his belly button. "Keep dreaming, you manwhore."

He laughed, squeezing her tighter. "I think this will be a fun assignment."

"Me too. What do we do when we get there?"

"Hopefully Langley will have some more intel for us."

"And if they don't?"

Kane gave her a look as they approached the security line. "They will. There's no way that sweetheart of yours is going to leave us in Moscow as newlyweds for any longer than he has to. You might not be able to resist my charms."

She slapped his shoulder. "You're terrible."

He grinned. "Yes, I am. You're just lucky you're my best friend's girl, and the mission doesn't dictate I charm those pants off you."

She rolled her eyes. "You're not my type."

Kane thought of his friend, the polar opposite of him in so many ways. "Clearly. But as a master of disguise, I can be anybody you need me to be."

Sherrie eyed him. "I think we better update our cover."

Kane's eyes narrowed. "To what?"

"To a newlywed couple that had their first fight, and needs separate rooms."

Kane laughed. "I can see why Chris loves you so much."

"And don't you forget it."

He smiled, handing over his passport and boarding pass while lifting his bag onto the scanner. "Trust me, I won't."

Mountain View, California

Temple drove his car, the same Mercedes his daughter had died in only a week ago, the memories of her panicked breathing, then silence, haunting. He had intended to get rid of it, but he hadn't yet had time to go through the brochures Davis had already provided him, too preoccupied with bringing those responsible to justice.

God, she's efficient.

She was his rock, and had been for years. Through his wife's sudden illness then death, she had kept him together, kept the company running smoothly, allowing him time to grieve. She had filled the hole left in Angela's life, giving her a strong, caring female figure to lean on when her dad was hurting so bad he couldn't bear to be with his own daughter because of the memories she forced to the surface every time he saw her.

Davis had been there through it all.

And he was determined to save her, whatever it took. Even if they asked him to sell his company, he'd do it.

In a heartbeat.

He cared for Davis. Deeply. It wasn't romantic. He didn't know what it was. It was more than family, more than a friend. It had developed into something more with each crisis he faced.

Could it be love?

His stomach flipped at the thought, guilt sweeping over him as he thought of his wife, and the betrayal it would mean if he had developed feelings for another woman.

She would want you to move on.

He shook his head. It was just emotional weakness. He was still overwhelmed with his daughter's death, and was searching for something to fill the void left behind by her loss, and Davis was the only person in his life that had the potential to fill it. If Davis were a man, he'd be filling the void as well, just in a different way. They might be out drinking, playing golf, or talking cars and smack about their college days.

No, it couldn't be love.

Yet the guilt he felt at this moment suggested otherwise.

The phone delivered earlier rang, the Bluetooth pairing tying it into the car's audio system. He pressed the button on his steering wheel. "Yes?"

"Are you alone?"

"Yes."

"We'll kill her if you're lying."

"I'm not. I've left the building in my car, and nobody is following me."

"You know what we want."

"No, I have no idea. Tell me, I'll do anything."

"We want Donald Penn."

A wave of nausea swept through him, his worst fears confirmed. This *was* all about Penn, and that meant this had to be related to a foreign government.

And that meant they wouldn't hesitate to kill Davis if he didn't deliver exactly what they asked for.

"You can have him, but I want to talk to her."

"No."

"Proof of life, or there's no deal."

The phone call ended, and Temple screamed at the radio. "No!"

He slammed his fist several times into the steering wheel, his eyes clouding over with tears, the car correcting his drift with a beeped protest as the lanes became blurs. The phone rang again, and he hurriedly pressed the button. "Yes?"

"Sir, is that you?"

"Tanya, oh thank God! Are you okay?"

"I-I'm fine. I'm sorry, sir, I—"

She was interrupted, the voice from earlier replacing hers.

"Satisfied?"

Rage blazed through him. "If you hurt her—"

"I will do whatever I please to her. If you follow my instructions exactly, then that won't become necessary. Do we understand each other?"

Temple forced himself to calm down, nodding at the radio. "Yes."

"Good. Instructions have been sent to the phone. Follow them precisely, or your friend dies. But not before we've enjoyed ourselves."

The call went dead and Temple shouted a string of curses at the radio before pulling off the road and grabbing the phone, a text message received, the timeline horribly tight.

He grabbed his own phone, dialing Simmons. He answered almost immediately. "Please tell me you haven't killed him yet!"

FBI Field Office
Albany, New York

Dawson held up a finger, silencing the room, the interrogation having resumed on the other side of the glass after the abrupt beat-down he had given Penn. "Why?"

"They've taken Tanya."

Dawson's eyes narrowed at the desperation in Temple's voice. "Who took her?"

"I don't know. Four men came into my office, shot my security chief, shot out the windows, then jumped out with parachutes. They took Tanya! I just heard from them. They want Penn in exchange for her, or they'll kill her."

Dawson pursed his lips, staring at Penn through the glass, the man now going through photos of suspected North Korean agents, as the NSA tried to figure out who he was working with.

So far, he had recognized nobody.

Or at least hadn't admitted to any.

"How did they contact you?"

"Through a phone they had delivered."

"Are the police or FBI involved?"

"They were, but not anymore. They said they'd kill her if they were."

"Where are you now?"

"In my car. I don't know what to do!"

Dawson felt for the man. It was probably a situation Temple hadn't been in before. A man like that was rarely out of control, yet now he was being manipulated by experts.

It had to be the North Koreans.

"Can you describe the men who took her?"

"Why does that matter? They looked Chinese or something, though I suspect Korean. North Korean."

Dawson's eyebrows shot up, surprised Temple had made the connection. "What makes you say that?"

"They looked Asian, were *all* shorter than the Asian's I'm used to meeting, and I thought I heard on the news Penn's ancestry was Korean." Temple paused. "You're the expert. Did we just kidnap a spy?"

Dawson frowned, his mind racing as he debated what to tell the man. Yes, they had kidnapped a spy, and yes, Temple had put two and two together. Would telling him he was right or wrong change anything? "Yes, I think it's possible."

"What do we do?"

"Send me the instructions they sent you. I'll get back to you."

"Make it fast. They want this to go down in less than six hours."

Dawson ended the call as Niner pointed at the mirror.

"He just identified somebody."

Dawson glanced at their prisoner, some excitement on the other side of the glass. But none of that mattered now.

They had bigger problems.

Briefing Room C-6, CIA Headquarters
Langley, Virginia

Leroux sat in his chair, quiet, a mere fly on the wall, his presence only needed should Director Morrison be asked a question that he couldn't answer.

So far, there had been none.

Directors, chiefs, secretaries, and more were either in attendance in person, or via teleconference, Leroux waiting for the man himself to perhaps make an appearance at any moment.

For it was an important decision that needed to be made, and the President would have to sign off on whatever recommendation came out of this hastily called, late-night meeting.

Unfortunately, he wasn't confident that any agreement would be reached, the finger pointing and blame-game underway for the past fifteen minutes, fifteen minutes they didn't have.

He checked his watch.

Sixteen minutes.

"He's a traitor," said the NSA's representative in the meeting.

"No, he's a spy." That was Morrison.

"Didn't you vet him before you hired him?"

Yet more criticism directed at the NSA.

"Of course we did, and everything checked out. Listen, this goes way deeper than someone infiltrating the NSA. His identity passed our deepest checks. Everything, right down to his high school yearbooks."

"You're suggesting he was here that long?"

"No, I'm suggesting he was surgically altered to look like the real deal."

"Then what happened to the real deal?"

"Probably dead. His parents, I mean the ones who adopted him, both died in a car accident a year before we hired him. He had just moved to DC, so he knew almost nobody, so his background check relied on old contacts who wouldn't be able to see him in person to know that anything was out of the ordinary. This was extremely well thought out. Christ, the guy has a wife and kid!"

"But the bottom line is he isn't American," said Morrison, interrupting the repeated information.

"No, he's not. He's already admitted that under interrogation. An interrogation he's been fully cooperative in."

Morrison leaned forward slightly. "And that is the crux of the matter, isn't it, ladies and gentlemen? Penn is a North Korean spy. Tanya Davis is an American citizen. Isn't it our duty to try and save her?"

"And give up this resource? Penn could give us invaluable insight into the North Koreans."

Morrison shook his head. "How? He's been out of there for at least a decade. What could he possibly know that they can't change tomorrow? They know he's been compromised. Hell, they sent a team to take him out. He's useless to us now. Any codes or contacts he may have had will already have been changed, and the most we can hope for is that he might be able to identify some faces that he saw a decade ago." Morrison leaned back in his chair. "Listen. While we debate this, the life of an innocent American citizen is at risk. I say we make the exchange, then try to get him back as soon as she is safe."

The NSA chief waved a hand. "Not so innocent, Leif, and you know it. She and her boss got themselves into this when they kidnapped Penn. Now they're mixed up in something far bigger than them, and only have themselves to blame."

Leroux had to agree with that observation. If Davis and Temple hadn't interfered with their own brand of justice, then none of this would be happening. Though Davis was probably only guilty of participating. Temple was the man who called the shots. And from what his team had put together from media reports, Davis was an extremely loyal employee, and a close friend of Temple's.

She was the only thing left in the poor man's life that he probably cared about.

"She's just a pawn."

Everyone stopped their bickering, turning toward Leroux, who sat aghast that he had vocalized his thoughts.

Morrison waved a hand at him. "Explain."

Leroux gulped, now committed. "Well, my team has been putting together a profile on Temple and Davis. It's our belief that Davis is so loyal to Temple, that she will do anything he asks of her, including breaking the law. She was a friend to the family for years before Mrs. Temple died from ALS a year ago. The amount of time the two have spent together outside of company business, has increased significantly based on news and social media reports. She became a sort of surrogate mother to the daughter."

"What are you saying?"

"I'm saying we shouldn't be so quick to condemn the woman. She was acting out of loyalty to a man she has been very close to for years, who is responsible for making her very wealthy, and whom some have speculated actually loves Franklin Temple."

Morrison's eyes widened slightly. "Do we have any proof of that?"

Leroux shook his head. "No, though the possibility can't be dismissed. We have no evidence that anything has ever happened between them, but with the amount of time they spend together, there is definitely a bond there. That could have led her to do things she normally wouldn't have done. I don't—" Leroux stopped, not sure he should finish his thought.

"What, son?"

Leroux sighed. "I don't think she deserves to die because she works for a man who lost control in a moment of grief, and turned to the one person he thought he could trust."

Morrison turned to the display showing the Delta commander. "Sergeant Major, how confident are you that you can retrieve Penn after you hand him over."

"Sir, if anyone can do it, we can. However, keep in mind that the North Koreans will have planned this out extremely well. I expect they'll have snipers in position, and multiple means of egress. I'd like to suggest something different."

Over Colorado, United States

Dawson stared at the prisoner, handcuffed to the seat across from him. For a man about to be handed over to "his" side in the dispute, he didn't seem very chipper.

In fact, he seemed downright depressed.

Maybe it's the two black eyes and broken nose I gave him.

It could have been a lot worse.

Atlas could have hit him.

He checked his watch. They were still two hours out from California. To make his life easier, he had demanded radio silence from Temple, otherwise the man would constantly be hounding him, requesting an update as to when he'd arrive. Unless the hand of God intervened, they weren't getting there any quicker.

He had instructed Temple to return home, and Washington had arranged for a security detail to watch the house, with any interrogations to be delayed until the morning.

After the handover.

Penn caught him staring. "What?"

Dawson shook his head. "Nothing. How's the nose?"

"It hurts like a mother."

"Pyongyang taught you well. You speak English like you grew up with it."

"I did."

Dawson's eyebrows rose slightly. "Really? How's that?"

"We have special schools where children who show certain attributes are placed. We're taught foreign languages and customs. Those who excel are trained to become foreign agents."

"Sounds like a fun childhood."

Penn shrugged. "If you know no different, it is. You serve the state, and you end up eating a lot better than your friends. If you truly do well, your family gets treated better too."

Niner turned in his seat. "What a wonderful country you work for."

Penn stared at him. "You're Korean?"

"American born and bred. My folks were Korean. *South* Korean. Now they're American citizens."

"When the war comes, and Korea is united under the flag of the Democratic People's Republic, whose side will you be on?"

"Whatever side America is on." Niner smiled. "And don't think for a moment your side would win."

"We would because we are more committed than the south is, or its allies. Do you really think America will shed the blood of its young men and women for brown skinned people?"

Dawson grunted. "You don't know us too well if you have any doubt about that. We fought you once, we'll fight you again."

"No, you fought the spread of communism once, not the spread of what you ignorantly call North Korea. This time we would be reuniting the peninsula. Your domino theory wouldn't apply anymore. Do you really think you could get the American people riled up enough to spend hundreds of billions, sacrifice tens of thousands of lives, all to stop a war on a peninsula thousands of miles away? I think you're being naïve."

Dawson shrugged. "I'd go in a heartbeat."

"Me too," agreed Atlas, the others echoing the sentiment.

"Oh, I have little doubt the average American soldier will want to fight, but the public won't."

"Again, you're sadly mistaken, and if that's the message you're bringing back to your Dear Leader, that America doesn't have the will to fight, you're putting your nation at great risk. If your country decides to attack, it will be decimated, your Dear Leader and his family will be dead, your military crushed, and your people freed. You've lived among us for years. Surely you must realize that your people would be better off free."

Penn laughed. "You're not free. That's just an illusion. Police can stop you at any time, you don't have freedom to cross the border without proper documentation, your press is a joke, your politicians can't get anything done, and freedom of speech died with the advent of the Social Justice Warrior. Your country is a lot more like mine than you may think. The difference is we understand the realities of today, and are willing to sacrifice to achieve our goals."

"And just what are your goals? Complete domination over the world?"

"No. We want to reunify the Korean people, then be left alone."

Niner chuckled. "Yeah, right. Your God, miraculously born without an asshole, won't be happy until everyone has ridiculous haircuts and a photo of him over every headboard."

"It's easy to insult what you don't understand."

Dawson nodded. "True, but understanding requires access to the facts, which your country doesn't permit. Why did the Soviet Union collapse? Part of that was the growing access to Western culture. When people started to realize we weren't the evil bastards depicted by their

215

propaganda machine, and when they started to realize that living a meager life, lining up for food each day, wasn't the way things were supposed to be, they demanded change. Do you really think if your people had any idea what life was like outside North Korea, that they'd want to keep things that way?" Dawson leaned closer. "*You've* lived here, you've seen what it's like. Hell, you even have a wife and kid here. Can you honestly tell me you'd rather have your wife and kid join you in North Korea, to live out their lives there, starving and ignorant, than to live here, in America, where things aren't necessarily perfect, but are a hell of a lot better than 99% of the world?"

Penn's face clouded over at the mention of his family. "It would be home," he murmured.

Dawson shook his head. "You keep up that talk, and Pyongyang might just believe you. But I think you're all talk. You don't sell state secrets for millions of dollars if you're loyal to the Dear Leader. You do that because you're setting yourself up for the good life in the good ol' US of A."

Niner held up his laptop, showing a zero dollar balance on Penn's Bitcoin account. "Looks like your nest egg is all gone, though, so if you have plans to return to America, you're going to have to start all over."

Penn frowned. "You didn't take my money, you took my son's."

Dawson stared at him. "Excuse me?"

"Why do you think I did it? I didn't do it for me, I did it for them. For my wife and kid. I knew they'd be calling me back at some point, and you don't say no to them. When they order you back, you go. No questions asked. That money was so that if anything happened to me, they'd be taken care of."

Atlas grunted. "Touching. A spy with a heart of gold."

216

Penn glared at him. "How is what I do any different from what you do? Yes, I'm a spy. I'm a spy for your enemy. And guess what? You have spies in my country too, doing their job. Don't for a minute mix up spies with traitors. Traitors should be shot. Traitors betray their country. Spies don't. Spies *serve* their country. I love my country just as you love yours."

Dawson nodded. "That's true, yes. But you're forgetting one thing."

Penn stared at him. "What?"

"You've betrayed your country. You spent hours spilling every secret you knew before you got on this plane. What will Pyongyang think about that?"

Penn paled slightly. "They'll never know."

"You managed to steal the ToolKit from NSA headquarters. Do you really think your people won't pick up chatter about your interrogation?"

He paled a little more, leaning toward Dawson. "Listen, I don't care what happens to me, but you have to protect Grace and my son."

Dawson sniffed. "Sorry, but you expect me to believe your wife isn't a North Korean agent as well?"

"Have you looked at her? When's the last time you've seen a five-foot-eight black woman in downtown Pyongyang?"

Dawson chuckled. The man had a point. "So you're telling me she doesn't know?"

"She hasn't a clue. The poor woman has probably been calling my phone non-stop, wondering what's happened to me. There's no way she hasn't heard about the attack on the house."

"Ask the Dear Leader for a phone call when you get back."

Penn stared at him. "Are you really that heartless?"

"Buddy, I don't know what to believe, but I can assure you your wife is already being checked out by the FBI and every other acronym you can think of. If she's involved in any way, she'll be heading to prison, and your child will be taken care of by the system."

"His grandparents. Make sure he goes to his grandparents. They live just outside New Orleans."

Dawson paused for a moment. The man seemed genuinely concerned for his child. He wasn't sure why that was surprising. Perhaps his prejudices against the North Korean regime were transferring to this man who was a spy on their behalf. But the North Koreans were people too. They married, they had children. They loved and hurt, just like everyone else. They worried about their children, about their future, and the policies of their leaders shouldn't be held against people struggling to be good parents.

Penn was a victim of his own government, though that didn't excuse his selling the ToolKit for profit. But at the same time, it didn't negate the fact he was a father, and that an innocent child's future was at stake here.

Dawson sighed. "Look, if your wife is innocent, she'll be set free, and your kid will be fine."

Penn shook his head. "That's not enough. If they decide to punish me, they could do it through my family. Grace and my son need to be put into Witness Protection. That's the only way they'll survive. If I ever hope to come back, I need to know they're safe. If they're not, they'll kill them the moment I leave."

Niner frowned. "You're going to try and come back?"

"Wouldn't you if you had a wife and kid out there?"

Niner shrugged. "I suppose so. But the question is, *how* are you coming back? Are you escaping, or are you coming back on the job?"

Penn smiled slightly. "Whichever is necessary."

Dawson chuckled. "Well, at least you're honest about one thing."

Atlas shook his head. "Yeah. *One* thing. All this bullshit you've been feeding us about how North Korea is better than America, and will conquer South Korea, is just that. Bullshit. You're already talking about escaping and coming back to this horrible country. If you truly loved *your* country so much, you'd just have your government kidnap your wife and kid. God knows they've done it before."

Penn turned away, staring out the window, the stars in full force. "I couldn't do that to them," he whispered, his voice cracking. "My wife wouldn't be able to handle it."

Dawson pursed his lips, staring at the man. "You said in your debrief that the marriage wasn't sanctioned."

Penn shook his head. "No. I was almost terminated when they found out, but because of the cock-up on the Hummel investigation, I was on the outs at the NSA regardless. The only thing that kept me alive was that I had delivered them the ToolKit, which was enough to save me."

"So it's love?"

Penn stared at Dawson. "Yes. Have you ever loved someone so hard that you can't imagine life without them?"

Dawson thought of his fiancée, Maggie. "Yes."

"Then imagine living your life, knowing that any day you could be taken away from her, just because you were part of something bigger, something you were born into." His voice cracked. "That's been my existence every single day since I met her. And today is that day."

"You sound like you're having doubts."

Penn sighed. "I don't know anymore."

Dawson stared at the man. That was perhaps the first truly honest thing he had said so far. Penn was having doubts. These were the kind of doubts that could be used to turn a spy to become a double-agent, or simply a traitor to his own country.

Unfortunately for Penn, he was worth more to them as a pawn in this situation, the life of Tanya Davis more important than what few secrets he may still have to spill.

Penn stared at him. "Listen, I know you're going to try and get me back. I understand that, and you know what? I can't promise which way I'll run when given the chance. I just don't know. But whatever choice I make, I need my wife to know that I love her, and that I love my son. I need them to know that if I end up running back to where I came from, it's because at that moment, I felt it was the best thing for them." A tear rolled down his cheek. "I just don't know what to do. I don't know what will protect them."

Dawson felt for the man. For the *man*. He hadn't understood true love until Maggie had entered his life, and couldn't imagine making the choice now facing Penn. Stay with the woman you loved, and the child she had given you, risking their lives in the process, or leaving them, possibly forever, to save them.

It was a choice he was certain he'd never face, his country free enough for him to be able to say no, should the choice be demanded of him.

Though what would happen should some foreign power target his family, and the only way to save them was to renounce them?

It had happened before with the Rosicrucians, but rather than capitulate, he and the others had taken the fight to them, and won.

It was why their identities were so secret.

Dawson regarded the man as Penn wiped the tears from his face. "I'll tell you what. I'll let you record a message to your wife and kid, and I'll give it to the powers that be. They'll analyze it six ways from Sunday, and if they find nothing, no hidden messages, they'll probably pass it on to her." He held up a finger. "*But,* if they find anything, and I mean anything, your wife will be sent to prison for the rest of her life, and I guarantee you, you'll never hear from your child again. Understood?"

Penn's eyes brightened, and a hopeful smile spread, his entire demeanor changing, exactly as it should have for any honest man given this opportunity. The reaction reaffirmed Dawson's decision in his own mind, now almost certain he hadn't just been snowed by an expert manipulator.

"You'd do that for me?"

Dawson shook his head. "I'm not doing it for you. I'm doing it for them."

Operations Center 2, CIA Headquarters
Langley, Virginia

"I've got him!"

Leroux turned in his chair to see a triumphant Randy Child performing his customary victory spin. "Got who?"

"His name is Colonel Park Ji-Sung. He's a cultural attaché at the North Korean Embassy in Moscow."

Leroux pointed at the large displays, and Child brought up the file, the details sparse. "This is the guy Penn identified before he left for the exchange?"

"Yes. The only one he recognized. He didn't know the man's name. He just said he recognized him from when he was being trained at Bureau 121."

Leroux frowned. "Doesn't look like we know much about him."

Child shook his head. "No. Just when he arrived in Moscow, and the fact he's still there. With your permission, I can try to hack the Russian's and grab their file on him. It's probably more extensive."

Leroux held a finger up over his shoulder. "Just hold off on that. Tensions are high enough already without us hacking their systems and getting caught."

"They'll never catch me!"

It sounded like a maniacal comic book villain, though Child was probably right. He was good at his job. Very good.

"Well, if he's a colonel, and in Moscow as part of Bureau 121's operations there, then he's either in charge, or pretty close to the top.

It's a good starting point for Kane. Get that info to him ASAP. I'm going to talk to the Director and see what he says about probing a little deeper."

Palo Alto Airport

Palo Alto, California

Temple tapped his watch. "You're cutting it a little close, aren't you?"

Dawson stepped toward the man still operating under the false assumption that his name was Simmons, and that Simmons worked for him. "That's the idea. They knew exactly how long it would take us to fly here. They don't want to give us any time to set up."

Temple's eyes narrowed. "Set up? What do you mean, set up? What needs to be set up?"

"We need sniper coverage in case something goes wrong." Dawson gestured toward two SUVs parked nearby. "Are those ours?"

Temple nodded, then pulled his phone from his pocket, the display lit up. His eyes widened. "It's them!"

Dawson cursed, motioning toward the Mercedes parked nearby. "Let's take it inside." He led the shaking man to his car as he scanned the airport for anything out of the ordinary, knowing he'd come up empty. The North Koreans had obviously followed Temple here, and had been waiting for the plane to arrive.

Dawson closed the door and turned to Temple. "Put it on speaker."

Temple did then took the call. "Hello?"

"We see your team has arrived. If any of them leave the airport, she dies. Take him to the address we just sent you. Alone."

The call ended and the phone vibrated. Temple held it up, and Dawson entered the address in his phone.

"What are we going to do?"

"You're going to follow their instructions, as will we."

"But they might kill us both."

Dawson stared at the terrified man. "Yes, that's a distinct possibility. Do you want to change your mind?"

Temple pulled in a deep breath, shaking his head. "No. I have to save Tanya."

"Good." Dawson checked his watch. "You better hurry." He stepped out of the car and motioned toward his men. "Put Penn in the back seat. Cuffed behind his back."

Sergeant Eugene "Jagger" Thomas led Penn toward the car. "We're not going?"

"Nope. They've got eyes on the airport."

Jagger pushed Penn into the back. "Clever, those North Koreans."

Dawson leaned into the back, staring at Penn. "If I find out you caused any problems, I'll make sure you never see your wife and kid again. Understood?"

Penn nodded. "Don't worry about me. I'll play my part."

Director Morrison's Office, CIA Headquarters
Langley, Virginia

"Russia was hit just as hard as us. That's the problem with these types of untargeted attacks. Sometimes your friends get stung as well."

Leroux nodded at his boss' observation. Morrison was right. Targeted hacks could be as focused as a single machine, but these blanket attacks, where millions of emails were sent out in the hopes of infecting as many machines as possible, were uncontrollable. It was why even the hackers sometimes built in shutdown protocols, like in the May 2017 attack where the ransomware software would check for the existence of a particular website, and if it was there, shut it down. Another hacker discovered the shutdown code, registered the domain himself, and saved untold numbers of computers from becoming infected.

This time, if there was a shutdown routine, no one had discovered it yet. The ransomware attack was mostly over, but the cost to the economies of the world was in the millions, if not billions, either through paid ransoms, or through lost productivity as machines awaited reformatting and reinstallation.

It was why Leroux had some sympathy for Temple's initial position. If a hack could be linked to a death, then it should be treated as murder. If a hack cost millions of dollars to fix, then those responsible should be treated as if they had robbed a bank of that sum and be sent to prison as any thief would. Temple was right in one thing. Digital crimes weren't treated the same as physical crimes, and that had to change. Steal something digitally, treat it the same as physically stealing the equivalent value. Destroy someone's computer by encrypting their data, or worse, wiping it? Treat it as if you had broken into that person's home and smashed their hard drive with a hammer.

It was time to stop glorifying hacking. Yes, there were white hat hackers out there who thought they were doing good, and sometimes they were, but unfortunately, the majority of the activity was done by the black hat type, sometimes for their own benefit, sometimes on behalf of foreign governments, so they couldn't be traced.

Like in this case.

The Shadow Collective had known ties to the Russians. Serious ties. And now, one of their actions had cost the Russian economy billions of rubles. The Russians were pissed, but couldn't take action without revealing their connection.

After all, how could they know where the Shadow Collective was operating from without some previous association?

The Shadow Collective was good. Government good. And they had hidden their tracks extremely well. Those investigating knew they were responsible, but didn't know who they actually were, or where they were located, except that they *appeared* to be operating out of the Ukraine.

Yet that could be faked.

"Chris."

Leroux flinched, having drifted off in thought. "Umm, sorry, sir. I was just thinking."

"About?"

"Well, actually, the Shadow Collective. Just wondering if they're even in the Ukraine at all."

"I thought that was always a possibility?"

"It was. And I guess it's irrelevant. The Russians will know. Maybe they'll take care of them for us."

Morrison grunted as he leaned back in his chair. "Well, right now Washington is leaning toward sharing what we know with the Russians. They're pretty pissed about what's been going on, and DC is worried they might overreact and target some of our own assets if they don't have someone to blame soon."

Leroux's eyes narrowed. "I thought they knew the Shadow Collective was responsible?"

"I'm sure they do, but the Shadow Collective put out a statement denying they were responsible. They claimed they were framed and are blaming us."

Leroux chuckled. "Yeah, I saw that. I think they're getting desperate."

"Yes, but it's enough for the Russians to deny behind closed doors that their own people are responsible for the biggest cyberattack to ever hit their own country. But it creates another problem. We can't just go in and kill these guys now, without possibly causing problems with the Russians."

Leroux sighed. "It's never easy, is it? Good thing Temple has been stopped."

"Which is exactly why Delta was sent in undercover. We got lucky there. If Temple's security chief wasn't ex-military, God knows who he might have hired. A hit squad running wild in the Ukraine, killing Russian government assets? The tit-for-tat could escalate very quickly."

"If we want the Shadow Collective brought to justice, how are we going to go about doing it?"

"We're going to have to work with the Russians, by the looks of it. That will get resolved in time. The bigger concern is the North Koreans. They had a mole in the NSA, stole classified data, sold that data to the Russians or those acting on their behalf, conducted two armed operations on our soil, killed at least one American citizen and kidnapped another. Washington wants a message sent that this won't be tolerated."

Leroux chewed his cheek for a moment, staring at the far wall. "I can only think of one way to do it without causing bigger problems."

Morrison's eyebrows rose slightly. "I'm all ears. I haven't been able to figure out a way yet."

Leroux leaned forward in his chair. "Have the Russians do it for us."

Morrison's eyes narrowed. "Go on."

"Tell the Russians about Bureau 121's operation in Moscow, and tell them they're responsible for the cyberattack."

"But what about the Shadow Collective?"

Leroux shrugged. "It doesn't matter. All that matters is the code that was used. We tell the Russians about the mole, show them the interrogation tapes if we have to. We have proof the North Koreans stole the ToolKit. And we know, and can prove it to the Russians, that part of the ToolKit was used in the attack. They don't have to know about the sale of the data. That's never been proven in public. We can make them think the North Koreans did this, operating out of Moscow, and that we have reason to believe the story is about to hit the news wires at any moment, and they better get ahead of this before it's too late."

Morrison stared at him for a moment, then chuckled. "I'm glad you're on our side. That's pretty twisted."

Leroux grinned. "I learned from the best?"

Morrison wagged a finger at him. "Flattery goes nowhere in this office. Okay, I like it."

Leroux frowned. "There's just one problem, though."

"What?"

"If we're to believe Penn, Bureau 121 has the ToolKit on their computers in Moscow. If the Russians decide to go in, they could get their hands on it."

"Don't we think the Shadow Collective has already given it to them?"

A burst of air escaped Leroux's lips. "We think it's a possibility, of course, but we've seen no evidence that the Russians have used any of the exploits that were unique to the ToolKit. The Shadow Collective may have kept it to themselves, to make themselves even more indispensable to Moscow, without Moscow knowing how."

Morrison's head bobbed slowly. "So we still need to eliminate the Shadow Collective before they can spread the ToolKit, *and* somehow prevent the Russians from seizing it if they decide to deal with Bureau 121."

"Exactly. And I can think of only one way to deal with that second problem."

Morrison chuckled. "Even I can figure that one out. Kane."

Mountain View, California

Temple checked his rearview mirror for the umpteenth time, staring at the man responsible for his daughter's death. He couldn't believe he was going to just hand him over to the North Koreans, but he had no choice. He had to save Davis. She was all that mattered right now.

But once I have her…

He wanted Penn dead, and he wanted the Shadow Collective dead. Those goals hadn't changed. But he'd worry about that later.

"I'm sorry about your daughter."

Rage enveloped Temple as he glared at the man, his foot easing off the accelerator as he contemplated pulling the car over and delivering a beating.

Nobody said in what condition I had to hand him over.

He checked the display on the dash and pressed the accelerator harder. There was no time to waste.

"You killed her."

"In a way, yes."

"No, there's no sugarcoating it. You killed her, just as if you pulled the trigger yourself."

Penn sighed. "You're right, of course, but please understand I had a job to do."

Temple glared at him in the mirror. "Bullshit. Stealing the data was your job. Selling it was something entirely different."

Penn frowned. "I wish it were that simple. You'd never understand."

Temple turned, only a few minutes left until their destination. "Try me."

"I have a wife and child. A son. He's almost two."

Temple's rage eased slightly, but only slightly. "I *had* a daughter, and she's dead because of you."

"And as I said, I'm sorry. But what you don't understand is that I did it for them. I stole the data for my country, but I sold it for them."

"You keep telling yourself that. Maybe it'll ease your conscience a bit, but it won't change the reality of what you did."

"I understand your anger, and I don't blame you. Hell, I'd want to kill me right now if I were you, and again, I wouldn't blame you if you did. But we have to save your friend, and the only way to do that is to hand me over. But I need you to know something, in case something goes wrong."

Temple's eyes narrowed as he spotted the parking structure he had been instructed to drive to. "What are you talking about?"

The car announced they had arrived at the destination, and he canceled the route guidance before it annoyed the shit out of him.

"We don't know what's about to happen. I don't think they'll hurt you, as long as they don't spot any tricks and you remain calm. But who knows what will happen to me."

Temple tensed as he took the winding ramp to the top level. "Do you think they'll kill you?" The thought at once elated him, but also made him a little sick.

"Eventually, yes, unless your friends can rescue me."

"Why the hell would they do that?"

"I'm worth more to them alive."

"What are you talking about?"

232

"You don't know?"

"Know what?" They pulled onto the top level, two black SUVs parked at the far end, facing him.

"Simmons works for the government. He's been playing you this entire time."

Temple's jaw dropped as he spun around in his seat, staring at the man. "Bullshit!"

"Why would I lie?"

"To save your life."

"How could telling you that save my life?"

Temple frowned. The man had a point. How did this bit of information, whether true or not, change anything at this moment in time?

It didn't.

Headlights flashed at them three times.

He reached forward and repeated the signal, the sound of doors opening sending his heart racing. He stared at Penn. "None of that matters now. We're here for Tanya."

He opened his door and stepped out, the headlights of the SUVs turning on, blinding him for a moment. He held up a hand to block the beams as he opened the back door, pulling Penn out by the arm.

"Listen, you need to tell your friends something for me. It's important."

Temple said nothing, instead pulling Penn in front of the car and facing the half-dozen men now silhouetted by the lights.

"Listen, it's important. Tell them that I had a partner, and he's far higher in the structure than I am. If they want to know who he is, they have to save me."

Temple glanced at him. "Do you think I'm going to do anything to save you? You killed my daughter, and the only thing I want with respect to you is Tanya. Once I have her, I'm going to do everything in my power to make sure you die." He turned toward the silhouettes. "Let me see her!"

Niner lay on his stomach, MP5 stretched out in front of him as he peered through the night vision scope, a clear angle on the proceedings laid out in front of him. "One-One in position, over."

Atlas' voice came over the comms as he confirmed he was in position as well, tucked out of sight behind a large HVAC unit to Niner's left.

Again with a clear shot.

"Copy that. Zero-Two and One-Zero in position," replied Red from the sniper position he and Jimmy were manning. Normally Niner and Jimmy would be sniper and spotter, but Red had tweaked his ankle when they were hoofing it into position, leaving Niner to take over. If there was any action, it would be in the parking garage, not on the rooftop across the street.

He just wished Dawson and the others were here. Eight against what he assumed would be eight, were odds he liked.

Four against eight, not so much, especially when one was a spotter.

Red, Niner, Atlas, and Jimmy had been dropped off at Moffett Federal Airfield before the plane carrying Penn continued on to Palo Alto, less than ten miles away. So far, it appeared the North Koreans were unaware of this, otherwise they would have called this meeting off, picking up on the fact they were twenty minutes late due to the layover at Moffett. Instead, they were here, their intel evidently entirely based upon eyes they had on Temple.

Still, those eyes were keeping Dawson and the others out of the game.

For now.

He watched as one of the rear doors of the waiting SUVs opened, a man stepping out, a woman following, then another man.

"Target sighted. Stand by."

His heart rate ticked up a couple points as he followed the woman, his weapon trained on the man holding her arm.

"Zero-Seven here, I've got the three on the left," said Atlas.

Niner waited for Red to confirm who he had a clear shot of, since he currently had a view of everyone.

"Zero-Two here. We've got the next two. No shot on the ones on the right. The SUV is in the way, over."

Niner adjusted his position slightly. "One-One here. I've got the other three. If you'd prefer, I can just take them all out. Let you ladies sit this one out, over."

"Cut the chatter, One-One. Stand by, something's happening."

Niner watched as Penn walked toward the North Koreans, Tanya Davis toward Temple. Niner stole a quick glance at Temple, the man nervous, fidgety. Exactly the kind of behavior men with itchy trigger fingers didn't like.

Calm down, buddy.

He returned his attention to the North Koreans, all armed with submachine guns, all very calm, at least outwardly.

Definitely military. Probably Special Forces.

He frowned, thinking how that could have been him if his grandparents had lived just a few miles farther north at the end of the war. Would he have joined the military? Probably. There wasn't exactly much choice on what you did in North Korea. Would he have excelled at it? Probably. Why would that have changed? And with the indoctrination from birth, he might have drunk the Kool-Aid and done his duty to the Dear Leader, as a good, loyal citizen should.

The very idea sickened him.

Penn and Davis passed each other, exchanging looks, but saying nothing.

"We've got a problem."

Niner frowned at Red's voice, quickly scanning the area, not seeing the issue.

"Local cops just arrived. Squad car is going up the ramp now. Control says they've picked up chatter that a police helicopter spotted the vehicles on the rooftop."

Niner cursed.

That's why you don't use the top level!

"What are your orders?" he asked.

"Wait for the exchange to complete. If things get ugly, eliminate the North Koreans. The civilians and law enforcement must be protected. If we lose Penn, then so be it."

"Copy that."

Niner tensed as the engine of the squad car revved below him.

One of the North Koreans turned toward the sound.

This is about to get ugly.

Temple reached out for Davis and she rushed toward him the last few steps. He drew her into his arms and held her tight as she did the same, her shoulders shaking as she sobbed with relief. He lowered his head, whispering in her ear. "Calmly go and get in the passenger side. Don't say anything."

She nodded, breaking away from the hug and doing as he said.

"Are we done here?" he asked.

A tire squeaking on pavement cut off any reply, the North Koreans all turning toward the sound of an approaching vehicle making its way up the ramp.

One of them drew a handgun and fired two shots into Penn's chest, the man collapsing, his body silhouetted by the lights. Davis screamed and Temple felt all his energy drain as he watched the gunman step over the body, putting two more in the head.

They're going to kill us all!

He sucked in a breath, heading off the fainting spell, and stepped to the side, slowly backing toward his door. "Get in!" he hissed at Davis, frozen with fear on the other side. "Now!"

A police car appeared to his right and he cursed as the lights on the roof kicked in, announcing they were here on business.

The North Koreans opened fire.

Niner was already cursing as he saw Penn taken out, the locator chip with a time delayed trigger implanted in the North Korean spy on Dawson's suggestion, no longer necessary. He squeezed the trigger of his MP5, taking out the first man in his arc. Atlas' position opened fire, and a sniper rifle from across the street barked its participation.

The police car was torn apart, the fate of the two officers inside unknown at this point, Niner not taking the time to look, instead calmly selecting his next target and eliminating it.

And it was over.

The North Koreans never stood a chance, the surprise total.

A good day.

Niner rose from his position. "United States Federal Agent! Let me see the hands!" He advanced toward the squad car, his submachine gun directed at the windshield, the last thing he needed was terrified cops opening fire on him. He had no intention of shooting them, even if they opened fire, but they were a lot less likely to do so with a heavy weapon trained on them.

Four hands appeared, empty, as the one man and one woman slowly rose from their position crouching behind the dash.

"Are you two okay?"

"Y-yes," replied the woman, her hands pressed against the roof.

"I'm a Federal Agent." He pulled his ID, flashing it at them. "I'm going to check on the hostiles. Radio for backup, and secure the area. Understood?"

They both nodded, their hands still up.

Niner turned his back to them, no longer concerned as he pushed toward the bodies of the North Koreans. None were moving, none were moaning.

All were dead.

Not *a good day for them.*

Two hit teams eliminated in one night.

"Somebody in Pyongyang is going to be swinging tonight."

Niner glanced over at Atlas. "Yup."

A woman screamed behind them.

They both spun toward the sound, then sprinted toward Temple and Davis, Temple on the ground, Davis at his side. Niner dropped to his knees, skidding to Temple as he pulled his med kit off his back. He tore Temple's shirt open, revealing a nasty gunshot wound to the right shoulder, blood oozing out steadily.

"We're going to need paramedics here, stat," radioed Atlas as he provided cover, there no certainty more hostiles weren't positioned nearby.

"Is he going to be okay?" asked Davis, tears streaming down her face.

Niner applied a pressure bandage, causing Temple to gasp. "He'll be fine, ma'am. I've patched up worse than this." He jerked a thumb over his shoulder at the big man. "That big lug got shot in the ass once. I saved him."

Atlas smacked his ass. "And the ass."

Niner grinned at Davis. "And that's a lot of ass."

Temple reached up and grabbed him by the vest. "He had a partner."

Niner's eyes narrowed. "What?"

"He told me to tell you he had a partner."

Temple dropped to the concrete, unconscious.

Palo Alto Airport

Palo Alto, California

"Zero-One, Zero-Two. Be advised, shots fired. The hostiles are all down, as is Penn. Davis is safe, Temple has been shot. Paramedics inbound, over."

Dawson cursed at Red's update as he rushed toward the SUVs left for them. "Everyone take cover, now!"

As if on cue, a bullet ricocheted off the pavement where he had been standing, another a moment later, a sniper dialed in on their position. The others pressed against the side of the SUV as several more shots slammed into the opposite side of the vehicle.

Dawson's trained ear listened to the impacts, followed by the shockwave of the shot, the bullet traveling faster than the sound. "I'd say he's about a mile out."

"Agreed," said Jagger. "That means he'd really have to move to try and get an angle on us."

Dawson frowned. "It also means with our equipment, we have no hope of hitting him."

Two more shots slammed into the SUV, then there was nothing.

Jagger glanced at Dawson. "Do you think they're done?"

"Why don't you poke those big ass lips up there and check?"

Jagger flipped him the bird, opting instead to stay put.

Dawson pulled the ball cap he'd been sporting as part of his cover from his head, and put it on the barrel of his MP5, raising it up over the hood of the SUV.

Nothing.

"Maybe they know that trick."

Dawson glanced at Jagger. "Would they? It's not like they've got a lot of movies in North Korea."

Jagger nodded. "Imagine dating a North Korean woman? All the jokes would be new!"

Dawson slowly rose, prepared to drop at any moment back to safety, but if the sniper were worth his salt, it would be too late.

Still nothing.

He stood all the way, then stared down at the others. "You ladies going to just sit there?"

Jagger looked up at him. "If it's okay with you."

Outside the Embassy of the Democratic People's Republic of Korea
Mosfilmovskaya Street, Moscow, Russian Federation

Kane sat across the street from the North Korean embassy in Moscow, sipping a cup of coffee and chowing down on his McDonald's breakfast as any good American tourist should be. It was so stereotypical, it would raise zero suspicions with the North Koreans—no spy would label himself American so obviously.

And none would proudly sport a New York Yankees ball cap.

He didn't care if he was spotted, that was the point. What he did care about, was spotting Colonel Park Ji-Sung. He was the only man Penn had identified, and he had said he was part of Bureau 121 when he had seen him years ago. And if he was a colonel like Langley said, and he was stationed at a foreign post, he was certainly high enough up in the chain of command, and in the good graces of the Dear Leader, that he might actually know something worthwhile, including how to wipe the ToolKit from their computer systems.

Washington also wanted Park interrogated to find out what other moles might be operating on behalf of Bureau 121 or the North Korean government. By grabbing him here, and interrogating him here, there would be few ramifications, as long as the Russians didn't catch wind of it.

When they had arrived and checked into their hotel, a care package from Langley was waiting for them under the bed, including all the comms and weapons any good spy would need, along with all the known information on Park.

And that was nothing beyond his name and photo, and the fact he was at the embassy.

He and Sherrie had set up surveillance on the embassy within an hour, and before staff should normally be expected to arrive, hoping to spot Park before he made it inside. There was no way they'd be picking him up now, but if they could track his movements after he left at the end of the day, they could grab him without the benefit of the North Korean security detail.

"I have him."

Kane casually glanced to his left, sipping his coffee, spotting Sherrie heading away from the embassy, several dozen people walking in both directions. He scanned ahead as he took another bite of his McMuffin, scanning the crowd.

His eyes came to rest on a short Asian man, standing out from the others. He was wearing civilian clothes, though there was no doubt it was Park.

Sherrie turned her head, waving for a cab. She slammed into him. Kane couldn't hear the conversation, but she was sufficiently animated for him to guess apologies were exchanged, though one sided, before Park continued, and Sherrie resumed her search for a cab.

"It's done."

Kane swallowed the last bite of his sandwich as Sherrie climbed into a cab. He stood, tossing the wrapper and bag into a nearby bin, then slowly strolled toward their hotel as Park entered the embassy.

With a tracking device that would allow them to follow his every move.

Colonel Park strode into his office, Captain Tann rushing in a moment later, closing the door before Park had a chance to remove his jacket.

"Sir, we have a problem."

Park tensed before forcing himself into his chair. He wasn't about to let a mere junior officer affect his routine. There was a knock on the door.

"Yes."

His secretary entered, his morning coffee in one hand, his morning briefs in the other. She said nothing, instead delivering the items then bowing before beating a hasty retreat at Tann's impatient stare.

Park held up a finger, cutting off Tann. His first sip would not be interrupted. He put the coffee aside and leaned back in his chair. "What is it, Captain?"

"Agent K is dead, and so is the retrieval team."

Park closed his eyes as he sighed, his entire body going numb. "How?"

He heard Tann drop into the chair. "We don't know. Initial reports are that local police showed up, but I can't believe they managed to kill eight highly trained soldiers."

Park opened his eyes. "I would tend to agree. But Agent K is dead?"

"Yes."

"You're certain?"

"Yes. The members of the team assigned to watch the airport were able to observe the aftermath. Agent K is dead."

"And the woman?"

"She is alive, but Temple was severely wounded. I don't have a status on him."

Park batted away the words. "It doesn't matter. None of it matters anymore. Agent K is dead, so any secrets he may have had are now safe."

"But what of the team?"

"They're untraceable, right?"

"Yes."

"Then we won't worry about them. The Americans will have figured out by now that our ambassador's son was involved in the initial retrieval attempt, meaning they know it was us that was after him. They will look at eight Korean bodies and know that again, it was us after him. We are in no worse position now than we were yesterday."

Tann nodded, though not convincingly. "I can't believe you are so calm, Colonel."

Park shrugged. "My fate is sealed already. At least Agent K is dead, which may buy some leniency, but I expect to be recalled at any moment." He sipped his coffee, better than anything available back home. "Has Pyongyang been informed?"

Tann stared at his shoes. "Umm, I felt it should come from a senior officer, sir."

Park chuckled. "Very well. Place the call."

Moscow Marriott Royal Aurora Hotel

Moscow, Russian Federation

The coded three-one-two knock at the door had Kane drawing his weapon and heading for the peephole, Sherrie taking up position around the corner with her own weapon. He eyed the man wearing Aeroflot coveralls.

Kane opened the door, and a suitcase was handed to him.

"Your lost luggage, sir. We're terribly sorry for the inconvenience."

Kane signed the clipboard shoved in his face. "No problem. At least you found it."

The man smiled then disappeared down the hallway as Kane closed the door. He locked it then carried the suitcase to the bed, tossing it on the mattress with a bounce. Sherrie placed her weapon on the nightstand as he opened the case. He removed a large manila envelope, handing it to her, then smiled at the Russian officer's uniform neatly folded underneath.

Sherrie pulled out two sets of identity papers and a briefing note. "Looks like the Russians have been informed about Bureau 121 operating out of the embassy and they're pissed. Langley says they'll be hitting the embassy in an hour to arrest the 'spies,' and they want us to get in there and wipe the ToolKit from their computers if possible."

Kane's eyebrows rose. "Oh, is that all?"

"I'm to play a moron millennial tourist, applying for a visa to visit the wonderful Democratic People's Republic of Korea."

"If it's safe for Dennis Rodman, then it should be for you too."

"It's so sweet how you care about my welfare."

Kane stared at her with a smile. "It is, isn't it?" He opened his new wallet filled with ID. "And apparently I am Major Igor Vasiliev." He tossed it on the bed then unbuttoned his shirt. "Anything in there about how the Russians are justifying breaking international law by entering the embassy?"

Sherrie grinned as she pulled out a lighter and lit the paper on fire. "Apparently they kidnapped the North Korean ambassador a few hours ago and got his permission in writing to enter."

Kane shook his head as he pulled off his pants. "Gotta love the Russians."

Sherrie gestured toward his underwear. "Need me to step outside?"

Kane's eyes narrowed. "Why would I want you to do that?" He hopped on the bed, bouncing on his side with an elbow already cocked under his head. "It is our honeymoon, after all."

Sherrie picked up her weapon. "This is the only gun I'm touching today."

Kane rolled off the bed. "Oh well, you don't know what you're missing."

Sherrie headed for the bathroom. "Hurry up, we don't have much time."

"Are we still talking about the same thing?" called Kane after her. "I can be quick."

Sherrie groaned. "I don't think that's something you want to be advertising."

Embassy of the Democratic People's Republic of Korea
Mosfilmovskaya Street, Moscow, Russian Federation

Sherrie sat patiently in the waiting area, her trained eye taking in everything with the innocent look of a wide-eyed naïve little girl. In reality, she was counting the number of armed guards, taking note of those who appeared bored or tired, where the exits were, what type of physical security was present—anything that might help her fulfill her task.

A task that just might get her killed.

She was using an American passport that would come back valid should anyone check—Langley was excellent at its job. Her cover story was well rehearsed and simple. She was here with her husband on their honeymoon, and as a surprise to him, she wanted to extend their trip and visit North Korea, a place that had always fascinated him.

She knew she'd be turned away, but by arriving only a few minutes before the Russians' planned raid, that was irrelevant.

"Mrs. Ryan?"

She rose, smiling at the short, plain woman standing before her. "Yes. A pleasure to meet you," she said, extending a hand.

The woman shook it firmly, a single pump, exactly how Sherrie suspected was taught at whatever military finishing school the woman had been sent to, handshaking not a common practice in Asian cultures.

"As my colleagues have informed you already, we aren't issuing any travel visas to American citizens at this time."

Sherrie clasped her hands under her chin. "Pleeease, is there any way you can make an exception? My husband has always been fascinated by your country, and I would love to surprise him with a trip there. There's no embassy in Washington, and you're my only hope."

The woman didn't appear moved, her face expressionless. "I'm sorry, Mrs. Ryan, but there are no exceptions." She held a hand out, her arm extended toward the doors. "I'll have to ask you to leave now."

Sherrie's shoulders slumped, and she delivered an Oscar-worthy pout. "He's going to be sooo disappointed."

"If it is a surprise, then simply don't tell him of your failure. He will never know." The woman's voice was slightly softer in tone, and Sherrie smiled.

"You're so right." She threw her hands toward her feet. "I'm such an idiot sometimes." She suddenly wrapped her arms around the woman and squeezed her tight before letting her go. "You're so nice."

The woman said nothing, too busy trying to remove the shocked expression from her face.

A commotion at the entrance caused them both to stare as someone in uniform rushed toward them, shouting something in Korean. Sherrie turned to the woman. "What's happening?"

"You must leave, now!"

Colonel Park flinched at the sound of a loudspeaker. He rose from his chair and stepped over to the window, looking out at the street below.

And nearly soiled his pants.

Hundreds of Russian troops and police were surrounding the embassy, tanks, armored personnel carriers, and other heavy equipment rolling into position as embassy personnel scrambled inside the walls, clearly uncertain as to what to do.

There was a quick rap on the door behind him, and it opened before he could say anything. He glanced over his shoulder to see Tann hurrying toward him. "What's going on?"

Tann pressed against the window beside him, pointing toward the gate. "They're claiming the ambassador gave permission for them to enter the embassy and conduct a search for evidence related to the recent ransomware attack."

Park watched as two Russian soldiers accompanied a man in a business suit to the gates. A paper was handed through the bars to one of the guards, who took it and promptly sprinted inside the building. Park cursed. "I find that impossible to believe. Where is the ambassador?"

"He is not in the building."

"Find out what happened to him."

"Yes, sir." Tann headed out the door, and Park picked up the phone on his desk.

"Initiate Protocol J-Seven. I repeat, initiate Protocol J-Seven."

"Yes, Colonel!"

An alarm sounded moments later, and Park sat in front of his computer. He double-clicked an icon then entered a code, initiating a complete wipe of his computer and any networked files it could access, similar actions being taken throughout the building. He unlocked all his desk drawers then rose and did the same with the filing cabinets as his secretary and several aides rushed in with large carts, immediately filling them with his files.

"Everything must be destroyed. Bureau 121 has priority on the shredders and incinerators."

"Yes, Colonel!" cried his flustered secretary.

"Remain calm, everything will be fine. They won't dare break international law."

Gunfire erupted from outside, making a liar of him. He rushed to the window and peered out. A guard was down, two of his comrades hauling him to safety as the thunder of helicopters sounded overhead. He twisted his head up and his heart hammered as at least a dozen Mil MI 24 Hind helicopters thundered past, weapons pods bristling.

The roar of a tank engine drew his attention back to the front gate, a burst of diesel exhaust filling the air as a massive T-80 tank surged toward the gate, shoving it aside like balsa wood.

Kane watched as the troops poured through the gates, automatic weapons fire filling the air as the North Koreans fought back valiantly but uselessly, the Russian's numbers too overwhelming. This fight would be over quickly, then the Russians would have full access to the embassy staff and computers.

He had to act quickly.

As the Russians continued through the gates, he stepped from the shadows across the street, and walked with purpose toward the action. He wore the uniform of a major, high enough that few would question any action he took, but low enough that he wouldn't be looked to for leadership.

He passed through the gates, unnoticed, the bodies of several North Korean guards scattered among at least a dozen dead or wounded Russians.

This is not going to go down well in Pyongyang.

Embassies were always hotbeds of international intrigue and espionage the world over. The Russians spied on the Americans, the Americans on the Chinese, the Chinese on the Russians. It was the way the game was played. Information gathering was what embassies did, consular services a secondary function.

The key was not being too obvious about it.

Or causing too much trouble.

Gathering information was one thing. Conducting cyberwarfare on the host country from within one's embassy? That was crossing the line.

If it had happened in America, diplomatic credentials would have been revoked and people sent home. At worst, utilities might have been cut off in some "accident." In Russia? Anything was game, including, apparently, kidnapping the North Korean ambassador and forcing him to give written permission to enter the embassy, thus not violating international law.

How they'd get away with the kidnapping, he wasn't sure, but if he had been running the op, he would have made sure to use private contractors who couldn't be traced back to the government. It would have been criminals that kidnapped him, forced him to sign an already prepared document, then released him after the operation was complete.

The Russians would deny involvement, pleading ignorance to the fact the ambassador's request for assistance in apprehending the criminals responsible for illegal activity at the embassy, was obtained under duress.

The world wouldn't buy it, but the Russians wouldn't care.

They never did.

They lived in a country where the press was controlled, the message was managed from the top, and the people, desperate for a strong leader, ate it up.

Kane stepped through the front doors of the building, unchallenged.

Now to find Sherrie.

Sherrie had headed for the exit as ordered, then feigned fright and curled up in a corner, covering her head as consular staff ran about in all directions, shouting orders to underlings. From what she could tell, computers were being wiped and papers shredded, standard practice at any embassy under attack.

Nothing suspicious here.

If data were being wiped, that was a good thing. That's why she was here, to make sure the Russians didn't get the ToolKit. But she couldn't rely on the North Koreans to actually accomplish the task in time.

Gunfire shattered the glass and the civilians hit the ground, the armed soldiers returning fire. Something clattered to her left and she spun toward the sound, gasping.

Grenade!

She lunged forward and swatted it back toward where it had come from then covered her head. A massive explosion tore through the room, screams of terror and agony overwhelming her as she scurried back into her corner, checking for wounds.

She was good, but she had to get out of here—the next time she might not be so lucky.

Park checked his computer, confirming it was wiped, then headed out the door, Tann rushing toward him. "What did you find out?"

"Nobody knows where the ambassador is, sir. He left for work this morning, but never arrived."

Park cursed. "Those damned Russians must have kidnapped him. That's the only explanation."

"What are we going to do?"

"We're going to get out of here and report back to Pyongyang."

"But how? The building is surrounded."

"Leave that to me."

Park headed for an interior stairwell, shoving the doors open. He raced down the stairs toward the basement, their only hope of escape probably minutes away from being overrun.

Kane strode deeper into the building, the fighting still ahead of him, Russian guards at each entrance snapping to attention as he passed. He had never been an officer, but he could understand the appeal.

Respect.

He followed the signs in Korean and Russian toward where he expected Sherrie to be. If she had managed to accomplish her task, they should be in and out in no time.

He pushed through another set of doors and into what appeared to be a waiting area. There was heavy damage at the entranceway from an explosion, probably a hand grenade. Who had thrown it was anybody's guess, several Russians and Koreans apparently having borne the brunt of it.

His chest tightened as he spotted Sherrie, curled in a ball in the corner, her clothes suggesting she had been caught up in the explosion.

Chris is going to kill me if anything happens to her.

He ignored his sense of urgency and strode toward her calmly. She spotted him and rose, rushing toward him. In flawless Russian, she said, "Oh, thank God, an officer! Is it over?"

"For you, child, it is."

She hugged him, the Russian soldiers giving them a look. He rolled his eyes and they grinned. She pressed something into his hand.

"Come, let's get you someplace safe."

He led her deeper into the building, keeping an eye out for any North Korean personnel that weren't already dead.

Someone whimpered from a room to his left. He drew his weapon and opened the door. He scanned the room but found no one.

But he had heard something.

"Come out, or you die."

A pair of shaking hands appeared from behind a desk, a woman slowly rising to her feet.

"Where is the server room?"

She stared at him, confused.

Kane aimed his weapon directly at her. "Server room. Now."

She pointed down the hall. "Take the stairs to the basement. Go right. You can't miss it."

Kane clicked his heels and bowed slightly. "Thank you. Now I suggest you resume your hiding."

The woman nodded, dropping to the floor and out of sight. He closed the door and headed farther down the hallway, sticking to Russian. "Good work on the pass."

"It's amazing what a little hugging can do."

"Ooh, should Chris be jealous?"

"It was a woman."

Kane grinned at her. "Wish I was there."

"It's not like we were naked."

"Too bad." He spotted the stairwell and cautiously opened the door. He could hear footsteps below them as at least two people hurried somewhere. He peered over the railing and silently cursed.

It was Colonel Park.

But there was nothing they could do about that now. He was their secondary target, their primary was the data.

Shouts behind them erupted, and he ducked back into the hallway to see half a dozen Russians making their way down the hall, searching each room as they passed. Kane stepped out and pointed toward the door where the woman was hiding.

"There's a civilian in there. Unarmed. Try not to kill her."

"Yes, Major!"

They burst in as Kane returned to the stairwell, following Sherrie to the basement level. They came through the doors and found a deserted corridor, no sign of Korean defenders, nor Park and his companion.

Park swiped his pass, entering a highly restricted room, then closed the door behind them. He stepped over to the far wall and opened a panel, entering a six-digit code known only to the senior officers. There was a clicking sound, and a door to his right opened.

"What's this?" asked Tann.

"Escape route. Something the Russians know nothing about."

Park stepped through, followed by Tann. He pressed a button on the other side, and the door closed behind them. He pulled a flashlight off the wall and turned it on, then rushed forward through the dark, damp tunnel, every sound amplified by the confined space, the thud of weapons fire acting as a deadly bass drum to their journey.

It took only a few minutes before they reached the other end. He entered another code, and a door clicked open. He pushed it aside slightly and peered into a perfectly normal bedroom.

Empty.

He pressed the flashlight into an empty holder on the tunnel wall, then stepped into the bedroom, a stunned Tann on his heels. Park pushed the door closed, a door disguised to appear as a wall panel.

He walked over to a wardrobe and threw open the doors, his fingers sorting through dozens of plastic covered sets of clothing, spotting his ID number on one of the tags. He lifted the bundle off the rack and headed for the corner of the room. He pointed toward the closet.

"Find something that fits."

Tann, wide-eyed, nodded, grabbing the first set as Park stripped out of his uniform and changed. Within minutes, he was a South Korean businessman, replete with identification.

He glanced at Tann as he slipped on a pair of shoes. "Does it fit?"

"Yes, sir. A little tight in the chest, but the overcoat will cover it."

"Excellent. Let's go, we have little time."

Kane pointed. "This must be it." There was a large set of double doors with a security panel to the right. He swiped the ID, and the panel flashed at him, expecting a code. "Lovely."

He reached into his pocket and pulled out several bricks of plastic explosives, handing two of them to Sherrie. They placed them on the four hinges, inserted detonators, then ran toward the end of the hallway.

"Ready?"

Sherrie nodded.

"Fire in the hole." Kane triggered the devices, and a deafening roar overwhelmed them, dust and debris rolling down the hallway toward them with nowhere to go, threatening to swallow them whole. Kane covered his mouth and pushed through it, the dust so dense he couldn't see if they had succeeded in blowing the doors.

He reached a gaping hole in the wall where the doors had been and smiled. He stepped inside to find a room with rows upon rows of racked hardware, the ventilation system visibly exhausting the dust from the hall outside, allowing them to breathe and see clearly. He pointed to a terminal and Sherrie dropped into the chair. He handed her a USB key provided by Langley, and she plugged it in. The security lockout was quickly overcome, and they watched as Langley's virus hunted for the ToolKit.

Kane sat at another terminal and inserted a second USB key. As soon as the security was bypassed, he found the personnel files and transferred the data to the USB key, then swapped it out for another, copying the files once again.

"Got it."

He glanced over at Sherrie's terminal. "How much longer?"

"Just a few minutes. It's copying then wiping everything it can."

Shouts from the hallway indicated the Russian's search had finally reached the basement. "We're out of time."

Sherrie nodded, executing a final command that would eat through the entire network independently, then repeatedly overwrite all storage with ones and zeroes over and over until stopped by someone.

She pulled the USB key and stuck it in her bra.

Kane grinned. "If you forget where you put that, I'll help you find it later."

"I'm telling Chris every single thing you've said to me on this mission."

Kane laughed as he straightened his uniform for the impending confrontation. "Now, remember, you're a scared American who ran from the bullets and found your way in here. The doors were already blown before you got here. Oh, and you don't speak Russian. Understood?"

"Da."

He smiled. "Now hug me like you mean it."

She wrapped her arms around his chest, and he led her toward the door, soothing words delivered in Russian as four soldiers appeared in the doorway, weapons raised.

"Lower your weapons!" he barked, the men immediately complying. "Search the entire area. I saw a North Korean colonel run down here, but when I reached the doors, he was gone. All I found was this poor tourist."

"Yes, Major!"

The four men continued their search as Kane calmly led a "terrified" Sherrie to the stairwell. They climbed the steps in silence, arriving at the landing of the main floor. Kane looked at Sherrie.

"Ready?"

"Yup."

"Remember, if anything is said other than English, pretend you don't understand, and just cling to me like I'm your knight in shining armor."

"Got it. Damsel in distress routine."

Kane pushed open the door, startling two Russian guards who snapped to attention. Kane ignored them, instead leading Sherrie by the shoulder and elbow down the hallway and through a succession of doors before reaching outside. Scores of North Korean staff and soldiers were lined up against the wall, weapons trained on them, a Russian major with a megaphone shouting at them in Russian.

"Anyone who is a member of Bureau 121, step forward immediately!"

Unsurprisingly, nobody did.

Kane stopped. "Wait here."

Sherrie nodded, and Kane strode quickly toward the major. He handed him the second copy of the personnel data he had made. "Major, a copy of their personnel records. Anyone reporting to Colonel Park is a member of Bureau 121."

The man's eyes widened slightly as he took the memory key. "Excellent work, Major. How—"

"Never ask a question that might have a dangerous answer."

The major smiled slightly. "Understood."

Kane turned and walked directly back to Sherrie, the major shouting for someone to bring him a computer. As Kane and Sherrie walked through the twisted gates of the embassy and out onto Russian soil, they turned right, clearing the cordon of security, just as names were called out, the major apparently finding a computer.

Bureau 121 in Moscow was finished, their data wiped. Any risk they had posed was over, and any chance of the Russians gaining access to the ToolKit through the North Koreans had been eliminated.

But they still didn't have Park, and he was key. If he had planted Penn in the NSA as a mole, he might have others. Capturing him could prove invaluable, and their only hope of doing that was the tracking device Sherrie had planted on him earlier.

Let's just hope he hasn't changed clothes.

Sherrie pulled some keys from her purse and unlocked a nearby Renault, the lights flashing and the alarm chirping. She climbed into the driver's seat as Kane closed the passenger side door. She started the car and pulled into traffic, Kane tossing his Russian Army hat into the back seat, then removing his jacket. Sherrie dialed Control as he lost the tie and removed any insignia from the dress shirt.

"This is Control Actual. Status?"

Sherrie smiled at the sound of Leroux's voice. "We're clear. The ToolKit has been wiped, we've got a few gigs of data, and the worm is chewing through their entire system. The Russians won't get anything—nothing of value, anyway."

Kane thrust his hips up off the seat and yanked at his pants, Velcro strips down either side separating, the distinctive slacks stripped away, a thin pair of black pants revealed. "Your lady did great, buddy. Fooled everyone."

Sherrie grinned. "Was there ever any doubt?"

"I know I had none," replied Leroux. "We tracked Colonel Park out of the embassy. We lost his signal for a few minutes, and judging from where he came out, I'd say they had some sort of escape tunnel. He's now located in an apartment building across the road. Looks like a basement unit."

"Send us the location, we'll go pick him up," said Kane as he reached behind him and retrieved a bag. He pulled out a light jacket then struggled into it.

"Done."

Sherrie glanced at her phone. "Confirmed. We'll double back and come in from the rear. There're too many Russians in front of that building, and me thinks they'll be there for a while."

"Copy that."

Kane retrieved a pair of sunglasses and planted them on his nose, then stuffed the uniform into the bag before zipping it up. "How do I look?"

"I'm sure your mirror would tell you you're the fairest in the land."

Kane made a loud kissing sound for Leroux's benefit. "She's a wonderful girl, buddy, a wonderful girl."

"He knows that."

"Umm, yes I do. You better hurry. Park's signal hasn't moved in over fifteen minutes. If he's waiting for a pickup, it has to be arriving soon."

"Copy that. We're boogying."

Park stepped out the rear entrance of the large apartment building, Tann in tow, and climbed into the cab he had ordered. He gave the driver a destination about ten minutes from their current location, then they drove in silence, Park warily eying every police and military vehicle he spotted along the way.

They weren't safe yet.

Not by a long shot.

The cab pulled to a stop. "Here you go." Park handed over the cash to pay the fare as Tann stepped out onto the street. Park led them casually toward a nearby café, but ducked into an alley before entering. He dialed the emergency number he had memorized for just such a situation.

"Go ahead."

Park steadied his voice. "Asset Six-Four-Seven-One-One-Alpha. I need extraction for two. Myself and Captain Tann. The embassy was attacked."

"Current location?"

"Lao Lee Café, Tsvetnoy Boulevard, Moscow."

"You will be contacted in exactly thirty minutes with instructions."

The line went dead, and he sighed.

"What now?" asked Tann.

"Now we wait."

Kane took only seconds to pick the lock of the basement apartment, a quick search finding it empty, though there was evidence that at least two men in uniform had used it as an escape route. He was certain one of those was Park.

He dialed Leroux and delivered the news as Sherrie cursed, holding up her tracking device, still tucked into Park's jacket pocket.

"Control Actual here."

"We found the tracking device, but Park is long gone. Are you guys listening in on the Russians?"

"Hi, you've reached the CIA. How may I help you?"

Kane grinned at his buddy's flat delivery. "Yeah, okay, stupid question. Any indication Park's been picked up by them?"

"None. My guess is he's gone to ground, awaiting extraction by his people. They'll want to act fast. We'll start watching the airports and train stations."

"Copy that. We'll head to the hotel for some hanky panky, and await your call."

"Umm, what was that?"

"I said we're going to wait to hear from you."

"Before that."

"No idea. Can't remember."

Sherrie grabbed the phone. "Just ignore him, darling. If he tries anything, I'll castrate him and deliver you his nuts in person."

Kane didn't hear the response, but there was a twinge from down below.

Lao Lee Café

Tsvetnoy Boulevard, Moscow, Russian Federation

"I think that's it."

Park put his coffee down and glanced toward the street, spotting a black four-door sedan with a front quarter panel in a different color, as if undergoing repairs. "I believe it is."

Park threw some money on the table and rose, heading out onto the street, the instructions on their extraction received exactly thirty minutes after their initial call, this car arriving precisely fifteen minutes after that.

The People's Democratic Republic of Korea was efficient.

The car pulled to the curb and Park climbed in the back seat, followed by Tann. They pulled away, blending with the traffic. A woman in the passenger seat turned around, handing them each a large manila envelope.

"These are your new identities. You are South Korean businessmen on your way back to Seoul. Your plane leaves in two and a half hours, and you will be met at the airport when you arrive."

Park opened his envelope and found plane tickets, a passport, credit cards and cash, along with photos of him and his family in front of various landmarks in South Korea. Several hotel and restaurant receipts from the past couple of days were included.

Pyongyang had thought of everything.

"Memorize your identity summary sheet. Your lives may depend on it."

She then turned to face the front, leaving the two men to load their pockets with their new lives, and study the single page summary of who they were, what they had been doing, and any other thing a border official might ask them in Moscow, or upon arrival in South Korea.

Moscow Marriott Royal Aurora Hotel
Moscow, Russian Federation

Kane stepped out of the shower and wrapped a towel around himself, before sauntering out into the bedroom area. "All yours."

Sherrie rushed past him, already down to her skivvies, how much time they had before Langley would call, unknown. Kane quickly toweled dry as the shower fired up again, and within a couple of minutes was ready for action.

He lay on the bed, turning on CNN, the coverage now dominated by the "Embassy Invasion in Russia" story. Moscow's rhetoric and propaganda machines were in full swing, putting out the story about Bureau 121 operating there illegally, and how they were responsible for the ransomware attack a week ago.

Evidence would follow.

If they can find any.

In the end, it wouldn't matter. Bureau 121 had been shut down in Moscow, the ToolKit had been wiped so the Russians couldn't get it, and the North Koreans would be watched like hawks from now on. He had no doubt it wouldn't impact Bureau 121's abilities in the long run, this only one of their locations, he was sure. But losing Russia as a base of operations would be an inconvenience. They'd have to concentrate more of their efforts from China, Hong Kong, Ukraine, and other hotbeds of cybercrime.

It would never end.

And the ironic part was that they weren't even responsible for the ransomware attack, though the fact their agent had stolen then sold the ToolKit to the hackers, did sort of make them culpable in a roundabout way.

The shower turned off and the curtain slid aside.

"Need some help drying yourself?"

"Yes. Can you get me my gun first, though?"

Kane grinned. He had really enjoyed working with Sherrie. In his business, he usually didn't have a partner, and when it was a woman, too often there was too much sexual energy for it to remain platonic for long. But things were different now that he had Fang, and even if he were partnered with someone willing, he'd never betray her trust.

He had been forced to sleep with women since he'd been with Fang, though that was part of the job, not casual sex for the sake of sex. Fang understood that, and had even been relieved when he had confessed to her what had happened.

He had felt so guilty, he began to distance himself from her.

And she was having none of that.

But with Sherrie, the banter was fun. She was his best friend's girl, and he would never betray Leroux, and neither would she. With the exception of Sherrie, he could think of no female friends he hadn't slept with, and those weren't really friends. His pattern of self-destructive behavior between missions, before meeting Fang, had been curbed, at least from the promiscuous sexual point of view, though he still enjoyed his Scotch a little too much on occasion.

Now his idea of unwinding was to spend time with the woman he loved.

His phone rang, interrupting his thoughts of Fang.

"Go for the Bedroom King."

"I'm not sure how I should take that, but stay put. And don't worry about the knock on the door. It's just room service, not a hit squad."

Kane laughed at Leroux. The guy was loosening up, the longer he spent with Sherrie, the more confident he was becoming. It was wonderful to see. "What's up? Have you found him?"

"Affirmative. There will be a car outside in five minutes to take you to the airport. Park and one of his men, a Captain Tann, were spotted at Sheremetyevo Airport. Looks like they're heading to South Korea under assumed identities."

Kane pressed the phone against his chest and called to Sherrie. "Four minutes!"

Sherrie cursed.

"When does their flight leave?"

"We've hacked the airport's system, so everything is delayed right now."

Kane grinned as he swung off the bed. "Nice. Our tickets and ID?"

"You're back to your newlywed covers. We couldn't put together new IDs quick enough. Your driver will have everything else you'll need."

"Understood. I'm enjoying the part. Your girlfriend's a good kisser."

"We'll be talking when you get back."

Sheremetyevo International Airport
Moscow, Russian Federation

Colonel Park sat on the toilet at Sheremetyevo International Airport, his ass killing him. He had been in here for almost half an hour, Tann in the next stall. Their flight had been delayed, as had every other flight on the board, apparently something wrong with the computer systems.

It sounded suspicious to him.

If he had to guess, the Russians had disrupted their own system to give them time to find those escaping the embassy. He had only spotted one other familiar face in the crowd. They had ignored each other. Part of him hoped others had escaped, and another part hoped Pyongyang hadn't put all of the eggs in one proverbial basket, sending everyone on the same flight to Seoul in a desperate bid to get them out on the first flight.

That would be foolish.

And Pyongyang wasn't foolish.

He had never been extracted before. He had been briefed on a regular basis on how to trigger the extraction, how to hide while waiting, often in plain sight, then what might be expected of them once the process started.

The problem with Russia was that it wasn't exactly a free country. Rights were violated all the time, and with it fairly homogenous, Koreans stuck out.

Fortunately, a flight to Seoul was expected to have lots of Koreans on board. A shorter flight to Western Europe might have seemed wiser, but there would be few if any Koreans heading in that direction. Not from Moscow.

An announcement over the PA system declared the computers had been fixed, and flights would be resuming departure shortly.

That probably still meant at least an hour.

An interminable hour.

Kane helped Sherrie out of the cab, driven by a CIA operative stationed in Moscow. The man helped with their luggage and Kane tipped him.

"Don't spend it all in one place."

The driver stared at the 50 ruble note. "Don't worry, I can't even buy a good coffee with that."

Kane grinned and followed Sherrie into the terminal. He noticed the boards indicating major delays, but the PA was announcing flights were resuming.

Leroux's delaying tactic was over.

Fortunately, their contact had provided them with boarding passes, saving them some time. Security hadn't been backed up, which was fortunate, but he noticed a significantly higher number of armed guards visible, eyeballing anyone who didn't appear European.

He and Sherrie breezed through, not matching the profile of fleeing North Korean spies. They reached their gate as the flight began boarding, and Kane quickly scanned the impatient crowd.

"Ten o'clock," he whispered, spotting Park and his minion that Langley had identified as Captain Tann, to his left.

"I see them. Let's hope he doesn't recognize me."

Kane nodded, handing over her boarding pass. "Try to stay behind me and out of sight."

Park and Tann were ahead of them, which was unfortunate. Depending on who was seated where, they might be forced to pass each other. They would have to remain vigilant the entire nine-hour flight, though Park and Tann had never seen him, leaving Sherrie the only one at risk.

He handed over his boarding pass and passport, then waited for Sherrie to do the same, before heading down the jetway toward their plane. He breathed deeply, the smell of aviation fuel filling his nostrils, a smell he'd never tire of. He loved flying, no matter what the circumstances.

He presented his boarding pass again, and was directed toward his seat. Sherrie was right behind him, and he quickly spotted Park and Tann several rows ahead. He reached out behind him and guided Sherrie slightly over, hoping she'd pick up on the cue.

A baby's toy dropped to the floor in front of him, and he bent over on instinct to pick it up.

And cursed to himself. He stood, handing the toy back to a grateful mother, but the damage had already been done.

Park was staring through Kane.

Sherrie handled it like a pro as they passed. "Oh my God! Twice in one day! What are the chances of that!" She patted Park on the shoulder then continued past, Kane taking his window seat, Sherrie the middle.

"Well, that was unfortunate."

Sherrie nodded. "He made me as soon as you bent over. I figured it was best to acknowledge it rather than pretend it never happened."

"You made the right choice, but we may be useless once we get to Seoul."

"You won't be."

Kane shook his head. "He saw me with you. We've both been made."

Park's heart hammered as he gripped the arm rests tighter. It was the same woman who had bumped into him this morning, minutes before the Russians had invaded the embassy. He didn't believe in coincidences, and he was certain he had caught a brief moment of hesitation in her eyes before she had thrown on the charm.

It was exactly as a trained, though perhaps inexperienced spy, might react. She knew she had been made, and tried to salvage the situation by acknowledging the fact with almost no hesitation.

She was good, but not that good.

Yet why was she here? And who was that man she was with? Were they here for him? Someone else?

It made no sense. If they were Russian, and they were here for him, then that would mean the Russians knew they were on board. Why not just arrest them now? They were out of uniform, flying under false identities. They could be arrested as spies with no problem. Following them to Seoul made no sense.

What if they're not Russian at all?

They could be Americans.

His heart slammed even harder.

Now *that* made sense. The Americans would want to avoid an incident on Russian soil, but they wouldn't hesitate in Seoul. They had tens of thousands of troops in South Korea, the country was a staunch ally, and would probably cooperate fully in his apprehension. As soon as they got off the flight in Seoul, they'd probably be swarmed by armed security, then whisked away for interrogation.

And as soon as he disappeared, his family would be arrested back home, his incentive to keep his mouth shut.

"Sir, are you okay?"

He glanced at Tann and shook his head. "Neither of us is."

Operations Center 2, CIA Headquarters
Langley, Virginia

Leroux glanced up from his workstation as Director Morrison entered the operations center, Leroux jumping to his feet before Morrison could wave him off. He returned to his seat, scrutinizing his boss' face.

"Something wrong, sir?"

Morrison dropped into a free chair and leaned closer to his underling. "Where's Kane?"

"In the air, heading for Seoul. Five hours out."

Morrison frowned. "Any way to contact him?"

Leroux shook his head. "No, we figured satellite phones wouldn't fit their cover, and we had them hand over their watches, just in case the Russians decided to pull everyone off the plane. We're still not confident they won't order the plane to land before it leaves Russian airspace." Leroux's eyes narrowed. "Why? What's wrong?"

Morrison sighed then stood, Leroux following. "Can I have everyone's attention please?"

Leroux's team fell silent, all heads turned toward Morrison. "The reports will start hitting the wires at any moment, but I wanted you to hear it from me first. The North Koreans have just launched a medium range ballistic missile over Russian territory, in protest of the attack on their embassy in Moscow."

Gasps filled the room, and Leroux's chest tightened. "Where did it land?"

"It landed in international waters, but missed a Russian naval task force by less than ten nautical miles."

"Holy shit!" exclaimed Randy Child. "Are they nuts?"

Sonya Tong grunted. "I think that's been well established."

Leroux held out a hand, silencing the chatter. "And it went *over* Russian territory?"

Morrison nodded. "Yes, and they're pissed. The Russian President just got off the phone with our President."

Leroux paled slightly and gripped the back of his chair.

Morrison looked about the room at the team of specialists, all now on edge. "The Russians have already launched over two-hundred cruise missiles at North Korea, and are sending naval, air, and ground assets into the region."

Somebody cried out. Leroux didn't bother checking to see who, the shock in the room universal.

Two nuclear powers were about to go to war. There would be no contest between the two. Russia would win, without a doubt. The problem was who North Korea would take with them. With their forces geared toward the south for an assumed future conflict with South Korea and the Americans, would they lash out in that direction, regardless of who was attacking them, taking possibly hundreds of thousands of lives with them?

Or would they launch their limited number of nuclear weapons? And with little to no population centers within range in Russia, would they target Seoul or Tokyo?

With a madman at the helm, there was no telling what might happen.

"Do the North Koreans know?"

Morrison shook his head. "We don't believe so." He gestured at Tong. "Bring up the NORAD tactical display. Authorization Alpha-Papa-Four-Seven-Six-Bravo." Tong's fingers attacked her keyboard, her entire body shaking. The large displays at the front of the room filled with a map of the world, thousands of pieces of data appearing. "Show us the Korean Peninsula." The display updated. "Show us all known North Korean rocket and nuclear installations." Several dozen dots appeared with data displays beside each. "Bring up live satellite coverage of each of those targets. Impacts should begin any minute now."

Leroux motioned toward the screen. "Are we sure this is all they're hitting?"

Morrison shook his head. "No. Based upon the transcript of the conversation, the *suggestion* is that only these targets will be hit, but the Russian interpretation of 'involved with' and ours, might be something different. If they think the leadership is 'involved with' the nuclear and rocket program, they might well hit Pyongyang and the Dear Leader himself."

Leroux cursed. "If they do that, then we're going to war for sure."

Morrison nodded. "I fear we may be going to war, regardless of what they hit."

"What's the President going to do?"

"Nothing."

Child's brain-mouth filter failed once again. "Nothing? Are you kidding me?"

Morrison glanced at him. "The Joint Chiefs recommended we do nothing, and the President agreed. And frankly, so do I. The key here is to make it clear we have no involvement in this strike whatsoever. If we put our forces on alert ahead of the strike, then North Korea might retaliate in our direction. If we do nothing to provoke them, then condemn the attack loudly and publicly, we may just save the South Korean people from nuclear annihilation."

Leroux shook his head, staring at the displays.

All because of a ransomware attack.

One of the satellite images showing a North Korean facility flashed, a massive explosion filling the screen.

There's no way we're not going to war.

Aeroflot Flight 250 to Seoul
Over Russian Airspace

"Ladies and gentlemen, if I may have your attention, please."

Kane glanced up at the ceiling as if it would help him hear better, elbowing a sleeping Sherrie.

"What is it?" she asked groggily.

"Something's going on."

She immediately became alert, sitting straight as the flight attendant continued in Russian.

"We regret to inform you that due to events beyond our control, we will be diverting to Tokyo. This will add about two and a half hours to our travel time. Once on the ground, arrangements will be made for you to continue to Seoul as soon as possible. Again, we apologize for the inconvenience."

The announcement repeated in English then Korean, the passengers becoming increasingly irate as more were let in on the news.

"Something's wrong," said Sherrie. "You can hear it in her voice."

Kane agreed. "I'd kill to have a laptop with a satellite connection."

"I've got one, dude."

The man in the aisle seat stood, retrieving his carry-on bag from overhead and removing a laptop. He sat and lowered his tray table. Moments later, he was connected to a brutally slow, but functional, CNN.

"Holy shit! The Russians have attacked North Korea!"

Kane would have preferred it if there was a mouse rather than a lion sitting next to them, as the news spread like wildfire throughout the plane, dozens leaving their seats to crowd around as their seatmate read the headlines.

Headlines that were terrifying.

Headlines that meant war.

Park exchanged a nervous glance with Tann as someone shouted out the news about their homeland. The Russians were attacking, but beyond that, the details were sketchy. Though not as powerful or advanced as the Americans, the Russians had the capability of targeting their attacks, or not.

The question was what was actually being hit.

He would hope it was only military targets and not civilian populations. But if utilities or factories were hit, it could mean prolonged hardship for his people, people already facing lives far tougher than they should.

I wonder if they'd dare target the Dear Leader.

If the Russians did, the results could be disastrous, depending on who took over. If enough of the leadership remained, and that leadership were members of the fanatical group surrounding the leader, then all-out war could be declared, and millions would die.

The Russians have to know that!

But it wouldn't be millions of Russians. It would be few, if any. Most likely, the Russians were using missiles, putting little if any of their personnel at risk, and his country's ability to strike back was range-limited. There was little within range that Russia prized besides the naval base at Vladivostok.

And what of the Americans? What would they do?

Or the Chinese?

North Korea had few friends beyond the crazies, and if the Chinese didn't support his country, they were doomed.

And it was all his fault.

This was because of the embassy. Because of Bureau 121's set-up there. It had been his idea to set up a branch inside the embassy, the grounds a perfect cover for their operations. Russia was already a hotbed of cybercrime, and a little more added to the mix would go unnoticed. Bandwidth into North Korea was so limited, no operations of any significance could be conducted from within.

But Moscow?

It was perfect.

And it had been perfect.

Until today.

The Russians had somehow found out about the operation, and because of how severely they had been impacted by the ransomware attack, had taken unprecedented action. His country had retaliated with a relatively harmless missile launch that had come uncomfortably close to the Russian Pacific Fleet, and the Russians had escalated.

If it had been anyone else, there would merely have been strong diplomatic condemnation.

But not with the Russians.

His homeland was under attack, and it was his fault. If he had never suggested Bureau 121 set up in Moscow, none of this would be happening.

He sighed. He was doomed. He could try to escape when they reached Tokyo, but if he did, his family would be immediately executed. This had always been made clear to him. Every North Korean knew this when they stepped across the border. It was the only way the government had of ensuring the return of its citizens.

The only hope his family had was for him to return home and face the consequences.

Assuming there would be a home to return to.

Tokyo Narita Airport
Chiba Prefecture, Japan

Kane hung back in the line with Sherrie, Park and Tann visible ahead. The airport was slammed, what with so many flights diverted from South Korea, though the Japanese were handling things fairly well— better than the visibly frustrated passengers. Too many didn't know why they had been diverted, but once they found out, tears and fear abounded.

He didn't blame them. Most of these people were South Korean, and they knew full well the dangers of a rattled North Korea. As they waited to clear customs, their seatmate, several paces in front of them, continued to give updates.

"It looks like North Korea is getting pounded by the Russians. Just military sites, apparently."

Kane glanced at Sherrie, saying nothing. If the Russians stuck to military targets, then things might not escalate if they took it easy on them. A proportional response might be tolerated by the North Koreans. After all, they had launched a rocket over Russian territory, and it had almost hit one of their ships.

But keep pounding them, they might wonder when it would stop, and if they had any doubt it might not, a further response from Pyongyang might become necessary.

And that was when war could break out.

"Have they attacked South Korea yet?" asked somebody, the woman's voice quavering, her accent thick.

"No. The American President apparently issued a statement condemning the Russian attack, but told the North Koreans that if they attacked any American or ally target, he'd immediately respond with nukes."

Kane's chest tightened. Strong rhetoric like that might work with most leaders, but how the North Koreans would respond was anyone's guess. The advantage the rest of the world had was that the Dear Leader had no desire to die.

His life was too good.

If he knew he'd absolutely die, one had to think he'd back off.

"Has the Dear Psycho responded?" asked another.

"No. According to CNN, there's been no reaction by the North Koreans except the normal insanity that they usually broadcast. It's as if they're ignoring the attack."

Kane smiled slightly. That made sense. If the Russians were sticking to military targets away from population centers, then the North Korean public might have no clue what was actually happening. And if things could remain that way, the Dear Leader could pretend it had never happened, saving face, and was probably delusional enough to think the world would eventually come to believe the same.

It might just head off a war.

Why go to war over something that never happened?

Kane and Sherrie cleared customs with no problem, Park and Tann only minutes ahead of them with only one direction to go. They hurried toward the exit when a man approached them.

"Excuse me!"

Kane looked at the man holding out a cellphone. "Yes?"

The man gasped, out of breath. "Thank God I caught you." He handed Kane the phone. "You left this on the plane."

Kane sighed, kissing the phone. "Thanks, man! I don't know what I'd do without this baby!"

The man grinned. "I know how you feel! Enjoy Tokyo!" He disappeared into the crowd, dragging a carry-on.

The phone vibrated in Kane's hand and he swiped his thumb. "Yes?"

"Leave Park alone, your job is done."

Kane frowned at Leroux's voice as he spotted Park about to exit the terminal. "Are you sure? He could be able to name every mole they've placed."

"Washington doesn't want to risk any further provocations."

It made sense. If the North Koreans were playing possum right now, taking their beating like most schoolyard bullies eventually received, capturing one of their agents connected to the entire mess could inflame things. He sighed. "Understood. We'll head home as soon as possible."

"Negative. The Director wants you to wait twenty-four hours, just in case."

"Copy that. Should we keep Park under surveillance?"

"Negative. Let him go. If you're made, there could be consequences."

"Yeah, well, we were already made, so it's probably a good thing you're calling it off."

"What happened?"

"I'll let you know in the debrief."

"Copy that. We've got a hotel arranged for you. Details have been sent to the phone. *Two* rooms."

Kane grinned. "What? Don't trust me?"

"Not for a second."

Kane laughed, ending the call before stuffing the phone in his pocket.

"What's up?" asked Sherrie as they cleared the doors, stepping into the fresh air.

"Op is off. We're letting him go. Washington doesn't want to risk provoking Pyongyang."

Sherrie frowned as Park stepped into a waiting car with Tann. "That's too bad. I'll go get us some tickets."

Kane shook his head. "Nope. We've been given an extra day here in case things changed." His eyebrows bobbed suggestively at her. "I can think of some ways to kill a day in Tokyo. We never did get that honeymoon."

Sherrie laughed. "You're incorrigible!"

Park glanced over his shoulder as he climbed into the car sent to collect them, and his heart slammed. It was the woman again, not fifty feet from where he sat. There was no doubt now that she was following him. She and the other man were definitely spies, probably American, and absolutely after him.

And he couldn't let them succeed.

If Americans kidnapped him, his family would certainly be killed. Pyongyang would assume he was a double agent and had been extracted by the Americans for a debriefing.

He had to stop them, he had to get home.

He turned to the driver. "Are you armed?"

"Yes."

"Give me your weapon. Now!"

"Sir?"

"Now! That's an order!"

The driver retrieved a handgun from a shoulder holster, then handed it back. Park pushed Tann aside and shoved the barrel into the sunlight.

And fired.

Kane spotted the barrel of a weapon emerge from the darkness of the car's interior, and shoved Sherrie to the side as he dove in the opposite direction. A gunshot rang out, followed by two more, as Kane rolled to the left then to his feet. He grabbed the submachine gun from a stunned Japanese guard, and aimed at the car as it pulled away, Tann diving in before the rear door slammed shut.

Kane squeezed the trigger, emptying the magazine into the rear of the car to no effect, the skin probably armored. He shoved the confused guard to the ground while Sherrie sprinted into the road, forcing a cab to a stop. Before the driver could react, Sherrie had yanked open his door and hauled him to the pavement before hopping inside. Kane grabbed a handgun off the guard as others rushed toward them. He sprinted for the cab, jumping inside the right-hand drive vehicle.

Sherrie hammered on the gas as alarms sounded. Kane rolled down the window, checking the weapon as Sherrie closed the gap with the North Koreans. She stole a glance at Kane.

"Should we be doing this?"

Kane looked at her. "Huh?"

"I mean, we've been ordered to let him go."

Kane grinned. "You're the one driving."

"I'm operating on adrenaline and instinct. You're the seasoned agent. What the hell do I do!"

Park slid to the far side of the seat, his heart hammering as Tann picked himself up off the floor, taking a seat beside his superior officer.

"What was that all about?"

Park turned, staring out the rear window, a cab driving erratically behind them, this clearly not over. "She's been following us since Moscow."

"What?"

"She bumped into me yesterday morning before I arrived at the embassy, then I saw her on the plane."

"That woman who spoke to you?"

"Yes."

"If she was a spy, why would she admit to having seen you earlier?"

"She knew she had been made, so she did what was necessary to salvage her mission."

"Which is?"

"To capture me, obviously."

Tann frowned. "For all you know, they could be tourists."

Park glared at him. "Haven't you been paying attention? Would tourists return fire?"

Tann's jaw dropped slightly. "Umm, you're right, of course. What are we going to do?"

"We need to lose them." Park turned to the driver. "Can you?"

"We will. I've called for backup."

"Good. ETA?"

"Three minutes."

Park sighed, leaning back in the seat as the driver continued to swerve back and forth through the traffic of the loading zone.

"We heard there was trouble at home," said Tann, leaning forward. "Is there any news?"

"I'm not authorized to brief you," replied the driver. He looked in the rearview mirror at Park. "All I can say, Colonel, is that they are not pleased with you."

Park's cheeks flushed, and his heart hammered at the implications of what was just said. For the driver to say such a thing, a junior officer at best, he had to feel confident enough there would be no consequences. And that meant Park truly was in trouble.

He was already dead.

He thought of his wife and children. He hadn't seen them in years, and he was desperate to see them one last time, just to tell them he loved them, and to hold them in his arms before saying goodbye.

But he wouldn't be given that chance.

He knew that now.

He had failed the Dear Leader.

And there was no coming back from that.

"I understand."

He held the gun to his head and squeezed the trigger.

Sherrie locked up the brakes as a body was dumped from the car ahead of them. Kane gripped the dash, narrowly avoiding his head slamming into the unforgiving surface as they came to a halt. He jumped out and rushed toward the body, flipping it over.

It was Park.

"What the hell happened?" asked Sherrie as she rushed up beside him, a crowd gathering. "Did they kill him?"

Kane shook his head, pointing at the head wound. "No, this is self-inflicted. He shot himself."

"Why? They still could have gotten away."

"He knew what was coming." Kane stuffed the weapon he had taken from the guard, under the body. "Come on, let's get the hell out of here." He took Sherrie by the arm, pulling her into the crowd as police converged on the area. Spotting a cab dropping off a pair of passengers, he hauled Sherrie silently through the throng, beating out what appeared to be a husband and wife.

"Hey, that's our cab!" cried the man in the Queen's English.

"Sorry, too slow," replied Kane in Russian as Sherrie slammed the door shut.

"Those bloody Russians! So rude!"

The cab pulled away, Kane dialing for extraction instructions.

There'd be no 24-hour layover in Tokyo now.

El Camino Hospital
Mountain View, California

The sounds of machines beeping and droning, of voices in the background whispering, slowly drew Temple out of the deep sleep he had been in. He blinked, everything a blur, all he was aware of at first the fact he was lying on his back, and someone was holding his hand.

He turned to see a dark shadow leaning over him. At first, fear commanded him, his mind filled with the last images he could remember.

The hostage exchange gone terribly wrong.

"Tanya!"

He bolted upright, immediately regretting it as pain racked his shoulder, surging through his entire body.

"It's okay, I'm here."

The room snapped into focus, and he sighed as he sank back onto the bed, Davis at his side, holding his hand.

"You're okay?"

She smiled. "Thanks to you." She glanced toward the other end of the room. "And him."

Temple looked over to see Simmons standing in the doorway.

"Mr. Temple, how are you feeling?"

Temple shrugged and gasped. "I'll live, I think."

Davis smiled, patting his hand. "You're going to be just fine."

Simmons stepped over to the bed. "So you're good enough to remember what I'm about to say?"

Temple eyed him. "Yes. What's this all about?"

"My name isn't Simmons. I'm with the United States government."

Temple frowned. "Penn said the same thing before they shot him." He glanced at Davis, his heart hammering. "I don't understand. What's going on?"

She shook her head. "You better listen to what he has to say."

Simmons stepped closer. "Your late security chief called us in when he found out what you wanted to do."

"That bast—"

Simmons raised a finger. "Shut the hell up and listen!"

Temple shut up, genuine fear gripping him, the man he had hired appearing very intimidating now that he was no longer on his side.

"Only a handful of people outside of this room know what you did. With what has happened over the past few days around the world, the last thing we need is the truth about your involvement getting out. It will just muddy the waters."

Temple's eyes narrowed. "Why? What's happened?"

Simmons motioned toward Davis. "She'll explain it to you." He leaned in closer. "But here's how it's going to go down. You never hired anyone. You had your tech teams try to track down who was involved, with the intention of handing that data over to the FBI to take action. Miss Davis here has already disbanded the team and handed over everything they've found. As far as you are concerned, this is over, you were never involved, and you never met me. Understood?"

Temple nodded, then gestured at Davis. "But what about her? She was kidnapped. How do we cover that up?"

"We don't. She was kidnapped by hackers pissed off at your press conference. She was rescued and the perpetrators killed. Case closed."

Simmons leaned over him and pressed a finger on his wound, a hint harder than gently. "Consider yourself lucky, Mr. Temple. You should be in prison for what you did, but instead, you just got away with murder." Simmons lifted the finger and Temple sighed with relief.

"I understand. Thank you." He reached out and grabbed Simmons by the arm. "But they're dead, right? Those responsible?"

"That's no longer your concern."

Simmons pulled his arm free and left the room. Temple stared after him then sank into the bedding, finally realizing how tense he was. He turned to Davis. "You're going to have to explain to me what the hell is going on."

She smiled, squeezing his hand. "Later. All that matters now is that you get healthy."

He stared into her eyes, eyes that were glistening, smiling at him as much as her mouth was.

And he couldn't look away.

He drew a deep breath.

And took a leap.

"When did things change between us?"

Her smile spread, and she leaned in closer. "I don't know, but it has, hasn't it?"

He nodded, and he raised his head from the pillow. She pushed him back, lowering herself closer to him, then gently kissed him on the lips. He closed his eyes and smiled as she drew away. He opened them and gazed at this woman he finally realized he loved.

"How about when I get out of here, I take you out for dinner?"

"I'd like that, sir."

He reached up and caressed her face. "How about you call me Franklin?"

She smiled, pressing her cheek into his hand and closing her eyes. "I'd like that too."

Kane/Fang Residence
Falls Church, Virginia

"Do you think the couch is good here, or would it look better over by the window?"

Kane wagged a finger at Fang. "Sorry, darlin', but you've got this all back-asswards. *First,* you figure out where you're putting the TV, *then* you arrange all the furniture around that."

Fang stared at him, her hands on her hips. "Ah, I'm the one who has to live here for 365 days of the year. *You* will rarely be around."

Kane felt butterflies and reached out, pulling this incredible woman closer. He wrapped his arms around her. "You know what? You're absolutely right. You choose where the couch goes."

She smiled at him and popped up on her toes to give him a peck. "Good boy."

He let her go. "We can always rearrange things when I'm back."

A sidekick lashed out, stopping an inch from his nose.

He kissed her foot, then made to suck on her toe when she bent her knee, denying him.

"Don't start something we don't have time for you to finish."

He grinned. "I can be quick."

There was a knock at the door and Kane's eyes narrowed. "Expecting someone?"

Fang gave him a look. "Do you have any clue who you're living with? Your girlfriend has no friends, no colleagues, and no family she can ever see again."

Kane tried to smile, but couldn't, her words breaking his heart. She had no one except him, which was one of the reasons he had wanted to move.

He headed for the door and peered through the peephole.

And smiled at two of the reasons for picking this location.

He opened the door. "Hey, buddy! Good to see you!"

"Sorry, I would have called, but Sherrie insisted we surprise you."

Sherrie lifted a pizza over her head with one hand, a bottle of wine with the other. "We come bearing gifts."

"Come on in, come on in!"

Leroux followed Sherrie inside, and Fang rushed over, taking the pizza from Sherrie's hand. "It's so good to see you two."

Sherrie gave Fang a hug, the two having been through hell and back together, a bond like that hard to break or replicate. "I hope you don't mind."

"Not at all, not at all." Fang glanced at the wine. "But we haven't unpacked any dishes yet!"

Leroux held up several grocery bags. "Plastic plates, cutlery, and glasses." He leaned toward Kane, whispering loudly. "And a bottle of Glen Breton Ice."

Kane grinned, slapping his friend on the back. "A man after my own heart." He pointed at the couch. "Grab a seat, but don't be surprised if Fang moves it with you in it."

Fang swatted him. "Dylan! Don't be silly. Let's eat, get them drunk, then get them to do all the moving for us."

Kane roared with laughter as he emptied a love seat of several boxes stacked atop it, then hauled it over to where the food and drinks had been laid out. He sat beside Fang and goose bumps washed over his body at the smile on her face.

She was happy.

Truly happy.

And he realized at this very moment, that Leroux and Sherrie were probably the first houseguests she had entertained since her exile in America.

That was exactly why they had moved into the same building his best friends lived in.

He wanted her to have someone she could turn to if she were bored or lonely. Leroux lived at the office, and Sherrie was on assignment often as well, but just knowing they were close, he hoped would be enough to make her feel a little more at home than the isolation of Philly had.

At least Leroux and Sherrie knew who she really was, and she could be herself around them.

He sighed.

"What?" asked Fang, staring at him.

Kane waved at the gathered friends. "*This*. This is good. This is what I've always wanted."

"What's that?" asked Sherrie.

"Good friends. Good friends that you don't have to lie to all the time." He looked about the apartment. "A sanctuary from the craziness out there." He put an arm around Fang and squeezed her tight. "A place where we can all feel at home."

Fang smiled at him. "I feel at home already."

Kane sucked in a breath then pushed her away. "Somebody pour me a scotch before I start getting all teary eyed."

Fang patted his shoulder, smiling at Sherrie. "He's really just a big teddy bear at heart."

Leroux snorted as he handed a scotch to Kane. "Now *that's* something I have *never* heard him called."

Kane sipped his scotch, enjoying the bite. "Okay, I'm starving. Let's break out the 'za."

Sherrie flipped open the lid, revealing sixteen inches of cheesy goodness.

"It's a thing of beauty," sighed Kane, wiping a fake tear from the corner of his eye.

Sherrie rolled her eyes. "*This* you get emotional over."

"Hey, Russia, Japan, Korea, and how many other places have we been the past two weeks? I haven't had a good pizza in I don't know how long."

Fang handed him a piece. "Enjoy, my little pooh bear."

Kane eyed her. "We're going to have to have a discussion about boundaries when friends are over."

"Eat your pizza, dear."

"Yes'm."

Fang turned to Leroux as she took a piece for herself. "Any luck tracking down Tann?"

Leroux swallowed, holding a hand in front of his mouth. "No. He's gone to ground. But I don't think it really matters anymore. Park is dead, Bureau 121 is dismantled in Moscow, the North Korean rocket program has been hammered back into the Stone Age, for a little while at least, and the world has moved onto its next problem."

Fang smiled at Sherrie. "I'm just glad you're all back in one piece." She took a sip of her wine. "It must have been fun, though, going undercover together."

Kane grinned at Sherrie. "It was."

Leroux jabbed a finger at him. "That reminds me. I've gotta bone to pick with you."

Kane leaned back, putting some distance between him and his friend. "Umm, what?"

"If I ever see you kiss my girlfriend like that again, I'll put a hit out on you."

Kane roared with laughter, Sherrie joining in. He glanced at Fang, who wasn't laughing, instead staring at him, giving him a look.

"Umm, I guess I better explain that, otherwise this is going to be a very short cohabitation."

Boulangerie Klara

Luhansk, Ukraine

Pro-Russian Militia Controlled Territory

Captain Tann knocked on the door buried at the rear of a humble bakery, the aromas intoxicating, yet not enough to distract him from his mission. A Judas hole slid open, a pair of eyes staring at him.

"Agent K?"

"Yes."

For today.

The hole slid closed, the sound of bolts on the other side echoing through the thick metal door. It swung inward, and he stepped through, the door closing behind him. He was patted down, Tann not worried—there was no way he'd be foolish enough to bring a weapon.

"Is everyone here?"

"Yes."

He stepped further inside, navigating a cramped hallway before coming out into an equally cramped room, half a dozen young men and two women sitting behind computers, turning to stare at him.

His eyes narrowed. "So few?"

"The Shadow Collective is the best. We only need a few."

Tann nodded, putting his briefcase by the wall and removing his gloves. He smiled at those gathered. "And this is everyone? My employers want all who have helped us to hear what I have to say."

"Yes, everyone is here."

"Even those of us who are sick," said a nasally voice from the corner.

Tann smiled. "I will be brief, then." He handed a USB key to the man clearly in charge. "First, you will transfer my share."

The man took the key, handing it to one of the others who plugged it into his terminal. The display updated, and millions of dollars' worth of Bitcoins were transferred into his account, his private key on the memory stick ensuring only he could ever access his share of the ransomware attack's proceeds.

The USB key was removed and handed back to him. He placed it in his pocket and smiled at the total on the screen.

Enough to disappear forever.

He had planned this for most of his life. The only means of escaping the tyranny of North Korea was through foreign service, and that was usually only given to family men. His parents had died young, so he had taken a wife he didn't love, and had two children in rapid succession.

It had taken years of hard work, studying at the University of Automation, and finally getting his assignment to Bureau 121, a branch he knew out of necessity would deploy him in theater.

Yet he couldn't simply defect.

He was of no value to anyone. He was too junior. But when the ToolKit had been stolen, by an agent he had direct access to, an agent that had already broken the rules by taking a foreign wife, he realized there was an opportunity here to fulfill his dreams.

He had approached Agent K, Donald Penn, and together, they set the plan in motion.

Only Penn hadn't known the endgame.

Selling the ToolKit wouldn't be enough. Not for what he wanted. But using it to hold the world ransom? That was an entirely different level of money.

Tens of millions at least.

Enough to disappear and never be found, and to enjoy that new life to the fullest.

He looked at the criminals who had helped him achieve his dreams, and smiled. "It has been a pleasure doing business with you all, people who truly appreciate the value of discretion. My employer hopes to once again make use of your talents."

Their leader bowed slightly. "Thank you, sir. We look forward to that day as well."

Tann smiled. "I, of course, don't need to remind you that I was never here, and you have never heard of me or my employer."

"Of course. We are all professionals here."

"Yes, absolutely." Tann bowed to the room. "I shall take my leave of you."

He was led down the hallway, and the door was unlocked. He stepped through and into the bakery, eyeing fresh rolls being placed on a cooling rack. He bought a dozen, unable to resist.

He stepped out into the cool evening air and strolled down the street, chewing on one of the still piping hot concoctions as he reached into his pocket and pulled out his phone. He hit number 9 on the speed dial as he stepped into an alleyway.

The massive explosion from his briefcase bomb tore apart the bakery and its secret backroom operation, sending debris and a fireball in all directions, ending the Shadow Collective once and for all.

And leaving him a very rich man.

Janine Graf Residence
Odenton, Maryland

Graf plunked onto her couch, exhausted. It had been a good day. Several weeks had passed since the excitement surrounding her former partner, and now that anyone who mattered knew he was a North Korean spy, and the source of the leak, she had been completely cleared.

In fact, she had been told by her supervisor she was already up for promotion.

A good day.

She had toughed it out, never giving up hope, despite the whispers and dead-end assignments.

And it had paid off.

She was no longer persona non grata, smiles now greeting her at the office, invites to after-work gatherings extended once again.

It was as if the past two years had never happened.

And she wouldn't want it any other way.

Except for one thing.

She wanted to share her happiness with someone, anyone. Someone she could be herself with.

And she could think of only one person.

But it was idiotic.

Insane.

She stared at her iPad sitting beside her on the couch.

Don't do it.

She closed her eyes and reached out for the tablet, then sighed.

What's the worst that can happen?

She had a hole in her life that she hadn't been able to fill. But there was someone else out there with the same hole.

Perhaps they could help each other.

She opened her eyes and logged in.

Clayton Hummel Residence
Annapolis, Maryland

Hummel stared at the television, his favorite Battlestar Galactica episode, 33, about to finish. He loved the first couple of seasons of this show, though he felt it dropped off a bit in the last two. Still fantastic television, but 33, the first regular season episode, was incredibly entertaining, and he never tired of watching it.

His laptop beeped, and he glanced at it.

His chest ached and his stomach flipped.

He pressed pause on the remote, staring at the screen as his jaw dropped.

A rush of emotions swept over him as he read the short, simple message from someone he had never thought he'd hear from again, someone he had tried to forget, yet couldn't.

Someone he didn't even really know.

The past few weeks had been horrible, but nothing like two years ago when his heart had been shattered, permanently. The press had finally stopped hounding him, government officials were no longer questioning him, and the delivery guys had tired of asking what had happened.

Life, such as it was, was returning to normal.

He stared at the message, unsure of what to do, though as he read it, over and over, he realized there was only one thing he *could* do.

Take a chance.

He read the message one last time.

I miss my friend.

He closed his eyes, then hit Reply.

So do I.

THE END

ACKNOWLEDGEMENTS

Those of you who followed the WannaCry story, and dug a little deeper into the backstory of the NSA leak, will recognize a lot of elements from that reality embedded in this work of fiction. If you're not familiar with what happened, and how close we came to it being far worse than it actually was, it's worth digging into.

This book is dedicated to a man named Dave Camp. He was a colleague of my father's, and a good friend to the family. When I was younger, we traveled to Switzerland with his family, and I have fond memories of that trip, and some great photos hidden away somewhere.

Dave's name came up when I was discussing who I should dedicate this book to. I decided to go ahead, because there is an interesting story to tell with him.

When I started out writing, my father used to send copies of my books (in eBook form) to friends that he thought might enjoy them. As time went on, many of them became fans, and told him they had already bought the books. Dave was one of them.

Little did I know, he was a huge fan of my writing. A couple of years after I really got into this business, he sent me an email, out of the blue, through my website. I had never heard from him in my life, as he was my father's friend, not mine, and he addressed me as "Robbie," which was what I was called when I was a kid.

He mentioned who he was, that he enjoyed the books, then asked about The Arab Fall and when it would be coming out.

It was a heartwarming email to receive, and I replied back right away.

That was June 29, 2013.

He died July 5th.

It was almost surreal to receive this email from someone from my past, making him a topic of conversation for the first time in probably decades, then to find out less than a week later he was dead.

A fitting dedication, I believe.

As usual, there are people to thank. My dad for the research, Chris Holder and the real Chris Leroux for some hacking info, Ian Kennedy for some explosives info, Brent Richards for some weapons info, the proofing team, and of course my wife, daughter, mother, and friends.

To those who have not already done so, please visit my website at www.jrobertkennedy.com then sign up for the Insider's Club to be notified of new book releases. Your email address will never be shared or sold, and you'll only receive the occasional email from me, as I don't have time to spam you!

Thank you once again for reading.

ABOUT THE AUTHOR

With over 800,000 books in circulation and over 3000 five-star reviews, USA Today bestselling author J. Robert Kennedy has been ranked by Amazon as the #1 Bestselling Action Adventure novelist based upon combined sales. He is the author of over thirty international bestsellers including the smash hit James Acton Thrillers. He lives with his wife and daughter and writes full-time.

Visit Robert's website at www.jrobertkennedy.com for the latest news and contact information, and to join the Insider's Club to be notified when new books are released.

Available James Acton Thrillers

The Protocol (Book #1)
The Final Skull Has Been Found. Now All Hell's Breaking Loose.

Brass Monkey (Book #2)
Will a Forgotten Weapon and an Uncontrollable Hate Unleash the Ultimate War?

Broken Dove (Book #3)
Will a Secret Desperately Hidden for over One Thousand Years by the Roman Catholic Church Finally Be Revealed?

The Templar's Relic (Book #4)
The Church Helped Destroy the Templars. Will a Twist of Fate Let Them Get Their Revenge 700 Years Later?

Flags Of Sin (Book #5)
China is About to Erupt in Chaos!

The Arab Fall (Book #6)
The Greatest Archaeological Discovery Since King Tut's Tomb is About to be Destroyed!

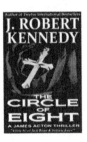

The Circle Of Eight (Book #7)
Abandoned by Their Government, the Delta Force's Bravo Team Fights to Not Only Save Themselves and Their Families, but Humanity as Well.

The Venice Code (Book #8)
A 700-Year-Old Mystery Is about to Be Solved. But How Many Must Die First?

Pompeii's Ghosts (Book #9)
Pompeii is About to Claim Its Final Victims—Two Thousand Years Later!

Amazon Burning (Book #10)
In the Depths of the Amazon, One of Their Own Has Been Taken!

The Riddle (Book #11)
The Russian Prime Minister Has Been Assassinated. The World Stands on the Brink of War.

Blood Relics (Book #12)
A Dying Man. A Desperate Son. Only a Miracle Can Save Them Both.

Sins of the Titanic (Book #13)
The Assembly is Eternal. And They'll Stop at Nothing to Keep it That Way.

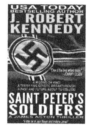

Saint Peter's Soldiers (Book #14)
A Missing Da Vinci. A Terrifying Genetic Breakthrough. A past and Future About to Collide!

The Thirteenth Legion (Book #15)
A Two-Thousand-Year-Old Destiny Is about to Be Fulfilled!

Raging Sun (Book #16)
Will a Seventy-Year-Old Matter of Honor Trigger the Next Great War?

Wages of Sin (Book #17)
When Is the Price to Protect a Nation's Legacy Too High?

Wrath of the Gods (Book #18)
A Thousand Years of History Are about to Be Rewritten!

The Templar's Revenge (Book #19)
Are Eight Centuries of Duty and Honor About to Come to an End?

Available Special Agent Dylan Kane Thrillers

Rogue Operator (Book #1)
In Order to Save the Country he Loves, Dylan Kane Must First Betray It.

Containment Failure (Book #2)
The Black Death Killed Almost Half of Europe's Population. This Time It Will Be Billions.

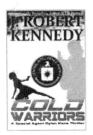

Cold Warriors (Book #3)
The Country's Best Hope in Defeating a Forgotten Soviet Weapon Lies with Dylan Kane and the Cold Warriors Who Originally Discovered It.

Death to America (Book #4)
Who Do You Trust When Your Country Turns against Itself?

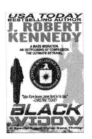

Black Widow (Book #5)
A Mass Migration. An Outpouring of Compassion. The Ultimate Betrayal.

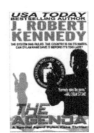

The Agenda (Book #6)
The System Has Failed. The Country Is on Its Knees. Can Dylan Kane Save It before It's Too Late?

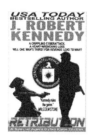

Retribution (Book #7)

A Crippling Cyberattack. A Heart-wrenching Loss. Will One Man's Thirst for Revenge Lead to War?

Available Delta Force Unleashed Thrillers

Payback (Book #1)

The Vice President's Daughter Is Kidnapped. Delta Is Unleashed on Those Responsible!

Infidels (Book #2)

Islam's Holiest Relic Is Stolen. America Is Blamed. Chaos Erupts.

The Lazarus Moment (Book #3)

Air Force One Is Down. But Their Fight to Survive Has Only Just Begun!

Kill Chain (Book #4)

Will a Desperate President Risk War to Save His Only Child?

Forgotten (Book #5)

One of Their Own Is Dead. Now It's Time for Revenge.

Available Detective Shakespeare Mysteries

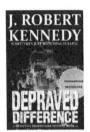

Depraved
Difference (Book
#1)
Sometimes Just
Watching is Fatal.

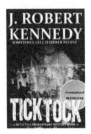

Tick Tock (Book
#2)
Sometimes Hell is
Other People.

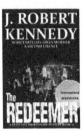

The Redeemer
(Book #3)
Sometimes Life
Gives Murder a
Second Chance.

Zander Varga, Vampire Detective

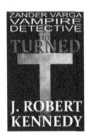

The Turned (Book #1)
Zander has relived his wife's death at the hands of vampires every day for almost three hundred years, his perfect memory a curse of becoming one of The Turned—infecting him their final heinous act after her murder. Nineteen year-old Sydney Winter knows Zander's secret, a secret preserved by the women in her family for four generations. But with her mother in a coma, she's thrust into the frontlines, ahead of her time, to fight side-by-side with Zander.

Made in the USA
Monee, IL
29 December 2022

23927374R00194